Murder
is in
the Air

Also available by Frances Brody

Murder
is in
the Air

A Kate Shackleton Mystery

FRANCES BRODY

**CROOKED
LANE**

NEW YORK

Published in the United States by Crooked Lane Books, an imprint of The Quick Brown Fox & Company LLC.

Crooked Lane Books and its logo are trademarks of The Quick Brown Fox & Company LLC.

Library of Congress Catalog-in-Publication data available upon request.

ISBN (paperback): 978-1-64385-807-4
ISBN (hardcover): 978-1-64385-466-3
ISBN (ebook): 978-1-64385-467-0

Cover illustration by Helen Chapman

Printed in the United States.

www.crookedlanebooks.com

Crooked Lane Books
34 West 27th St., 10th Floor
New York, NY 10001

Trade Paperback North American Edition: December 2021
First North American Edition: October 2020

10 9 8 7 6 5 4 3 2 1

To my readers and to booksellers everywhere.
Thank you and happy reading.

Chapter One

My name is Kate Shackleton. I am a private investigator. Although I could stretch to an office, Batswing Cottage remains our centre of operations. We are close to Leeds city centre, yet near open countryside for dog walks and thinking time. Jim Sykes, my assistant, lives a short walk away in Woodhouse.

For my meeting with William Lofthouse, the informality of being 'at home' would suit us very well. William and I first met at the opening of an exhibition in a London art gallery, before he married Eleanor, his much younger artist wife. I am the proud owner of an early Eleanor Hart painting, from her time at the Royal Academy. The painting depicts a shepherd and his dog herding a flock of sheep through a snowstorm towards a distant glimmer of light. My housekeeper, Mrs Sugden, calls it bleak. I think it optimistic.

William owns Barleycorn Brewery in the North Riding market town of Masham, locally pronounced Massam. He and Eleanor live a stone's throw from the brewery, at Barleycorn House. In anticipation of today's meeting, I did my homework. He inherited land in the North Riding of Yorkshire, as well as inns and alehouses in Masham and surrounding villages and hamlets. He and his late wife were childless, but there is a nephew, James Lofthouse. In a rare burst of poetry, Jim Sykes told me that Barleycorn Brewery is renowned for its luscious and richly flavoured Nut Brown Ale.

The doorbell rang promptly at 2 p.m. Mrs Sugden showed William Lofthouse in, and then went to invite his chauffeur into the kitchen for tea and cake, and probably to find out everything she could about his life and times.

William's secretary made the appointment for him to see me. He had come from attending an old schoolfriend's funeral at Lawnswood Cemetery. Having seen his friend's obituary in the *Yorkshire Post*, it did not take a high degree of skill to pinpoint William Lofthouse's age at sixty-two. Today, he looked older. His greying hair still showed signs of having once been coppery. More lines etched his face than I remembered.

'William, hello. Come and sit by the fire.' I felt a clamminess as we shook hands.

'Hello, Kate. A change to see you somewhere other than a picture gallery.' William moved towards the chair like a man carrying a burden. I rang the bell for tea, but William's pinched look prompted me to offer whisky, which he gladly accepted. I was curious to know why a brewery chairman needed a private investigator.

As William sipped his whisky, he talked about the funeral and his old schoolfriend. I sympathised, saying how sad to have a death in April when spring bursts into life.

After Mrs Sugden had settled the driver in the kitchen, she brought tea, sandwiches and cakes.

As pre-arranged, after setting down the tray, Mrs Sugden said, 'Oh and here's the diary, madam.'

'Thank you, Mrs Sugden.'

My visitor did not hurry to the point. After talking about his boyhood friend, he enlightened me about this morning's weather, and the state of the roads.

It was time to give William an opening, and a little prompt. I asked did he still play an active part in the running of the brewery, adding that my assistant sang the praises of Barleycorn's Nut Brown ale.

William came to life, telling me about working with his head brewer on a new beer that would top the lot. 'We'll be flooded with orders.'

I congratulated him. At a time when so many companies were laying off workers, here was a man providing employment.

After a moment or two of hearing more about the new brew, I realised that he was reluctant to tell me just why he was here. Perhaps I was on the wrong tack. Did Eleanor want to buy back her painting? Had I been crossed off the list for the garden party?

There was nothing for it but to stop dancing around the maypole. Just as I was about to form the direct question, he crept up on his topic.

'Eleanor and I were chatting the other day, and she gave me your card.'

This was not a moment to let slip. 'Eleanor believes you need an investigator. Do you think so too, William?'

'I wouldn't go as far as that.'

'What then?'

I waited until he filled the silence. 'As often happens, you hear of a person once, meet that person, and hear more about them. People have very good words to say about you, Kate.'

'I'm glad to hear it.'

'You've a right good reputation for discretion, for tackling all sorts of tricky business. My insurance agent mentioned you as having a chap on your books who looks into the business side of things.'

'Mr Sykes, Jim Sykes.'

William snapped his fingers. 'That's the fellow my agent mentioned.' He set his whisky aside for a moment to take a gulp of black tea. Dry throat, clammy skin, unhealthy colour. Here was a man feeling his age, with a wife in her thirties, something going wrong in his business, and suffering from a bout of jaundice.

If William Lofthouse worried himself to death, Eleanor may shortly become an independent and wealthy woman, never having to think twice about the price of oil paints.

'How may our agency help you?' I asked.

'The business is going through an uneven patch, let's say. It's worrying but these things happen. We have some good people working for us, and I ought to know. I was brought up to it. There's nothing I haven't done. I shovelled barley into the kiln during school hols, groomed the horses, shadowed the head brewer. Father encouraged me, showed me how to do every job. Mother didn't like it. A brewery can be a dangerous place.'

I perked up at the word dangerous, but he did not expand. 'What exactly has gone wrong?'

'If you blink in this business, something goes wrong. I took time off to be with Eleanor after our marriage. She wanted to get to know the area and see some of the places I went as a boy, and then she was making changes in the house and I enjoyed being with her. There was a bit of a muddle in the accounts. The accountant was a young man when he started working for my father. Out of decency, I had to wait until he came to me and said he planned to retire.'

A litany of minor business mishaps followed. William went on to explain that his secretary attended a lecture by a know-it-all businessman. 'She came in the next day, after listening to this fellow, still wet behind his ears, and told me that we needed an outside eye on our doings.'

'You have a nephew in the business I believe.'

'That's right. James is my right-hand man. He's away in Germany, picking up new ideas from the brewers there.'

'When will James return?'

'There's the question. In our trade, we send our youngsters to learn from another brewer. James had all that, years ago, in his twenties, at the Anchor Brewery in Southwark.'

He leaned forward, his frown giving him a slightly anxious look. 'He ought to have been back a month ago. He ought to be with me at the Barleycorn helm by now but he's flitting about Germany; Dortmund, Münster, Munich. Tells me we have to keep up with the times and that we have a thing or two to learn. He has written about his big plans for when he returns. But it's him I want back. Now letters have stopped. We get a weekly postcard.'

There was yearning in William's voice when he spoke of James. A prodigal son situation?

'You miss James.' I smiled. 'I won't promise to go to Germany and bring him back, but if you give me his itinerary, I'll see what I can find out. Discreetly, of course. I have contacts there.'

He smiled back. 'Thank you but I don't want to check up on him. I don't mind if he's taken up with a German lass, as long as he brings her back here.'

Until that moment, I was finding it hard to grasp just what William wanted from me, thinking that perhaps he was one of those men who likes to work with chaps. He had perked up at the mention of Jim Sykes.

Now I realised that there was something else going on. The way he moved betrayed him. He shifted his position in the chair, pressing his hands on the chair arms. It was one of those sudden insights that could be wildly wrong.

He has lost his grip, lost his confidence. Expecting James to take over, William had been winding down, got into a bit of a mess, and was embarrassed about it.

'You want everything to be ship-shape for when James returns?'

'Just so, Kate.'

'Then Jim Sykes is the man for the job.'

'Yes, I should like him to come out and see us. What will his daily rate set me back?'

Being used to blunt Yorkshiremen coming straight to the point, I told him. He did not blanch.

'It'll be worth it to me. When could he start?'

I reached for the diary. 'The timing is perfect. Mr Sykes could start on Monday. We would send a letter of engagement with our terms. I'm sure you and Mr Sykes will pinpoint where he may be most helpful to you.'

I hoped Sykes would be more successful in this regard than I had been so far.

'So, what are the terms, Kate?'

'The daily rate, based on an eight-hour day, travel and accommodation and necessary disbursements. Any additional outside expenses incurred in connection with the assignment, would be payable at the rate charged to our agency by a third party. We work with an excellent solicitor.'

'Hadn't thought of that sort of malarkey, just a general tidying up operation.'

'That would be your choice to be made at the time. Your company has a good name and a reputation to protect. Now, will you arrange accommodation for Mr Sykes, or shall we?'

'I'll book him into the Falcon. It's our own public house, much favoured by commercial travellers. It's on the town square, brewery right behind it.'

'And motoring expenses, unless you have a rail service?'

'We do but it's being run down. Blighters intend to close it, except for freight.'

'Then there will be travelling time above thirty miles, and petrol.'

'You drive a hard bargain, a woman after my own heart!' He reached for an iced bun and popped it into his mouth.

'The letter, in duplicate for signature, will be in the post today. I'm sure Mr Sykes will have everything in order very soon.'

'That's reassuring.' He rose to go. 'Oh, and Kate, perhaps you and Mr Sykes would like to come over if you can spare the time on Friday afternoon. You could take a look at the brewery. We've a lad coming out of his cooper's apprenticeship, so there'll be a trussing and a bit of a do.'

'Cooper—that's a barrel maker? But what's a trussing?'

'Ah, you'll have to wait and see.'

I walked him into the hall. 'Will Eleanor be there?'

'She hasn't said. But if you do see Eleanor, she may bend your ear about our wages clerk, Ruth Parnaby. Miss Parnaby won the Brewery Queen of the North Riding contest. You'll have heard of it.'

'How exciting! I read about it in the local paper. She will be a sort of ambassadress for your industry?'

'So I understand. The idea came from some of the bigger brewers in the North, starting on the other side of the Pennines. Good luck to them, I thought. That won't reach Masham.'

'But it has?'

He sighed. 'The local papers invited young women with a connection to the industry to send in their pictures. Readers voted as to which one went forward. Long story short, our wages clerk—good brass poured into her training and qualifications—suddenly finds herself Brewery Queen of the North Riding, more absent from work than present. You could have knocked me down with a stick of liquorice.'

'Did you know she'd entered the contest?'

'I wasn't consulted. Nor was her father, our head cooper. Girls these days, they dress like film stars and do as they please. Eleanor is cock-a-hoop about it.'

It is sometimes necessary to state the obvious. 'You're not cock-a-hoop?'

'No disrespect to your sex, Kate.' He sighed and shook his head. 'Four years ago, I asked the headmaster who was his best lad among the school leavers. He said his best lad was a lass. Ruth Parnaby. She should have gone to the grammar school, but her father wouldn't hear of it. Against my better judgement, I took her on. Should've known it would end in marriage or some sort of goings on. She's too good-looking.'

'How long will she reign as North Riding Brewery Queen?'

He gave a bitter chuckle. 'A year and a day would you believe? Some people have stopped believing in the real world. Think they live in a fairy tale.'

'I'm sure it will be manageable.'

'That's what my wife claims. Says it will be good for business. What's more, she wants Miss Parnaby to have a chaperone and move out of the family home.'

'I can understand the chaperone part, but why move away from home?'

'Oh, her father, Slater Parnaby. He is an odd man but the stories about him murdering his wife were discredited years ago. And I have no grounds for supposing that Slater knocks his youngsters about. Neither Ruth nor her brother George ever come into work with a black eye.'

As the car drove off, I wondered whether Eleanor had given William my card for an entirely different reason than muddles at the brewery and an errant nephew.

Of course, that nephew would be near Eleanor's age. That thought set off a whole new line of possibilities about why James Lofthouse may be staying away. James and Eleanor had fallen in love.

Before becoming an investigator, I never attached underhand or wicked motives to people. Now the thought fleetingly crossed my mind that William's anxiety about his business combined with his clammy skin and touch of jaundice might be a result of Eleanor fiddling the books and slowly poisoning her husband before James returned from Germany. I immediately felt ashamed at such a melodramatic thought. Eleanor was genuinely fond of William, perhaps even in love with him. Put those thoughts aside, I told myself. Stick to business.

But what was the business? There was something William was deliberately holding back or did not want to face.

Sykes and I would certainly attend the apprentice's trussing. I wanted to know what was really going on in Masham.

Chapter Two

George Parnaby waited in the wood stores among the stacks of new cask-staves that he'd brought down yesterday from the drying loft. He breathed in the familiar smell of the wood that had come all the way from Quebec. Wood never hurt anyone. Wood had no temper. Wood had no vicious streak.

The trussing wouldn't last long. The other coopers, Tim and old Barney, they'd see to that. They would make sure George came out in one piece. They had cleared a space in the cooperage, pushing trestles and saw-horses against the far wall. Each man's saws, planes and hammers hung in their proper places. Chairs and bar stools were set out for the spectators who might need to sit down. They'd swept the floor. That was usually George's job, the apprentice's job. Who'd do it now, he wondered? Would they take turns sweeping? If he had courage, he would say to his old man, I'm a cooper now, like you. The old man would laugh.

George heard the voices as people arrived. Why did they come? It was no one's business but his that this initiation had to happen. They were laughing and talking, waiting for the show to begin. I'm not a show, George said to himself. I'm not a circus animal. He wanted to yell at them. Go away, the lot of you.

He closed his eyes, breathing in the mellow smell of wood, planks and sawdust shavings. You are in a forest, he told himself. Shut your eyes. Go to the forest in Quebec. When your eyes open, you will have a bad dream of a trussing with people staring. Then you can be in the forest again.

Old Barney had said, 'It's nothing. Everyone goes through it. You'll look back and wonder what all the fuss was about.'

George pressed his hand on his chest, to slow his heart. He ran his tongue around dry lips. Looking at himself in the cracked mirror, he smoothed his hair. He admired his shirt, ironed by his sister Ruth the night before. 'This is your big day,' she whispered. 'I have my start as brewery queen, now you'll have yours. Our new beginning.'

This morning, when George put on his clean shirt, the old man sneered. 'You're not off to a wedding.' And then he laughed his nasty laugh, which was the only laugh he had.

As George waited, something was happening in his head, a thump, thumping at the front of his skull. He listened to people coming into the workshop, footsteps and low voices.

He made himself look through the crack in the door. The audience made a horseshoe-shape at the far end of the room, so many of them, too many. 'Don't come, Ruth,' George willed. 'Don't come, don't watch.' The feeling came to him, like a blow in his solar plexus. George had imagined something like a trophy, or a badge, now he knew that it would not be like that at all. He should have tried harder to find out what was going to happen at this trussing.

Suddenly, the audience cheered. Why?

George realised that Barney was speaking to the crowd that had come to ogle, that's why they cheered. Barney always stole the show at the Christmas pantomime. He'd played the bailiff in *Mother Goose*, wearing a yellow and purple jacket, red trousers, and a collapsible hat. Here Barney was, in well-worn trousers, old jersey and leather apron. But because Barney was Barney, master of ceremonies, the watchers thought they were in the upstairs room at the Town Hall, expecting a jolly time.

That's it, George told himself. I am playing a part. My show won't last as long as *Mother Goose*.

Through the partition wall, George listened to the bouncing hailstones of Barney's words.

'Cooperage—fine and ancient trade—long line of craftsmen—apprentice George Parnaby—apprenticed to his father, Slater Parnaby, also known as Sniffer.'

At the nickname 'Sniffer', a single cheer rose from the audience, amid many boos. The old man was cast as pantomime villain.

Barney had not quite finished. He always went on too long.

'. . . final ceremony—George's glorious initiation—the Society of Coopers—trussing in his own barrel, to complete his apprenticeship.'

George heard his own beautifully crafted cask being rolled across the floor, now knowing it would be placed where the watchers would have the best view.

Everyone went quiet.

In they came to fetch him, Barney pulling a funny face, soft Tim with an apologetic smile, and the old man, already in his cups, with that gleam of spite George knew so well.

George moved towards them, wanting it to be over and done with, wanting to show them that it didn't take three of them to fetch him.

The old man scoffed. 'Thick as two short planks. He knows nowt. You don't walk. We carry you in.'

Before he knew it, Tim took hold of his ankles. Barney placed his big hands under George's back. The old man lifted him by the shoulder so suddenly his head dropped back. Being shorter than the other two men, Dad held him in a way that made George's head point at the floor, cricking his neck. George remembered carrying grandma's coffin last year. No one will bear me along like this until I'm dead, he told himself.

They carried him into the cooperage, towards the cask he had made.

A cheer went up from the audience.

A stink rose up to meet George, like fox droppings, like rotten eggs, like old yeast. At the last second, as he thought he would go headfirst, they righted him. Feet in the cask, he felt himself being squashed into stinking sludge. Out came their hammers, hammering around the top edge of the barrel, securing the iron ring encasing stakes of curved wood. George wanted to cover his ears with his hands, but his hands were trapped.

At him they came, their hands full of filth, spreading it over his neck and face, and hair, every part they could reach. He wanted to cry for the good shirt, for Ruth's ironing, for his own stupidity. From a rusty can, someone poured smelly water on his head. It ran icily down the back of his neck. He closed his eyes and mouth, but the taste of sugar kissed his lips. What was it? He opened his eyes. Someone split a pillow. Feathers tumbled onto him, sticking to the sugar on his skin and clothes. Something like a muddy piece of carpet was shoved down the front of him.

He blinked and looked out at them. Faces, laughing, smiling, but not all. Richard, George's school pal, was there. He had that look, like when he fell off that high wall and was trying not to cry. There was Ruth, ready to pounce, ready to rescue him. He stared to tell her no. No, no. It would be a worse humiliation to have his sister interfere.

Two hands on his skull pushed him down. He was deep inside the barrel, feathers in his mouth, up his nose, vomit at the back of his throat. He could no longer see or hear.

He felt the lurch as the barrel was tipped and began to roll across the floor

Chapter Three

So, this was the trussing. It made me feel sick to watch. I felt a creeping horror, particularly at the brutality of the father. William had pointed him out earlier, putting his age at forty, looking sixty. Slater Parnaby's thinning hair had turned grey and his skin was lined. He wore an open-neck shirt under bib and braces overalls, topped with a sagging woolly jumper. He moved like a boxer, light on his feet.

I glanced at my three companions. Our client, William Lofthouse, was to my left, the local police sergeant to my right, and next to the sergeant, Jim Sykes. They watched without turning a hair. William looked slightly amused. The sergeant saw my shock. He whispered, 'It doesn't last long.'

'This is common assault. If you saw it on the street, you would arrest them.'

'Ah, but it's not on the street. We're on private property.' He turned to Sykes, 'No worse than the initiation for police cadets, eh Mr Sykes?'

William bent down and whispered in my ear in a way that made me want to kick him in the shins. 'It's tradition, Kate. Young George won't be accepted into the Society of Coopers without his trussing.'

'He's just a boy!' The poor lad had looked so smart, and so puzzled, when the three men carried him in.

'It's nearly done,' William said. 'They'll roll the barrel back into the woodshed and he'll come out smiling.'

From the other side, Sergeant Moon also intended to keep me informed. 'There's Slater Parnaby's daughter,' he said quietly, 'Ruth Parnaby, brewery queen.'

I watched Ruth as she watched her father and the two other coopers rolling the barrel back towards the woodshed. They came to a stop, Slater Parnaby produced its lid. Spitting nails into his hand, he took a hammer from his pocket and leaned down, ready to knock in a nail, like a man closing a coffin.

A woman hooted, 'Slater's turning his lad into Houdini!'

The other two workmen paused, as if unsure what to do. Unless they were feigning, this was not part of the proceedings. How long would this go on?

As her father hit the first nail, Ruth stepped forward, whipping the hammer from his hand. Bobbing down, she used her foot and the hammer to force the lid from the barrel.

A breathless silence fell. Ruth raised the lid. Holding it like a shield, she turned to the audience. 'If there'd been a brewery queen in the fourteenth century, at the very first trussing, she would have had to play a part, and so must I!'

Tension evaporated. There were cheers as the barrel was righted. The men lifted George from it and tossed him in the air, once, twice, thrice.

But there had been a look of rage on the face of Slater Parnaby when Ruth thwarted him.

William was applauding. 'Now what do you think to it, Kate?'

'Barbaric.'

After being cramped in the barrel, it took George a moment to find his balance. One of the men produced a cloth and wiped his face. As the applause continued, he was urged to take a bow.

Looking bewildered, he forced a smile.

He was patted on the back, his filthy hands squeezed and shaken in congratulation.

The man who had spoken at the beginning stepped forward, inviting spectators into the bar of the Falcon for a pint on the house, thanks to Mr Lofthouse.

People began to disperse, for the promised glass of beer.

William and Sergeant Moon led Sykes and me up a flight of stairs, through a door and along a corridor. William opened another door and we found ourselves in the Falcon, in a large comfortable lounge. Across the bar, I could see another room, the snug. Several of the women from the trussing audience were already in there, deep in conversation. My side of the bar was entirely male.

'What will you try, Kate?' William asked.

Since the only title I could remember was Nut Brown ale, I asked for that.

William congratulated me on my good taste, and asked for a lady's glass, along with his order for Sykes and the police sergeant.

William excused himself for a moment while the beer was being drawn, made his way to the feathered and still bewildered young George. William shook George's hand, had a few words, and slipped him a brown envelope.

He left George looking still bewildered, but the lad drew back his shoulders and forced what's called a brave look on his face. In his case, the mask was a mixture of seeming pleasantness and miserable resignation.

Sykes also noticed this. 'The lad's stuck that look on his face like the froth to a glass of best bitter.'

When William came back, and we sat at a table with our drinks, I said to him, 'Did you ask Eleanor to come to the trussing?'

'Oh?' He looked up, mid-sip, a moustache of froth on his lips. 'She decided not to.'

It did not surprise me that Eleanor decided against watching this throwback of a spectacle.

'William, when you came to see me, you said that Eleanor believed that your brewery queen Ruth Parnaby ought to move out of the family home, and that she should have a chaperone. I can see why. The father is a sadist. According to what you told me, her mother is dead or missing. Eleanor is right.'

William was taken aback. 'She is eighteen,' he protested. He did that blustering thing some men do when they want a woman to believe she has entirely misunderstood. 'Kate, you saw Ruth Parnaby.' He lowered his voice as if what followed must be shameful. 'She stood up for George in public. Engaging a chaperone would be a waste of brass on a girl like her. Everybody knows she can stick up for herself. If need be, my wife or my secretary will accompany her to these events. But if you're volunteering?'

'William, I am not a volunteer. I run a business, just as you do.'

We were interrupted when a rumpus blew up at the bar. A loud voice said, 'Keep your snitch out, Joe Finch, before I flatten your ugly mug.'

A waiter called, 'Order, order! Ladies present!'

The room went silent, except for two men, facing up to each other. Slater Parnaby's fists clenched. The other man, who wore a drayman's uniform, rocked on the balls of his feet. The drayman's voice was indignant. 'All I'm saying is George needs a bath and his hand bandaging. My missus has his clean clobber ready.'

Slater Parnaby squared up to the drayman. 'I'll clean clobber you!'

Before either man had time to land a punch, both Sergeant Moon and Sykes were on their feet. For the first time, I grasped the meaning of the word 'collared'. The sergeant grabbed Parnaby, Sykes took Finch. Seconds later, they were through the door. A short quietness lasted, and then conversation resumed.

Sykes and the sergeant came back to our table.

William looked suddenly drained of energy. Speaking seemed an effort. 'Thanks, chaps. I would have had to sack them for fighting on works' premises. Two good men, Slater and Joe. Well, good at their jobs. I can't speak for their private lives. I'll send for them tomorrow and dock their wages.'

'You have a lot to put up with, William.'

William said, 'You were a nurse, Kate?'

'During the war, in the Voluntary Aid Detachment.'

'I'm under the doctor, for a touch of jaundice. Eleanor is taking care of me. I'll be back to my old self before long.'

I put my hand on his. 'Jim Sykes will be with you on Monday.' I stopped myself from saying that everything would be all right which, as things turned out, was just as well.

Sykes and I walked across the town square towards the car, ready for the journey home.

'Mr Sykes?'

'Mrs Shackleton?'

'How did you and Sergeant Moon know to jump in so quickly, before the fight started?'

'Slater Parnaby turned his empty glass upside down on the bar.'

'I'm no wiser.'

'It means he wants a fight. Might be with a particular person, or just a fight.'

Chapter Four

Ruth lay on the lumpy mattress, desperately wanting to sleep. The old man rolled in drunk. He stumbled about, making himself a sandwich, arguing with the cheese. As long as he didn't drag her from bed to do it, she didn't care. George had gone out with his mates, celebrating the end of his apprenticeship.

Even though her gran was dead, Ruth tried to keep to her own side of the bed, not slide into the centre where Gran always ended up. The sheet and pillowcase smelled of soap and had blown in the wind on the line. She had bathed with carbolic soap, washed her hair, brushed her teeth with salt and polished them with soot. So why did that stench of the trussing still fill her nose, throat, behind her eyes? The smell of whatever filth they found to daub on George would never leave her.

Downstairs, the old man poked the fire.

Her gran once said they should make allowances for their father and support him in his ambitions. Ruth understood, or thought she understood. A long time ago, when she was tiny, he carried her on his shoulders, her cheek against his hair. They walked to where a cottage once stood, to look for something among bits of rubble and tufts of grass.

She was too little to know what she was searching for and brought buttercups to her dad. He said that at least she tried, and the two of them would find gold one day. On that day they would have a lump sum. A person needed a lump sum to set up in business. No one ever made money working for someone else. Her dad called Mam useless at looking and called George lazy. What she found out later was that a chest of gold coins had been found in the thatch of one of the cottages. Their dad felt sure they would find a few coins if they looked hard enough.

He took them back again and again, making them walk, making them search the grass for gold.

George would not thank her for what she did today at the trussing, his sister coming to the rescue. The old man pretended it was a joke, a put-up job, but he would get back at her in his own sweet time for preventing him from tapping nails into the barrel.

She tried to make plans. There would come a day when she would call for her mother in a taxi. The plan had always been for the three of them. Mam, George, Ruth. When they made the plan, it seemed so clear. George would finish his apprenticeship and get another job, where the old man would never find them. She would do the same. That would not be easy. She knew that now, from the out-of-work men who came calling at the Barleycorn, asking for a job, any job.

It might be one more year, a year of being queen of the North Riding, before the three of them could escape. If she won the next round of the contest, Brewery Queen of all Yorkshire, there would be money in it. The old man knew that too. He was playing cagey. 'You'll have a lump sum, Ruth. We've never had a lump sum.'

Ruth had to think quickly. 'It won't come to me until I'm twenty-one.'

'It'll come to me then, to keep for you, to invest in a nice little business.'

Gran and Dad used to talk quietly, in a low whispering when they wanted no one to hear. But the whispering couldn't last because Gran needed him to speak up. Their voices floated up through the floorboards. He talked to Gran now, but the only voice Ruth heard was his. Buried deep in the churchyard, Gran wouldn't hear him, or would she?

The old man told his dead mother about his plans. 'I've made notes. A corner newsagent's shop, when I have the capital. That would do me nicely, no perishables. There's a good mark up on sweets and cigarettes. I've looked into it. George is an early riser. He's hopeless now but he has the makings of a man. He could see to the papers before work. Ruth will do the books.'

Ruth did not want to hear, did not want to listen, but she needed to listen. What were the makings of a man? She did not want George to have such makings.

He was still rambling about George. 'Ah keep him all these years and soon as he's out of his time, he'll be off and wed.'

Sometimes he acted as if Gran was sitting there, disagreeing with him. He would argue with her. 'Oh, he will. He'll stay with his dad and his old gran. He would never part from Ruth. She's the one to watch. She'll look to get her hooks into some rich man. As long as she knows which side her bread is buttered and realises no one ever made money working for a boss.'

Shut up, shut up, Ruth said to them without a sound. She looked at the clock. Ten o'clock. George wouldn't be long. The old man was waiting because Mr Lofthouse had given George money.

The door opened.

The old man put on a cheery voice. 'Here he is, my lad, out of his time.'

'Hey-up,' George said.

'So, where's my share?'

Ruth felt her body tense, all her muscles tighten, so much that her arms and shoulders began to ache.

'It's my money, Dad. I'm keeping it.'

A chair scraped. A chair fell. 'Yer bugger, hand it over. As long as yer under this roof you tip up.'

Don't answer, George, she willed him. But he did.

'I treated mi mates and they treated me.'

'And did you tell your mates you're tied to your sister's apron strings?'

Keep quiet, George.

'Oh, I don't think our Ruth will be wearing aprons, not her, not now.'

'Hand it over. Hand over a quid. You're not too old that I can't take my belt to you. You wouldn't be a cooper if not for me.'

He didn't want to be a cooper and you knew it, Ruth said to him, but in her head. She waited for George to ignore him. The only way to deal with the old man is to keep quiet until the madness passes. There are some people there's no arguing with.

George answered back. 'Touch me, or touch Ruth, and I'll kill you.'

The old man laughed.

Ruth wanted to get up, she wanted to run downstairs, she needed to do something. This was all because of the lid of the barrel, the hammer, the nails, and her stepping up and now George not backing down. A sick feeling came over her as she listened to the blows.

A sound from George. Something knocked over. The old man groaned. George had never hit back before. The outside door slammed.

By the time Ruth went to the window, George was gone.

She lay there, still, pretending sleep, dropping off, dreaming she heard her dead grandma on the stairs. Dreaming her smell, of rancid butter. Dreaming the poke in the throat, reckoning always to know when Ruth was not asleep.

It was the middle of that night when George came back. Ruth heard the window open. The old man, snoring in the next room, would have locked the door against him.

She went to the landing, avoiding the boards that creaked, and saw George at the bottom of the stairs. He turned round and went back down. Haversack on the table, he put in a pair of socks.

'Where are you going?'

'Will you get my stuff from the drawer? He has a skin on, he won't wake if you tread softly.'

The old man snored like a train. She did as George asked, treading softly. He is leaving. She knew this would come.

Quiet as a ghost, she carried George's few belongings in her arms, to the bottom of the stairs. He pushed them in his haversack. 'I won't be back this time.'

'Have you got your indentures?' she whispered.

He tapped his pocket. 'I'll find a job.' He paused. 'Tell them at work, I'm sorry.' Straightaway, he changed his mind. 'Best say nothing. Keep out of it.'

'Where will you go?'

'I'm thinking about it.'

'Go to Richard's or go next door.'

'And give the old man another reason to thump Joe Finch?'

Ruth guessed there were other reasons why the old man hated Joe Finch, but she was not able to fathom them. 'Night, night, George. Sleep tight, don't let the bugs bite.'

'You should go too.'

'Don't worry about me. The old man knows I'm the goose that will lay the golden egg.'

Ruth went to the window. George turned to wave, and then made a writing motion with his raised hand.

She watched her brother cycle into darkness. George believed he was going somewhere. Ruth knew that he would sleep at his schoolfriend Richard's house tonight, and perhaps the night after. He would be back at work on Monday, and home on Monday evening.

Chapter Five

The café on Ripon Marketplace is renowned for its delicious curd tart and homemade ice cream. Eleanor had suggested that she and I meet for afternoon tea on the Saturday after the trussing. She was already seated at a table when I arrived. She waved and I went to join her.

Eleanor was wearing a voluminous silk dress in purple and orange, leaving me feeling quite tame in my aquamarine dress and jacket.

'Kate, you look so elegant,' she said. 'Now I feel like a circus elephant.'

I sat down. 'Nonsense! You are the bird of paradise that rides on the elephant's back.'

She smiled. 'I've been to buy paints. There are colours that I love but for this country will never need, not unless someone asks me to paint a portrait of their Clarice Cliff tea service.'

The waitress had already brought the menu. I expected we would order afternoon tea but when Eleanor said she wanted egg and chips, I decided to join her. I did order curd tart and ice cream, just in case they ran out. When our order came, Eleanor asked for vinegar. She lathered her chips in salt and vinegar. 'It's a bit of a craving just now.' She pulled a face. 'I'll take the risk of having us barred from this bastion of gentility.'

'Your chips and salt and vinegar craving would be entirely normal if you'd order fish instead of egg.'

'It has to be egg.'

I had already noticed a bump in her dress. 'Is this your way of telling me good news?'

She smiled. 'I suppose it is.'

'Then congratulations!'

'Thank you.'

It was not until the last spoonful of ice cream that Eleanor said, 'I do hope my William and your Mr Sykes hit it off and that William will confide in him. I know things are going wrong at the brewery, but the poor dear doesn't want to talk about it, or face up to it.'

She was in need of reassurance. 'Jim Sykes and William got on very well at the trussing. I'm sure whatever is wrong, Sykes will find a way to make it right.'

'The troubles have all blown up recently, Kate. It's as if I came on the scene and turned into the brewery jinx.'

'It isn't you, Eleanor. Whatever is wrong is to do with the business. Jim Sykes will get to the bottom of it.'

Chapter Six

~

When he had come to Masham with Mrs Shackleton for the trussing at Barleycorn Brewery, there had been no time for Jim Sykes to explore the town. On Monday morning, arriving deliberately early for his 10 a.m. starting time, Sykes left his suitcase at the Falcon, and took a walkabout.

Truth to tell, he felt a little self-conscious. He had not felt so self-conscious since his mother sent him to his first day at work wearing short trousers.

It was all his wife's fault that he was kitted out in a new suit. Rosie had gone back to working in tailoring, at Montague Burtons. She said that if Jim did not invest in a new suit, she would make one for him. It would not be black, she said. He needed brightening up.

Sykes had no intention of wearing a suit made by his wife. He went to his old tailor, who in-between times had spent a year in America and come back with ideas. The result was very smart, the tailor assured him, beige with chalk stripes, high-waisted trousers, five-button waistcoat and a long wide shouldered jacket nipped in at the waist.

Now Sykes had the uneasy feeling that he had swapped his plainclothes policeman look for the American gangster look. He must brave it out.

Mrs Shackleton had described Masham town square as Georgian and well laid out. To Sykes's eyes, this was a quiet place, that may or may not come to life on market days. He found the war memorial, read the names, and felt that surge of sorrow and helpless rage at the loss of so many lives.

He located the police station and the church. Looking twice at the Town Hall, he supposed it would do well enough for a town this size, but it was a poor specimen compared with the grand town halls of the West Riding.

Sykes had spoken to the assessor at North Riding Assurance, to glean some background information on the brewery. The assessor told him that the brewery accounts people used ancient adding machines that would not look out of place in a railway signal box. Having an entrepreneurial streak, Sykes had brought with him half a dozen shiny brown Bakelite adding machines, on sale or return from a salesman friend. Spotting Masham's stationery shop on Park Square, he made a mental note to call on them, in case he did not make a sale at the brewery.

When investigating, there could be an advantage in paying a courtesy call on the local constabulary, but Sykes and Sergeant Moon were already on good terms from their joint chucking out of troublemakers at the Falcon on the night of the trussing. Sykes stepped in to say hello. As luck would have it, the sergeant was on duty. He was pinning a poster on the information board, giving the names of Urban District Council members and dates of their meetings. Sykes gave a little smile. Men on the force always liked to refer complainants to the right person and save themselves the paperwork.

'Good morning, Sergeant.'

'You're an early bird, Mr Sykes.'

'Looking for the best place to have breakfast.'

'Café, across and on your left.'

'Thanks.'

'Oh and good luck at the brewery. Let me know if you have any bother.'

They laughed. The sergeant knew full well that Sykes could handle his own bother.

Sykes finished his breakfast, checked his watch and made his way to the brewery, keeping its high tower in view. Drawing closer, he savoured the aroma of malt and hops. Not a bad way for workers to start a day.

He and Mrs Shackleton had entered the brewery from the Falcon, through the connecting door. Now he entered from the other side of the building, through a pair of large iron gates into the cobbled yard. He saw that the building, which might have been adapted from some other use, had a T-shape layout. A four-storey tower with hoist stood at the junction of the T, with buildings on either side. The structure had been added to over the years. There were yards and a straggle of buildings, some more like sheds. One was stacked with timber. Another contained old barrels in a kind of iron cradle. He could smell hay and horses.

The man who called a greeting and came towards Sykes with a bounce in his step, was Joe Finch, whose collar Sykes had grabbed after the trussing, when he and Sergeant Moon stopped the fight between Finch and Slater Parnaby.

Finch wore an open-neck shirt, bib and braces and long wellington boots.

'Mr Sykes?'

'That's me.'

'Joe Finch, at your service. Mr Lofthouse's secretary asked me to look out for you, and to show you round. Mr Lofthouse invites you to the tasting.' He glanced at the clock above the door. 'We're early, so would you like a look round?'

Sykes agreed that he would. A tour of the brewery would give him a feeling for the place.

'Follow me!'

On the right, steps led down from the reception area. His guide led Sykes to the left, through a door into a room high as some cathedrals, with iron and brass balustrading around galleries, and decorative spiral staircases. Someone was hosing down the floor.

'It's ninety percent heaving, shifting, cleaning, and delivering, and ten percent brewing,' Finch told him. In the next room, Finch pointed out a row of half a dozen casks of different sizes. 'We don't know what our new brew will be called, or when it will be on sale. You'll be tasting this at ten o'clock.'

'You're very open about all this, Mr Finch. I might be a competitor, here to learn your secrets.'

Finch laughed this off. 'Even if someone else reproduced it exactly, it wouldn't be the same. Different water, see. We have our own bore hole. And no one would buy just the same barley, because ours comes from local farmers.'

Whatever shenanigans might be going on in the offices—and Sykes felt sure he would not otherwise have been called in—the work of the brewery seemed to him to be carried on with a serious efficiency.

Finch led him past iron staircases, making way for a fellow carrying a sack, and finally came out through a door on the left into another cobbled yard. 'We'll start at the stables.'

'What's your job then, Mr Finch?'

Finch began to talk in the way of someone who lives alone, whose mouth bursts with words that demand to be said and repeated. 'I'm a drayman, but if you ask why I'm not dressed accordingly, I'll tell you it's because we deliver twice a week. My pal is out today. On Friday I'll be delivering at every watering hole between here and Ripon.'

Finch obliged Sykes by naming every hamlet and pub. 'The rest of the time, we muck in.'

The smell of horses and hay overtook the scent of hops and malt. The row of stalls was empty, save for two great shire horses with white fetlocks and white nose markings. Turn by turn, Finch patted their necks and stroked them. 'Cleopatra and Caesar. We work through the alphabet for the naming of the pairs. I'll be taking these beauties out to the field. They won't be needed until Friday.' He pointed out a 'hospital' stall where a sick horse could be isolated and treated, and a wide gallery over the stalls for storing forage.

From the stall next to the shire horses, a brown and white Shetland pony trotted out. Sykes smiled. 'He doesn't look up to pulling a dray.'

'Billy's mine. Billy Boy. He was in a poor way when I bought him off a horse dealer. He was matted, needed shoeing, been left in the cold and wet to fend for hisself, lost his sight in one eye. Look at him now!'

Sykes obliged. 'He's a bonny fellow, beautifully groomed.'

'He's come along a treat. Nobody bothers if I fetch him across and he has a share of fodder. The dealer I bought him from is back in the area, not far from here. He'll be after reclaiming Billy if he sees what I've turned him into. I'm not taking that chance.'

Sykes thought the bobbies round here must like their posting. An upsurge in crime would occur only if a horse dealer stole back a pony.

'You love your horses, Joe.'

'I was brought up to it. Hoss boy in the East Riding, till us and us horses was interrupted by the war. We're lucky to have these shires.'

Finch remembered that he was meant to be showing Sykes the brewery. They went back inside.

Sykes's new shoes played a tune on the iron staircase

Finch continued his monologue. 'It all works on gravity.' They passed men shovelling barley into a kiln, a mash tun where two men stirred milled and malted barley into liquor, and a shining giant copper that Finch warned him was too hot to touch.

'Old mate of mine, Jack Tickler, a bit of a nutter, he'd taken a drop too much to drink, took it into his head to climb up and walk round the ledge. Fell in. All we found when everything cooled down was the bits of metal from his bib and braces.'

Sykes changed his mind about practised efficiency. 'Anything else I should be careful of?'

'Only one man goes in the mill room. Dust from malted barley is inflammable. If he smokes, he might ignite the dust and set fire to hisself. I've seen it happen.'

'Right.'

He led Sykes back down the stairs to the reception area. 'Oh, and don't go down them steps.'

'Why's that?'

'It's the fermentation room. Five minutes in there and your worldly worries will be over.'

'But you'll keep it locked?'

'No need for that. Everybody knows.'

Sykes felt glad that he would be confined to the offices, which Finch pointed out in a diffident way, as if offices were of no account. He then led Sykes to the brewers' room.

William Lofthouse and three other men stood around a table. Today, Mr Lofthouse looked sprightly, and as cheerful as a boy expecting birthday gifts. He greeted Sykes and introduced him to the head brewer and the assistant brewer, both wearing white coats. 'And Slater Parnaby you met on Friday.' Friday night's fight was forgotten. Today, Parnaby was introduced as 'the best nose in the business'.

The men at the table shifted to make room for Sykes.

'Well, gentlemen. Let us begin.' Lofthouse turned to Sykes. 'This will be our finest brew.'

The assistant brewer produced five V-shaped champagne glasses.

The head brewer drew the first glass. He placed a glass under the barrel tap and drew the beer. He examined the dull liquid, holding it to the light. He frowned, sniffed and shook his head.

Reluctantly, he took a sip and spat into a bowl. A long silence held. With automatic movements, as if he knew not what else to do, the brewer half-filled four more glasses.

Sykes wondered if this might be some practical joke being played on him, the stranger. The look on Lofthouse's face told him this was not so.

Lofthouse lifted his glass, looked carefully, sniffed, tasted and spat, before seeming to explode. 'What the hell has gone wrong?'

Lofthouse looked to the head brewer.

'I don't know.' The man looked shocked. 'It's been on track since the green beer tasting.

Parnaby sniffed but did not taste. 'Someone's been at it. It's sabotage, that's what it is.'

The firkin, and remaining casks of new beer, were taken into the yard and drained. It was Parnaby who identified the reason for the spoilage. Rotten wood and bits of debris had been inserted into each cask. Parnaby had no doubt about the perpetrator. 'It's Finch. He's a cheating, thieving, jumped-up East Riding hoss boy.'

'Why would he do such a thing?' Lofthouse asked.

'To get at me. To put the blame on my cooperage.'

Sykes was glad when the head brewer stepped forward and spoke quietly and reassuringly to Lofthouse. 'It's a setback, but we've seen worse. Let's see where we go from here.'

Lofthouse nodded and then turned to Sykes. 'And what do you say, Mr Sykes?'

'I say we report this to the police.' Sykes knew that the chances of finding the saboteur would be slim, but to have Sergeant Moon's constables undertake the thankless task of fingerprinting casks and giving a general warning might scare off whoever did this from repeating their mischief.

Slater Parnaby's response was less measured. 'I wish we'd saved the poison instead of pouring it away. We should've teemed it into a butt and drowned Joe Finch.'

Parnaby turned his back on them. Muttering under his breath, he made his way back towards the cooperage.

Lofthouse sighed. 'Sykes, old chap, sorry for this bad start. I'll leave it to you to go to the police station, and then find your way to my office, on the top floor. Miss Crawford will look after you. She'll see you have everything you need.'

Chapter Seven

Mr Lofthouse's office was in the part of the top floor that extended across the brewery building to the adjoining Falcon, where Sykes was staying. The office windows overlooked the town square.

Miss Crawford, a middle-aged woman with tightly waved hair, endeared herself to Sykes by providing him with a cup of tea and sandwiches.

'I thought it was near enough lunch time, Mr Sykes. Oh and your evening meal at the Falcon is booked. I'm told they do a good steak and kidney pie.'

Sykes thanked her. He was curious as to whether Mr Lofthouse was still in the building or had gone home after the shock of the spoiled brew.

Miss Crawford did not offer any information about her boss's whereabouts. She struck Sykes as being one of those secretaries, crisp as a starched blouse and discreet as a clam. He had come across many like her during the course of his work. Often, such women worked for men who did not have half as sharp a brain as the secretaries they dictated to.

Miss Crawford left Sykes in Lofthouse's spacious office and disappeared into her adjoining office, just long enough for him to polish off the sandwiches and tea.

She returned with a diagram of the brewery's structure, a list of departments and employees, and a list of keyholders. 'I have set aside the documents that Mr Lofthouse wished you to look at.

They are in a locked office at the other end of the building. I will take you to it. Is there anything else you need to know before you begin?'

'I'm interested in security, especially since what's happened with the new brew.'

She nodded. 'It's shocking. One spoiled cask might be explained, but not the full batch.'

Sykes agreed. 'This list of keyholders, Miss Crawford, is it complete?'

'As far as I know, but locks have not been changed in the thirty years I have worked here.'

'Is there a night watchman?'

She hesitated. 'There is a night watchman.' She manged to convey that he was not the most watchful of watchmen. 'He has a hut beyond the stables.'

'His name?'

'John Tickler.'

'Ah.' Sykes remembered the name. 'Any relation to the Jack Tickler who fell into the mash tun?'

She nodded. 'Yes. He is Jack Tickler's father. Mr Lofthouse set him on shortly after the son's funeral.'

'I see.' Sykes did see. Mr Tickler senior would feel no great sense of obligation to the brewery where his son lost his life, even if that son had behaved idiotically.

'You are seriously concerned about security, Mr Sykes?'

'I am, Miss Crawford.'

She smiled. She almost beamed. 'I shall tell Mr Lofthouse that Mr Sykes recommends all locks be changed. He will know that makes sense, regardless of expense. It ought to reduce insurance premiums. Now if you'll give me a moment, I shall telephone the locksmith, and then show you to your office.'

Miss Crawford disappeared through the adjoining door. Sykes heard her being put through to a locksmith and asking for a survey to be undertaken.

Here was someone not simply efficient, but confident and formidable. If Lofthouse had set a greater value on this competent woman, Sykes thought, he might not be in his present pickle.

In the tiny office, at the solid old desk that had been set aside for him, Sykes got down to work. It puzzled him that the paperwork Lofthouse had asked to be set aside for him was the sort of stuff a good bookkeeper could check. He examined lists of income and expenditure, went through copy invoices, alert for the old trick of a paler or darker carbon copy, that might indicate payment going to an unauthorised account, or being settled in cash. Nothing.

At 5 p.m., Miss Crawford came in wearing her hat and coat. She brought him a cup of tea.

'Mr Sykes, is there anything you need before I go?'

'I need information, Miss Crawford, but it will wait until tomorrow.'

'Tell me quickly. I am usually here until half past five. On the first Monday of the month, I leave early to attend the Oddfellows supper.'

'Then let me walk with you to the door.' He followed her along the corridor. 'I've glanced at the paperwork you brought me, and the invoices. I will look at everything relevant to the company, and whatever Mr Lofthouse wants me to see. So far, there is nothing untoward. I understand that you said an outside eye was needed. Why?'

She waved at a door. 'That's your nearest way through to the Falcon. It's not locked.'

'Well I suppose in case of fire, that's a good thing.' He thought for a moment that the secretary was ignoring his question.

As they reached the door to the yard, she said, 'Mr Lofthouse wanted you to see the company accounts and so on, to make sure everything is in order for the AGM, and for when James Lofthouse returns.' Sykes caught a hint of exasperation in her voice.

'But?'

Sykes went with her into the yard. She walked towards a row of bicycles. 'Answers are not always contained in figures. Next month's invoices reflect lost orders. Sometimes it can be a good idea to look back over correspondence.'

'Then may I see any relevant correspondence?'

'I think you should. I am to give you whatever you require.'

'Is there a telephone I may use?'

'Use my office.' She took a key from her bag and gave it to him. 'I always keep a spare for emergencies, Mr Sykes.'

'Thank you.'

She donned a red cape before mounting a black bicycle.

'Do you live nearby, Miss Crawford?'

'Between Masham and Ripon, in West Tanfield. There is a train service but in the fine weather I cycle. I'll wish you good night, Mr Sykes.'

'Goodnight, Miss Crawford.'

Sykes watched her go. I don't think you need me, Mr Lofthouse, Sykes said in his head. You need Miss Crawford.

Sykes went straight back to the office. He put in a call to Mrs Shackleton.

It was reassuring to hear her voice after spending the day with strangers. 'How are you getting on?' Mrs Shackleton asked. 'And are you comfortable in the Falcon?'

'Very comfortable in the Falcon. It's been an odd start, but I do believe I'll now find my way through.'

'Who or what is going to help you?' she asked.

'A very good and efficient secretary who knows everything has decided to be my guide.'

'So what comes next?'

'Supper. My guide recommends steak and kidney pie. After that, I'll put a fine-tooth comb through books and paperwork.'

'Goodnight then! Don't work so late that you get bleary-eyed.'

Sykes did work late. If a thorough check of accounts would put Mr Lofthouse's mind at rest, that is what Sykes must do. A heavy desk lamp cast a perfectly round pool of light on ledger after ledger. He checked figures. He examined bindings, looking for evidence of a carefully removed page.

In the wages office, he examined time cards and entries. All were in order. Nor was anyone suspicious about a desk being searched. As far as he could tell, no item had been so placed that the opening of a drawer would be a give-away. No single strand of hair had been stuck across cupboard doors. It seemed treacherous to suspect such conscientious employees.

The accountant had made a couple of mistakes that the auditor failed to notice.

The drayman, Joe Finch, had a small fiddle going. A horse had died, yet the amount of fodder ordered had risen compared with previous years, more than could be accounted for by food for a stray pony. Joe Finch could be selling fodder on the side. Joe was also changing the figures on delivery notes. Some lucky person was receiving an extra firkin of beer every week on the Bedale run.

There was always a certain amount of pilfering. A firkin a week was a pittance in relation to the overall accounts, but it was best to nip that sort of thing in the bud.

At 11 p.m., as he made a note of his finishing time and prepared to leave, Sykes heard a noise in the yard below, near the stable block. The moon lit the yard, but he saw nothing. Locking the door behind him, he looked about for the night watchman, to tell him he was leaving. Once more he heard a sound.

A fox taking a shortcut.

And then he saw a passing shadow by the stables. He went to investigate. At the back of the second stall was what looked like a pile of blankets. He trod carefully, but not carefully enough. He shone his torch. A figure raised itself to a sitting position and covered its eyes against the glare. Sykes moved closer and saw that it was a thin man with protruding cheekbones and big hungry eyes. Sykes lowered the beam. 'Who are you?'

With the slightest movement, the man cowered for a second as if to avoid a blow. And then he stood. 'I'm nobody, just somebody out of the cold.'

'How did you get in?'

'A gap.'

'Somebody made the gap for you?'

'I did it meself. I'll be off in the morning. Leave me be this night.'

There was the slightest movement from under the blanket behind him. Sykes went closer.

'Leave it!' the man said.

Sykes averted the torch's beam. A thin woman, no flesh on her bones, raised herself, attempting to shield two sleeping children.

The man looked down at them, as though they were nothing to do with him, as though they came as a sudden surprise.

The woman, still heavy with sleep, propped herself up. 'We have permission.'

The man shushed her.

'Who gave permission?' Sykes asked, knowing that it would be someone who did not have permission to give. The night watchman, or some well-meaning fool.

Sykes did not know the woman was going to speak. The man did, and tried to shush her, but not quickly enough. 'We're doing no harm,' she said.

The man remained standing, bouncing a little on the balls of his feet, coming between Sykes and the woman, and the children under the blanket. Now Sykes noticed the man's arms through the torn shirt sleeves, thin as sticks.

'It's not my business,' Sykes heard himself say, 'unless you cause bother, and then I'll come looking.' But it was his business. This state of affairs was all of our business, but nobody knew what to do. He took a pound note from his pocket. He reached out and put it in the man's icy hand. 'There must be somewhere you can go.'

It was the woman who spoke. 'Only the Workhouse.'

'Workhouses are abolished.'

'The rules are still in place. They'll separate us.'

They were trespassing. They might be harmless, but if they could get onto brewery premises, so could a gang of thieves.

All the man had to do was light a smoke, drop a match, and the place would go up in flames. Sykes thought about it, warned the man against smoking, and wished them goodnight.

Joe Finch the drayman had shown Sykes round the stables with the air of a man who claimed this as his domain.

The watchman could work out for himself that Sykes had left the premises. It seemed suddenly unimportant that Finch had a fiddle on the Bedale run. If Finch gave this family shelter, perhaps he fed them too.

As to Mr Tickler the watchman, being paid for sleeping on the job, Mr Lofthouse would do better to give Mr Tickler a small pension and let him go on his way.

After a restless sleep in the strange bed, Sykes woke at 5 a.m. the next morning, disturbed by a chorus of birds. By 5.15 a.m., he was dressed, took a swig of water from the tap and went through the connecting door and corridor into the brewery.

From the office allocated to him, Sykes watched the brewery yard.

At 6.00 a.m., the gates swung open. Only one man would arrive at work with a Shetland pony in tow. Joe Finch.

Moments later, the vagrant family emerged from their hiding place and went to the gate. Finch and the parents exchanged a few words. They left the yard. The children turned to wave. Finch treated the premises as his own, yet Sykes could not help but feel touched by the scene. Finch might be risking his job to do this kindness, if kindness it was.

It occurred to Sykes that Slater Parnaby, 'the nose' of the brewery, held Finch responsible for contaminating the beer because of his cavalier attitude towards opening the gates and letting people in. Finch might inadvertently admit someone who bore a grudge.

On his way back to the Falcon for breakfast, Sykes promoted Joe Finch to first person of interest, both for his minor frauds with the fodder and firkins, and now as a security risk.

Chapter Eight

When Sykes arrived back at the brewery offices at 8.30 a.m. and knocked on the door, Miss Crawford called for him to come in. She was speaking on the telephone, put her hand over the mouthpiece, and indicated for Sykes to take a seat. From the gist of the ongoing conversation, Sykes gathered that Miss Crawford was speaking to her boss. Sykes had noticed before that if a firm runs smoothly, the top brass do not need to be there.

While the secretary spoke to her boss, Sykes went to look at a painting on the wall. He was not a great follower of art but took to this picture of a river on a misty morning, and a man fishing. He would have liked to be in that spot, to be that man. Another painting, unmistakeably by the same hand, showed the brewery, in a soft evening light. A workman was lighting a cigarette, hand cupped round the match. How did the artist manage to make the figure look lonely?

The signature was Eleanor Hart. Sykes could see why Eleanor Hart's work was praised. Mrs Shackleton regarded her work highly, as did a chap Sykes had met who belonged to the Arts Club, a painter who had more of the labourer than the artist about him. Sykes wondered whether Mr Lofthouse minded that to enthusiasts of art, his wife would always first and foremost be Eleanor Hart.

Miss Crawford was saying to her boss, 'There is something I want to talk to you about, but I'll wait until you come.' She paused. 'No, I would rather speak to you in person about this.' Another pause. 'Very well.' With a small sigh, she put down the telephone. 'Mr Lofthouse asks me to say that he will be in after lunch. Is there anything else you need, Mr Sykes? I'll get that correspondence out for you later this morning.'

Sykes had noticed that there were no financial records in relation to the brewery queen expenses. 'I'd like to take a look at the past twelve months' bank statements, please Miss Crawford.'

She walked round to the front of the desk. 'The bank statements are in the safe. Come with me. You might as well see the safe.'

He opened the office door. Miss Crawford stepped into the corridor and led the way. She stopped at the wages office, explaining, 'There must be two members of staff when the safe is unlocked.'

She tapped and opened the door. 'Ruth, do you have a moment to go with me to the safe?'

This was Sykes's first sight of Ruth Parnaby since seeing the trussing. Without knowing that this girl was North Riding Brewery Queen, Sykes may not have given her more than the usual second glance, or would he? She was dark-haired, tall, slim but shapely and with high cheekbones, a full mouth and long lashes. In spite of her good looks and stylish dress, there was something about her that said, Ordinary, something that said, The Girl Next Door. These days all young women had what he called That Look. They copied styles from magazines and from film actresses. His own daughter was the same, pins in her mouth adjusting a dress pattern, scorching her hair with curling tongs.

As Sykes, Miss Crawford and Miss Parnaby stood together in the tiny lift that took them to the basement, he noticed the way Ruth held herself, something stately about her, a stillness.

No one spoke.

Sykes registered the system for opening the safe: date in a book, signatures on opening, items taken, signatures on closing. Although Miss Crawford had called it "safe", it was a strong room, with shelving and cupboards all the way round. Two large safes stood by the wall. It was from one of these that Miss Crawford took two folders.

Ruth's lips parted slightly. Sykes had the feeling that she knew exactly what was in those folders. Bringing an employee to the steps of a brewery industry throne would not come cheap yet Sykes had not seen a penny in any column relating to that expense. Here was the missing link. It might be helpful to get to know Miss Parnaby a little better.

After Sykes took the bank statements to his allotted office, he came out again, locked the door and returned to the wages office, carrying one of his prized adding machines. He tapped on the door and waited.

A deep voice called, 'Come in!'

Sykes and the owner of the deep voice introduced themselves. Chief accounts clerk, Mr Beckwith, a stout elderly man whose beer belly and John Bull looks would make him a perfect advertisement for beer, welcomed Sykes into the office.

Sykes had already seen their files and ledgers, all in perfect order. He now showed them the little Bakelite machine with its dainty green keys. Mr Beckwith and Miss Parnaby were full of interest, and looked for somewhere to plug it in. When the connection on the electric lead did not match the connection on the office wall, Miss Parnaby climbed on a chair and plugged it into the ceiling light, causing a small spark and laughing off an electric shock.

Once the machine was connected, Ruth began to add, her fingers going at such a speed that Sykes and Beckwith simply stared.

Ruth's eyes shone. 'Give me some big numbers!'

Beckwith obliged. 'One hundred and nineteen pounds plus three shillings and sixpence halfpenny. Twelve pounds four shillings and sixpence minus eight and fourpence.'

She added, subtracted, multiplied and divided. 'It's wonderful!' She stared at the keys. 'Do you want a square root?'

Mr Beckwith did not want a square root. A man with fingers as big as well-filled pork sausages, he looked on in dismay. Gamely, he took his turn, treating the adding machine switch with as much caution as if it were the trigger of a gun.

Ruth said, 'I love the look of it, and you could work all day without growing tired or your fingers aching.'

Beckwith gulped. 'You won't be here, lass. You're having time off, remember?'

'Oh, I know, Mr Beckwith. I'm just saying.'

'And I don't know who'll step in.' He turned to Sykes. 'Ruth will be on what Mrs Lofthouse calls a sabbatical.' Then he gestured at the machine. 'These little items are too flimsy, designed for people with delicate fingers.'

Sykes saw that Ruth straightaway grasped the anxiety of the man who had taught her the job, and who lacked the confidence to learn new tricks.

She said, 'Shall we not bother, Mr Beckwith? No one would begrudge us keeping what we are used to, and you can do everything in your head anyway.'

Beckwith nodded agreement at this description of his expertise. He turned to Sykes. 'And don't forget, with these dinky items we'd be at the mercy of the electric supply.'

Sykes did not remind him that the whole brewery was at the mercy of the electric supply. He knew when he was beaten and accepted defeat gracefully. 'There's a lot of life left in these old adding machines of yours.'

'Sturdy,' said sausage fingers. 'You know where you are with them.'

Ruth climbed back on the chair, unplugged the adding machine and re-inserted the light bulb. 'It's very interesting to try these, Mr Sykes, like a glimpse of the future.' She put the adding machine back in its box. 'But what we have works perfectly, at present.'

At that moment, Sykes hoped that Miss Parnaby's reign would be victorious and glorious. It wasn't just good looks that the voting public and the judges saw in her. Sykes reckoned Ruth Parnaby was one in a million.

As he walked along the corridor, Sykes had a word with himself. You are not here to be impressed by the kind-heartedness of a drayman who gives shelter to a homeless family, or be impressed by the generous way a bright young woman treats her elderly boss.

Perhaps there was something about this place that knocked the hard edges off a person and barred good judgement.

Sykes found the bank account statements he was looking for. Eleanor Lofthouse had been given a special account to cover brewery queen expenses, and that account made interesting reading.

Sykes was watching out for Mr Lofthouse to arrive. Now, there he was, walking through the wicket gate. Sykes gave him time to take off his coat, and then walked along the corridor. He tapped on the door. Mr Lofthouse called for him to come in. He was standing by his office window, holding a child's decorative enamel watering can, tending overgrown plants on the windowsill.

Miss Crawford stood nearby. She said to her boss, 'What I wanted to speak to you about—'

Mr Lofthouse said, 'Ah, Sykes, just the man.'

Sykes said, 'Sorry, I'll come back.'

'No, no, let's hear what you've turned up,' and to Miss Crawford, 'We'll speak later.'

Sykes caught Miss Crawford's eye and felt guilty at butting in. She looked away, and went back to her office.

Mr Lofthouse said, 'Sit yourself down, Mr Sykes.' He set the watering can on the windowsill and came to the desk. 'How've you got on?'

'I've more to look at, but there a couple of things worth mentioning now.' Sykes glanced at his notes, though he did not need to. 'Number one is security. It's too soon for Sergeant Moon to have got far with the investigation into the spoiling of the new brew, but I'm sure he will agree that there is a security issue. There are doors that ought to be locked, and there are too many keys floating about.'

Lofthouse put down his watering can. 'We have always run on trust, Mr Sykes. I should hate for that to change too much.'

'Let's see what the locksmith says tomorrow. He will do a survey.'

'You're not talking new locks all round?' Lofthouse had the crestfallen look of a boy told that he would lose his pocket money.

'He'll submit a quotation. It will be up to you where to take things from there. Miss Crawford would then be able to talk to your insurance agent. As she pointed out, improved security could reduce your insurance premium.'

A man of mercurial moods, Lofthouse brightened.

Sykes hated to throw in the damper. 'There is the small matter of a fiddle going on.'

Lofthouse sighed. 'There's always something. Who and what this time?'

'Joe Finch, flogging a firkin on the Bedale round. Let's keep that under wraps for a few days now until I see what else might be going on.'

'And you're holding back the best or worst until last?'

It was too soon for Sykes to say that Barleycorn Brewery needed a new accountant. That would be best put in a report. 'Miss Crawford will be pulling out some files for me, so that I have a full picture before I make recommendations.'

'It's a relief to know we'll be on the straight and narrow when James comes back.'

That was the easy part. Sykes paused and took a breath. 'Now about this account, opened for the use of Mrs Lofthouse in relation to expenses connected with the brewery queen.'

Lofthouse smiled indulgently. 'I gave Eleanor shares when we wed. She's on the board and that's her contingency account.'

Make the most of your smile, Sykes thought. It'll vanish in a minute. He cleared his throat. 'There's an initial deposit of five pounds in that account, and then a subsequent transfer of forty-five pounds.'

Dismay replaced the smile, but Lofthouse stayed loyal. 'Ah, I did give the nod to the bank manager—'

'The brewery queen account has gone into overdraft.'

'Surely not?'

Eleanor Lofthouse chose that moment to enter the office, after a short tap. 'Hello, darling!' She paused in the doorway. 'Oh, I'm sorry, you have someone with you.' She stepped forward. 'You must be Mr Sykes.'

Sykes stood. 'How do you do, Mrs Lofthouse?'

William Lofthouse was still blinking at the expenditure of fifty pounds and the thought of an overdraft. He remained motionless, failing to make the introduction.

Sykes moved a chair to the side of the desk, for Mrs Lofthouse. She sat down.

Something had been niggling at Sykes. Now it clicked. Mrs Lofthouse's paintings were signed Eleanor Hart. It was the lace on the collar and cuffs of her navy dress that gave him the clue. Her face was familiar from Rosie's magazines, where she used to advertise Harts' Lace. She was Mr Hart's daughter.

Harts' lace manufacturers of Nottingham produced high-quality goods but went out of business when the lace market moved overseas. Mr Hart, a widower, ended up in the bankruptcy court and died soon afterwards. It may well have been the failure of exports and a weak home market that brought closure to one hundred and fifty years of Harts' Nottingham lace. Or it may have been Eleanor Hart opening contingency accounts.

Sykes could not decide whether to pity Mr Lofthouse or judge him. He had a wrong 'un for a drayman, an accountant losing his marbles, a nephew meandering across Germany, and a wife who came trailing bankruptcy and ruin. That might explain why Lofthouse was reluctant to be precise about what worried him. He was embarrassed by his own loss of control.

Mr Lofthouse croaked. 'Fifty pounds, gone?'

'Yes. Leaving a current debit of five pounds.'

'Shall I come back later?' Eleanor looked at her lace gloves, as if she suddenly spotted a flaw. 'I seem to be interrupting.'

Lofthouse leaned forward. 'Where has it gone, Eleanor, all that money?'

'There are expenses. And you know that James wanted to visit Vienna. I telegraphed money to him. I'm sure I mentioned it. You said you wouldn't want to deprive him.'

'That was before I knew how long he would stay.'

'Everything regarding the brewery queen business has been done without extravagance. We have a local dressmaker who charges modest prices. The stones in Ruth's tiara are semi-precious. The gold chain of office gives her dignity. It was the specially cast Brewery Society medallion that went over budget.'

'Budget?' Lofthouse reached for his glass of water. 'What budget?'

Sykes considered excusing himself but stayed put.

'I know it seems a lot,' Eleanor spoke soothingly. 'But look at it this way. We have had a huge amount of interest, and more to come with the big event in Scarborough. The works outing to see the all-Yorkshire final is already paid for. Everyone will know about us. People will be queuing up to invest in the company.'

'Eleanor, we're not that kind of company, we're too small.'

'At present, yes.' She stood. 'I only came in to say hello. I must go pay Miss Boland.'

'The music teacher?'

'A little more than that. Celia Boland toured extensively with the Merry Opera Company. She is a voice coach, helps Ruth with her breath control, pitch, delivery, deportment.' She tilted her head to one side. 'Now I feel I've undone the doctor's good work. I had no idea you wanted to be more closely involved, darling. But don't worry about the finance side.'

'Oh?' A smidgen of hope lit Lofthouse's right eye.

'There'll be a marquee at the garden party with my paintings on display, for sale.' She gestured to the painting of the brewery and the river scene. 'Not the brewery of course, but others. I'll sell the River Ure if need be.' She made for the door. 'There will be businessmen, and farmers, wanting their brewery or farm immortalised. The cream of the county will be there. Commissions are bound to follow. The income from that will be my contribution to the brewery queen funds.'

She closed the door gently as she left.

The elderly brewer gulped.

Sykes pitied him. Eleanor Lofthouse, née Hart, in her lace collar and cuffs, would bankrupt him. He would die of a heart attack. The wandering nephew would lose his inheritance. Eleanor Hart would come out smelling of roses.

There was something Sykes ought to say, and yet was reluctant. He had not been asked his opinion on the wisdom of the brewery queen scheme. Why should he rock the boat? He knew all about the importance of brands and creating a big name for something that would become the public's first choice, whether it was tonics, tea or beer. It would be easy to leave Mr Lofthouse with just the answers to the questions asked. Someone should have spotted what Sykes spotted.

Alongside the painting of the brewery was a portrait of the company's founder. It seemed to Sykes that there was a time when every man of note modelled his appearance on whoever was the present king. Over a century of hard work had gone into the making of this business. Sykes must speak his mind.

'Something else did occur to me,' he began, immediately thinking this was a great impertinence, a criticism of the board's judgement. 'It occurred to me that it could be a very good thing to have a Brewery Queen of the North Riding, where you have most of your customers.'

Lofthouse waited.

'Is there a plan to expand the business, if demand increases?' It had to be said. 'Will there be a disproportionate expense if your queen—and I met her briefly and she seems the perfect choice—becomes Brewery Queen for all Yorkshire, and perhaps may be crowned for the North of England, or for all England?'

Two deep tramlines dented Lofthouse's forehead. 'It seemed a good idea at the time. Eleanor had such enthusiasm. I suppose I thought of Ruth Parnaby as good at her job and a pretty girl. I didn't fully realise her potential.'

'You'll have come to some mutual arrangement with fellow brewers, to share the responsibility?'

'I was blinded by Eleanor's enthusiasm.' Lofthouse made a steeple of his fingers. 'I'm trying to remember what was said about the arrangements for the brewery queen business.'

He stood. Opening the adjoining door, he said, 'Miss Crawford, would you bring the North Riding Brewery Queen correspondence?'

She had anticipated his request and gave him the folder in an instant. The previously discreet Miss Crawford showed a sudden burst of liveliness. 'Everyone is so excited. Ruth will make a perfect all-Yorkshire Queen.'

'Thank you, Miss Crawford.'

She did not consider herself dismissed.

Lofthouse thumbed through a slim batch of correspondence, blinking as if he could not quite take this in.

Miss Crawford helped. 'The replies regarding other breweries' participation and contributions fall into the categories of no-reply; not putting anyone forward; will discuss at a later date; will meet costs within their own area—that includes Scarborough, York and Northallerton—obviously hoping their candidate will win through.'

'I see.' Lofthouse closed the folder.

Sykes took it from him. 'I'll take a look at this, Miss Crawford.'

'As you please.' She paused. 'No one has the vision and the enthusiasm of Mrs Lofthouse. She is the one who will carry this through. And Ruth of course.'

Lofthouse waited until Miss Crawford had closed the door between their offices.

'We're on our own.' He put his head in his hands. 'This is beyond your remit, Mr Sykes, but—what am I to do if she wins the next round and increases these duties of hers, leaving me without a wages clerk?'

'Offer Ruth promotion on the understanding that she will withdraw from the next round of the contest.'

Lofthouse lifted his head. 'Promotion, for an eighteen-year-old lass?'

Sykes said, 'She's good at her job, shows gumption. Increase her wages.'

Lofthouse frowned. 'How would I explain that to her elders and betters?'

'They don't need to know. She does the wages.'

Lofthouse stroked his chin. 'She does have an accounting qualification and gets on with people.'

'Promotion and an increase in wages. She would be mad to refuse.'

'I'll call her in and put it to her.'

'Carrot and stick, Mr Lofthouse. She can continue as North Riding Queen but stand down from the next round of the competition.'

Ruth Parnaby was sent for. Sykes felt pleased with his solution. Now, he waited with Mr Lofthouse. They heard footsteps somewhere along the corridor.

'Her father is against the business,' Lofthouse said. 'Her fiancé broke off the engagement. He's in line to inherit the family farm, wants a wife not a beauty queen. We may be giving her the opportunity she needs to withdraw.'

Sykes suddenly thought of his own daughter and was not so sure.

The footsteps drew closer. Lofthouse wiped his brow. 'Eleanor and Ruth. Two beautiful women. This malarkey could bankrupt me. What are they trying to do to us, the women of today?'

Sykes did not regard himself as a philosopher, but a sudden insight came to him. He thought of his wife, taking that job at Montague Burtons clothing factory when there was no need. She wanted the company. She wanted the wage packet.

'Perhaps they're not trying to do anything to us, Mr Lofthouse. Perhaps they want to do something for themselves.'

'Then God help us, because that amounts to the same thing.' The tap-tap of Cuban heels grew louder. 'What happens if she refuses?' Lofthouse asked.

'In that case, you must pray that she loses the all-Yorkshire contest.'

The door opened. Ruth filled the space. 'Mr Lofthouse, you sent for me?' She smiled.

'Ah yes, Miss Parnaby, do sit down.'

Sykes watched Ruth Parnaby lower herself into the waiting chair, as if the office belonged to her. She waited.

Lofthouse cleared his throat. 'It's about this brewery queen business.'

'Yes?'

Lofthouse leaned forward, palms together, in prayer, fingers pointing at Miss Parnaby. 'You've done very well, so far.'

'Thank you, sir. I've learned such a lot. When Mrs Lofthouse kindly came with me to the Merchant Adventurers in York, we talked to a professor, two brewers, the mayor, of course, and two landlords. I believe you may have had an order from one or both of them?'

'Ah.' Lofthouse raised his fingers to heaven. 'We did have orders from York. That was you?'

'I hope I played my part. I know Mrs Lofthouse didn't want to bother you, but the head brewer will have told you that she arranged for taster barrels of our Nut Brown to be delivered the day before the banquet.'

Sykes saw that Lofthouse was unsure how to answer this, leaving Miss Parnaby to continue.

'I carry a satin bag, especially for our beermats. The professor thought that was a very good idea, being as how alcohol consumption has been declining since the last century. It made me terribly sad when he said that during the war, a generation of drinkers sacrificed their lives. It made me cry, to be truthful. I thought of the names on our war memorials, all the brewery workers who died, and all the men who enjoyed a pint by the fire in their favourite pub on a cold night. Not to mention the beautiful shire horses who went to war and never returned. We have to keep the industry alive for the future, don't we, Mr Lofthouse?'

'Indeed, we do, and in our part of the county. But you see, in business it is sometimes better to consolidate, rather than spread the butter too thinly—'

Sykes saw that Miss Parnaby knew what was coming. She disarmed him, by speedily agreeing.

'So true, Mr Lofthouse. And after the Yorkshire finals, we may need to think again. But you'll wish me luck, for Friday, won't you?'

'Friday? I thought it was Saturday. Why a weekday, a working day?'

'People are publicity mad these days, sir. It will be in time for the weekend papers and Pathé News. Wouldn't it be wonderful if I could play my part, not just in the North Riding, where Barleycorn have sales now, but across the whole of Yorkshire, where we will have sales in the future?'

Sykes felt a great deal of pity as Lofthouse strove to hide his dismay. 'Of course. Yes, very good luck, Miss Parnaby.'

'Thank you, sir. And of course, there will be a cash prize for the brewery, as well as for the successful candidate.'

Miss Crawford emerged from her office, smiling at Miss Parnaby and Mr Lofthouse in turn. 'You've remembered that I'll be accompanying Ruth to Scarborough, Mr Lofthouse? We're booked into a boarding house for Thursday evening, so that she'll have a good start on Friday.'

Ruth rose. 'Yes, and I'd better get back to work if that's all right. Mr Beckwith will think I've got lost.'

'Yes, of course. Go back to work,' Lofthouse said lamely, with an attempt at authority.

Sykes could not tell whether Lofthouse knew he had been outmanoeuvred.

Miss Crawford waited. When Mr Lofthouse did not speak, she said, 'Is this a good time for our chat?'

Lofthouse looked at his watch. 'It's almost four. I must go home and take my tablets.' He stood. Sykes thought he detected a hint of malice in Lofthouse's parting sentence. 'We'll talk in the morning, Miss Crawford. Bring any post round, and I'll deal with it from home. Mr Sykes can attend to the locksmith.'

Miss Crawford was about to speak, but Lofthouse was already picking up his hat She leaned slightly towards the door, as if she might go after him.

When Lofthouse closed the door behind him, Sykes said, 'I'm sorry. You might have said more had I not been here.'

She shrugged. 'As Mr Lofthouse says, we'll speak tomorrow.' She moved to go back into her adjoining office, and then turned. 'The correspondence you wanted, it's on your desk.'

The telephone began to ring. Miss Crawford turned to answer it.

Chapter Nine

∽

Sykes, armed with millboard and list of keyholders, waited in the reception area. The locksmith cycled through the gates at 9.00 a.m., took off his bicycle clips and dusted down his trousers.

He was a cheerful man by the name of Malcolm Phelan, in his early forties with dark hair and light blue eyes. He perked up on hearing Sykes's suggestion about the need for certain parts of the premises to carry warning notices.

Mr Phelan was a man of ideas. 'What you want is a "No Smoking" sign by the stables and on the door to the mill room. You want "Danger Keep Out" on the door of the fermentation room.'

As they walked from one set of gates to another, Mr Phelan warmed to his theme. 'There should be signs for each department. Mr W Lofthouse certainly ought to have his name on the door.'

Sykes took the locksmith to entry points into the building and to the doors that connected with the Falcon.

It was 11 a.m. when the locksmith left the brewery premises, promising Sykes that he would have his recommendations and prices to Mr Lofthouse by Friday and could start work on Monday if his quotation was acceptable.

Sykes felt pleased with the morning's work. He went back into the building.

Sergeant Moon was coming down the stairs as Sykes went up.

'Ah, Sykes, just the man. Where's Mr Lofthouse? He's not in his office.'

'He planned to work at home this morning. He asked Miss Crawford to take correspondence there.'

The sergeant looked suddenly brighter. 'And did she?'

The brightness dissipated as soon as Sykes said, 'I haven't seen her.'

'Can we check, discreetly?'

Sykes nodded. 'Pigeonholes in the mailroom.'

Sergeant Moon followed him. They walked to the ground floor, to the room just beyond the reception desk. There was no one on duty, only a bell inviting any visitor to press for attention. The mailroom was just beyond, also unattended.

Mr Lofthouse's pigeonhole was first in the row. Sykes glanced at the morning's post, waiting to be collected. 'Miss Crawford hasn't come in yet.'

The sergeant sighed. 'I was grasping at a straw. A call came in from Ripon. Miss Crawford has been knocked off her bike.'

'Is she badly hurt?' Sykes read the answer in Sergeant Moon's face.

'I'm told she was killed instantly. The officer knew her, but I thought what if, by any remote chance, he was wrong.'

'What about the driver?'

'Didn't stop, but we'll find him.'

Sykes waited. He understood the sergeant's dilemma. It was one thing to break the news of a death when you had seen the body. People always hoped, hoped there was a mistake, hoped a blink would shut down a nightmare.

The sergeant straightened his tunic. 'I'm going out there now to see for myself, but what other woman would be cycling, wearing a red cape? I have to tell Mr Lofthouse first. Miss Crawford was such a good person, Sykes.'

'Do you mind if I come with you to the Lofthouses?'

'You should. Mr Lofthouse relied on her so much. He'll need all the support he can get, until James comes back.'

Sykes had grown tired of hearing about nephew James. The fellow was beginning to sound like a mythical beast.

The sergeant and Sykes made the short walk to Barleycorn House in silence.

Eleanor and William were in the conservatory. She was at a canvas, paintbrush in hand. He was reading the newspaper.

Sykes hung back. 'I'll wait outside, until you break the news, Sergeant.'

Sykes watched as the sergeant tapped on the door, entered the conservatory, and took off his cap. Eleanor turned to him.

William was still behind his newspaper. It was a moment before he lowered it.

Sergeant Moon, standing very still, began to speak.

Eleanor dropped her brush.

For several long seconds, they all stood still, and then Eleanor went to William.

Moments later, the sergeant came out. He said to Sykes, 'Mr Lofthouse has taken it badly. I suppose Miss Crawford was like a member of the family, someone you take for granted.' He put on his cap. 'Mr Lofthouse is upset about being short with her yesterday, something Miss Crawford wanted to say.'

'That's unfortunate. Mr Lofthouse is bound to blame himself for that.'

'Did she say anything to you, Mr Sykes?'

'No.'

'I knew Miss Crawford so will identify the body, save Mr Lofthouse the distress.'

Sykes took off his hat. 'I'll go in and see if there's anything I can do.'

'Right you are.' The sergeant walked away.

When Sykes went into the conservatory, Eleanor was holding William's hand. *The Times* had fallen to the floor, its great sheets scattered.

Sykes picked up the newspaper and straightened it. 'I'm so very sorry for your loss, Mr Lofthouse, Mrs Lofthouse, so tragic and sudden.'

He sat with them, while Mrs Lofthouse rang for the maid, asking for tea and brandy.

When the maid came, Mrs Lofthouse hesitated. 'I know what the doctor said, but drink the brandy, William. You need it, and so do I.'

Sykes poured, refusing a drink himself.

William picked up the glass. 'People say someone was a treasure, but Miss Crawford really was.' He took a drink. 'I should have listened to her yesterday.' He turned to Eleanor. 'I always told you didn't I, what a fusspot Miss Crawford could be sometimes. Now I'll never know what she wanted to say.'

His wife tried to reassure him. 'She wouldn't have minded. She knew you well enough, probably called you a grumpy old so-and-so more times than you called her a fusspot.'

'I hope she didn't suffer.' William reached for the brandy bottle and topped up his glass. 'I wish I could get my hands on the blighter that did it.'

Eleanor said, 'The driver must have been drunk or going at top speed. A sober motorist would have to be blindfolded to miss that great boneshaker with a basket on it. And didn't she wear a red cape?'

William nodded. 'She'd been cycling that road since she learned to ride a bike.'

'Darling, I'm going to leave you in the capable hands of Mr Sykes. I'll go out there, lay some flowers, see what I can find out. And she has a cat. The least we can do is make sure someone is taking care of it or find it a good home.' She stood.

Lofthouse shifted in his seat and looked straight at Sykes, pulling a face and shaking his head. Sykes saw the panic in his eyes, and the unspoken message. Keep her away from the scene.

Sykes was on his feet in an instant. 'Mrs Lofthouse, the police will have cordoned off the road. I know how they work. Let me go.'

Mrs Lofthouse glanced at her husband. 'Very well, Mr Sykes. William and I will go later.'

Lofthouse walked Sykes to the gate. 'I'll be waiting in the office for you.'

Chapter Ten

Along the quiet road, under a perfect blue sky, Sykes drove towards the scene of the accident. When he saw a police constable ahead, taking photographs, Sykes slowed to a crawl, and then pulled onto the grass verge. Beyond the constable with the camera, another PC was taking measurements of the road.

The road was straight at this point, with good visibility, no overhanging branches, no twists or turns. Sykes got out of the car and walked towards the constables. As he drew closer, he looked to see what the constable was photographing. In the ditch beyond the verge, among grass, churned earth and crushed wildflowers, lay a black bicycle, the front wheel buckled, its basket broken. The grass was flattened where Miss Crawford's body had lain. Sykes stared at a long blade of grass spattered with blood. He closed his eyes, surprised by the way that after all these years pity and rage could still make him tighten his fists to keep from shaking. He looked away. Poor Miss Crawford. Whoever did this must be held to account.

Sykes waited until the PC put the camera back in its case and then introduced himself, adding, 'Sergeant Moon broke the news. I'm here on behalf of Miss Crawford's employer.'

The young constable hung the camera around his neck. 'I believe the lady worked at the brewery?'

'Yes, as Mr Lofthouse's secretary.' Sykes could not yet bring himself to speak of Miss Crawford in the past tense. 'Do you have any idea how this happened, and who was involved?'

'Not yet. Whoever did it, didn't stop.'

'Who reported the incident?'

'A telephone call came into Ripon station.'

If the constable knew more, he wasn't saying. Sykes asked, 'Are we far from Miss Crawford's house?'

'She lived down the lane on the left. There's a block of eight cottages. One of her neighbours, a Mrs Rigg, heard something and came out to look. She held herself together long enough to go to a house with a telephone, and then came back to wait for us. Mrs Rigg and Miss Crawford were friends. She told us that in the fine weather, Miss Crawford cycled to work. We got that out of her, and then the poor woman went to pieces. I had to half carry her back to her door.'

'Which cottage?'

'The third one down. But you won't get much out of her, if that's what you're thinking, sir.'

'You're sure of the correct identity?' Sykes knew that he was letting hope overcome experience.

'Our sergeant came with the ambulance to remove the deceased. He and his wife knew Miss Crawford because she was a regular attender at Ripon Cathedral.'

'What now?' Sykes asked.

The constable indicated his colleague. 'We're to wait until the bike is taken away, and then back to the station.'

'I can continue up the road?'

'You can, sir.'

'Thank you, officer.'

As he drove by, Sykes glanced along the lane that led to the eight cottages. It was too soon to disturb Miss Crawford's distraught neighbour. He was not entirely sure what he was looking for. Had the motorist driven on, or turned around and gone back the way he had come? Certainly, the car would be damaged. If the driver went through a town, or passed by farms, someone would notice a damaged vehicle. How and why had this happened? There was good visibility. A bike that size and a woman wearing a red cape could hardly be missed, unless the driver was asleep at the wheel.

Sykes stopped the car when he saw a house on the other side of the road. It was a substantial stone-built dwelling, smoke coming from the chimney. The garden, full of tulips, sloped down to the road. This house had a telephone wire. There had been no wire to the eight houses nearer to the scene of the accident, if accident it was.

As Sykes crossed and opened the gate, he suddenly thought of Rosie. She would love a house like this. Of course, she would love it for five minutes before hankering after neighbours, shops and a tram stop. The place was too isolated.

He called hello to the little boy who lay on his tummy between beds of tulips, looking like a small dark elf. The child, of about four or five years of age, glanced at Sykes and then walked to the bottom of the garden and looked over the wall at Sykes's car.

Sykes's knock on the door was answered by a woman, whom he assumed to be the little boy's mother. She wore a flour-splattered pinafore over a blue and green sari, her dark centre-parted hair drawn back into a bun.

'Sorry to disturb you, madam. I'm Jim Sykes, here for Mr Lofthouse of the brewery.'

'Ah, and you have come because I made the telephone call.'

'I thought it may have been you, Mrs—?'

'Murthy.' She sighed. 'So very sad. Miss Crawford, such a perfect lady.' She opened the door wider. 'Come inside. Sit down over there.' She waved towards the kitchen table. Sykes was surprised to be asked in. He remained standing.

'Did you see what happened?'

'Sit, sit!' she ordered.

He sat.

'I saw nothing. I heard the sound. It is so quiet here and then something happens. Hardly any traffic. When I first came, a tractor went into the ditch. When I heard the sound this morning, I thought it was something like that, like the tractor. And then Mrs Rigg came running, which she should not do, all out of breath, and saying to call for help. I had to sit her down to get sense out of her.'

'You telephoned the police?'

'I did, and I telephoned my husband at the bank. He will speak to the police, and he will come home when he can.' Mrs Murthy picked up a cup and poured from a small metal pan on the stove. 'When the police call, I will give them tea.' She placed the tea and a plate with two sticky buns on the table.

Sykes thanked her and took a drink. He decided against saying that he was not with the police. The tea was sweet and milky, but oddly comforting. 'Did you know Miss Crawford well?' He bit into a sticky bun.

'We met occasionally, at parish events, and at the Barleycorn garden party each year. Once a month, my son Jagadeep and I wave to the ladies, Miss Crawford and Mrs Rigg, as the car passes.'

'Oh?'

'Miss Crawford and Mrs Rigg go each month to the Monday Oddfellows supper meeting in Ripon. My husband gives them a lift, that being his evening for attending the Philosophical Society lecture. To think, Jagdeep and I stood by the gate just two evenings ago, waving.'

Sykes drained his cup. 'Thank you for talking to me, Mrs Murthy, and for the tea.'

She walked him out into the garden, glancing about for her boy, spotting Jagadeep down by the wall. 'I will write our condolences to Mr and Mrs Lofthouse.'

'Do you know whether Miss Crawford had relatives?'

'She never spoke of family. Mrs Rigg would know, being her neighbour and knowing her much longer than I did.' She turned away. 'I left the pot on the stove. Goodbye, Mr Sykes.'

'Goodbye, Mrs Murthy.'

She called to the boy. 'Jagadeep, come in now for your milk!'

Sykes walked down the steep path.

The boy met him at the bottom, by the gate. Shyly, he held out his drawing book. Sykes looked at a passably good sketch of his own pre-war Jowett. 'That's very good. You like motor cars?'

The boy smiled. He turned back a page, 'Police car.'

'That's good too. What else?'

The boy turned back another page. 'Ambulance. It went too quick.'

'You're good at drawing.'

'Lots of cars.' Jagadeep turned back another page. The car that filled the space was big, and square, with huge mudguards.

'When did you see this one?'

'Today.'

'Is it your daddy's car?'

'Silly! His car is an Austin 7.'

'Tell me about this car. You've drawn it big.'

'Silly! It was big.'

'Did it go fast?'

'It went slowly. It stopped. It went slowly, and then fast.'

Sykes's fingers itched to take the child's drawing book, but he could imagine the rumpus that would cause and decided against it. 'That's a very precious drawing book. Take good care of it.'

'I will.'

'Ta ta, Jagadeep.'

'Ta ta, mister.'

Clutching his book, the child went up the path. His mother was standing by the door.

Sykes turned at the gate and waved.

He drove back in the direction he had come. The young constables had gone from the scene. Seeing a police car at the top of the lane that led to the eight cottages, Sykes parked by the verge, and got out to stretch his legs. The hedgerow was occupied by a blackbird, a robin and butterflies. The blackthorn was in flower, the hawthorn in leaf. Sykes remembered a nature trip from school. The blackthorn flowers before it comes into leaf. He felt a stab of sadness. Miss Crawford would miss the best part of the year.

Sykes suddenly thought that he ought to have taken his children out more, while they were still young.

As Sykes was walking down the lane, Sergeant Moon was coming back up. Sykes knew the fine line between investigating for the Lofthouses and sticking his nose in police business. He was on good terms with the sergeant. Wanting to stay on good terms, Sykes fell into step with him.

First, give Mr Moon what might be an important titbit, and then wait for what comes back.

'Something you might be interested in, Sergeant.'

'What's that then?'

'The Murthys' little boy, Jagadeep, has a drawing book. If you drive up there now, he'll bags you as his second police car of the day. He also has a crayoning of my car, the ambulance and a car earlier today that went slow, then stopped and then slowly and then quickly. That's the vehicle that might be of interest. It takes up more of the page than his other drawings. It's square, big mudguards, four doors, a badge on the front.'

'Interesting.' Sergeant Moon took out his notebook and pencil. 'Any idea what make of car? How well does he draw?'

'For a four-year-old, he is the Leonardo da Vinci of motorcars. He got the shape of my Jowett and the ambulance. The big car has the look of a Lanchester. The only person I know of driving a Lanchester is the Duke of York.'

'We don't get many Lanchesters around here.' The sergeant made a note.

It was the word 'many' that Sykes picked up on. If you don't have many, you have some, or one. Sykes reckoned that if he was right about the Lanchester car as deadly weapon, the sergeant would owe him a favour. It would be foolish to press a question of car ownership based on a four-year-old's drawing. Sykes would bide his time for a possible pay off.

For now, Sykes asked Mrs Lofthouse's burning question. 'Has anyone seen Miss Crawford's cat?'

They walked back up the lane together. 'Mr Rigg is bed-ridden. Mr White Whiskers is keeping Mr Rigg's feet warm.'

When they reached the road, the sergeant climbed into his car and set off.

Sykes walked to his own vehicle, a little way down the road. He stopped at the place of the Miss Crawford's death and took off his hat. The mangled bike had been taken away, leaving its trace on the ground. He noticed now what escaped his attention earlier, red campion and cowslips.

Miss Crawford fell among flowers.

Chapter Eleven

Sykes listened to his own weary steps as he climbed the stairs to the top floor offices of the brewery, making his way to the little office that had been set aside for him. He needed a few moments, to hang up his hat and coat, and to think.

He unlocked the office door and stepped inside. He hung his coat on the hook and set his hat on the windowsill, gazing out across the yard towards the stables. The room felt stuffy. He tried to open the window, but it had been painted shut.

As he turned from the window, he looked at the desk. The accounts files were gone. For a moment, Sykes felt a rising panic. He then remembered that Miss Crawford said she would collect them. That may have been one of the last things she did, but not quite the last. On the corner of the desk were manila folders of correspondence. Two folders bore the names of public houses, one folder the name of a brewery. Another was headed, AGM 1930. Sykes had asked the right question of Miss Crawford. She had obligingly slid slips of paper next to relevant letters.

He sat down to read. It did not take long.

Mr and Mrs Lofthouse were in the office, waiting for Sykes to return. He gave them an account of what he had seen and heard.

Eleanor leaned forward. 'Why on earth would the driver have gone on his way, not stopping to help, or to report the accident?'

William answered her. 'He must have been speeding or drunk.'

All Sykes could tell them was that the police were investigating. He thought it best to keep the story simple at present. He confirmed that Miss Crawford's cat was safe and well.

Sykes listened to the litany of regret as Eleanor described Miss Crawford as a lynchpin of the company. 'This isn't just a personal blow, Mr Sykes, although it is that. It's a direct hit.'

William looked pale. 'It's beyond dreadful. I feel so bad. She was loyal and conscientious. Yesterday she wanted to tell me something and I wouldn't listen.'

Sykes realised that Mr Lofthouse would go on saying this, aloud and to himself, for a very long time.

It was Eleanor who put the key question. 'Was it deliberate?'

Sykes had a gut feeling that the answer was yes. He said, 'We need to wait on police findings.'

If the hit was deliberate, the question would be why? Sykes had a sinking feeling that the letters he had just read held if not *the* answer, *an* answer. The letters would not explain why someone might see Miss Crawford as a threat, but they explained Lofthouse's worries about his business.

Sykes asked, 'Is this the time to tell me what else has been going on in the company, loss of orders that you might have put down to a run of bad luck?'

Eleanor looked at William. 'I told you, you should have been straight.'

'I was straight,' William said. 'Losing orders was a run of bad luck. What else could it be?'

'It would be worth looking into,' Sykes said.

'I asked the landlords about cancelling. It was a business decision, they each said that. I thought that when James came back, he could take it a step further, and meanwhile I'd make sure the accounts and paperwork are in order.'

It struck Sykes as odd that two landlords came up with the same reply, but he kept that thought to himself for now.

Eleanor said, 'What if James does not intend to come back? We had all those letters extolling the virtues of German brewing, and saying how well he got on with people, and went to the opera with Herr and Frau Mensing and their daughter. Don't you think that was his way of preparing us for the news that he would not come back? Perhaps he has heard something, perhaps he sees the brewery as a sinking ship?'

'Eleanor, we are not sinking. Mr Sykes here is going to steady the course. And this is no time to discuss it, with Miss Crawford dead.'

Sykes was growing impatient. 'It was Miss Crawford who pointed me in the right direction regarding the loss of orders.' He thought he understood why Mr Lofthouse did not want to admit to what might seem like his own failures. 'Tell me about troubles you have had recently, any setbacks, unexpected changes.'

Lofthouse took a deep breath. 'Very well.'

Sykes already knew from the correspondence, but he wanted to hear the words from Mr Lofthouse. Sykes wanted an acknowledgement from him as to the mess he felt himself to be in. A mess he must be ashamed of, perhaps blaming himself.

'Two public houses in Ripon that have taken Barleycorn beer for sixty years cancelled orders. There's a small brewery, the Little Ripon. It has no cooperage and bought casks from Barleycorn. They've switched to another supplier. These are business setbacks,' Lofthouse protested. 'The best thing is to move on. Normally I would have discussed it with two fellow board members, but they have put off talking about it—'

Eleanor chipped in. 'Darling, Mrs Tebbit and Rory—Mr Sykes, Rory is Mrs Tebbit's son—haven't answered your letter, or the request for items for the Annual General Meeting. They haven't returned your calls and Mrs Tebbit has not acknowledged my invitation to the garden party.'

'It's not yet a cause for concern,' Lofthouse said. 'It's three weeks until the AGM. They know my hand is on the tiller. They quite rightly leave things to me.'

Eleanor soothed her husband. 'It's out in the open now, let's see what can be done. Mr Sykes ought to know the background.'

'I'd like to hear,' Sykes said, wishing that he had dealt with Mrs Lofthouse and Miss Crawford from the beginning.

Eleanor continued. 'Barleycorn is a family business. For historic reasons, the Tebbit family, Mrs Tebbit and Rory, own a forty percent share in the company. They have gone quiet, not even responding to my invitation to the garden party, and that's on Saturday.'

William turned to Eleanor. 'I can't face going ahead with the garden party.'

Eleanor sighed. 'Three days' notice is too short a time to cancel. It's too late to send word to everyone. Marquees are booked, the band, catering. We shall have a tribute to Miss Crawford on the day.'

'Listen to me, Eleanor. James isn't back and—'

Sykes saw the danger of this conversation becoming a marital row. He steered them back to what seemed important. 'If I may interrupt?'

'Please do,' Lofthouse said.

Sykes would have liked more time before putting his thoughts into words, but time might be in short supply. 'Miss Crawford wanted to talk to you on Tuesday. She had been in Ripon at the Oddfellows supper the night before. The tribute we could pay to Miss Crawford would be to investigate, to try and find out what she intended to say.'

'How are we supposed to do that?' Lofthouse asked. 'Miss Crawford was the soul of discretion. She would not have talked to anyone about business matters.'

Eleanor cottoned on more quickly. 'She may not have talked, but she would have listened. Mr Sykes, are you suggesting that she heard something at the Oddfellows supper?'

'It crossed my mind, since cancellations from the public houses and the brewery are all from Ripon.'

Eleanor chewed her lip. 'Mrs Tebbit and Rory live in Ripon. They have gone quiet. William, what if Mr Sykes is right? The

Tebbits have heard something to the detriment of the Barleycorn? That would explain their silence.' William was about to interrupt, but she raised her hand. 'When our lace company began to lose orders, we thought it was just one of those things, and then it multiplied. William, I do think Mr Sykes has a point. And news travels.'

Lofthouse sighed. 'I have a feeling James will be back for Saturday, for the garden party. He'll surprise us.'

'We don't need more surprises, William.'

Sykes intervened. 'Let's look at the situation objectively. Loss of orders might simply be because a pub decided to change its beer. The Little Ripon Brewery found a cheaper supplier of casks. The Tebbits overlooked the invitation. James may have fallen in love and come back with a German bride.'

'That's what I wondered,' Lofthouse said, 'when he wrote about wanting to go to Vienna. This could just be an arbitrary string of events.'

Sykes waited for Lofthouse to finish reassuring himself. 'So, while not being alarmist, and hoping things will turn out for the best, we should prepare for the opposite. If a rival is gunning for Barleycorn Brewery, we must arm against that.'

Eleanor reached for her husband's hand. 'This is what I've been afraid of. I watched my father bankrupted. People he thought were friends looked the other way. If someone is trying to ruin us, we must fight back. William, I refuse to watch another business trickle down the drain.'

'Then what must I do?' Lofthouse's question was to Sykes, but Eleanor answered.

'Mr Sykes must stay on and see us through the crisis. What you must do now, William, this very moment, is pick up the telephone and call Kate Shackleton.'

Still, Lofthouse hesitated.

Sykes felt a sudden impatience. 'If there is even the remote possibility of a vendetta against Barleycorn Brewery, take this seriously, please, as Miss Crawford did when she telephoned the locksmith, and when she showed me the correspondence about the cancellations.'

Lofthouse opened his mouth to speak.

Eleanor put a finger to her lips. 'William, your next words must be to Kate.'

William picked up the telephone and asked to be connected.

Sykes and Eleanor listened as Lofthouse spoke to Kate, praising Sykes, admitting there had been unfortunate setbacks that could no longer be written off as coincidences. His voice cracked as he told Mrs Shackleton of the tragic death of his secretary. He waited. 'Thank you, Kate. I am relieved you are able to come.' He paused. 'Yes, I'll put him on now.'

Sykes took the telephone.

Mrs Shackleton said, 'Are you able to come back now, Mr Sykes? You could put me in the picture.'

'Yes, I can do that.' Sykes was relieved at the thought of going home, where he would be able to do background checks on some of the things that had begun to concern him. This was a two-person job. They would make a plan.

He was about to hang up when Eleanor Lofthouse said, 'Don't hang up, Mr Sykes!' She held out her hand for the receiver.

Sykes passed it to her. She began to ask Mrs Shackleton's advice about the Tebbits' failure to communicate. She paused and said, 'Yes that's the same Tebbit, her husband was a banker, died three years ago, full of charm on the outside, led her a dog's life. No, I take that back as being unfair to most dog owners.'

William pulled faces at his wife, indicating that operators may be listening.

She ignored him, while listening to Mrs Shackleton.

After a couple of minutes, she thanked Kate for the good advice and hung up.

Sykes and Lofthouse waited.

Eleanor Lofthouse took her time. 'I think Kate has made a very good suggestion.'

'What?' Lofthouse asked.

'I must totally forget about the Annual General Meeting and business. As a person who has never organised a garden party, I am to call on Mrs Tebbit this afternoon, and ask her advice.'

'But it's all planned,' Lofthouse said. 'Miss Crawford dealt with everything.'

Eleanor smiled, as if at a simpleton. 'Mrs Tebbit does not know that, and Miss Crawford left it to me to organise the flowers, and I forgot. So, it is not entirely a lie.'

'If they are not answering invitations and formal letters—' Lofthouse began.

Eleanor held up her hand. 'The son, Rory, is not answering. It would not surprise me if Mrs Tebbit has not even seen the invitation. I will call on her this afternoon. Rory will be at the bank.'

'Don't ladies usually make calls in the morning?' Lofthouse asked.

'Oh, for heaven's sake, darling, catch up!'

Sykes was reluctant to interrupt, but he thought he ought to warn Mrs Lofthouse. He was surprised that Mrs Shackleton had not thought of it. 'Mrs Lofthouse, I know the person in question. Mrs Tebbit is a notorious kleptomaniac. You will need to take precautions if she is coming to the house.'

Eleanor drew on her gloves. 'Mr Sykes, this is far too important for such niceties. I don't care if she turns up with a removal van and two heavyweight boxers. We must get to the bottom of this.'

Chapter Twelve

Ruth Parnaby was alone in the office. Mr Beckwith had gone for his afternoon perquisite of Nut Brown ale.

Ruth's thoughts were on Friday's All Yorkshire Brewery Queen competition in Scarborough. She sat at her desk, pen in hand, writing employees' names and Friday's date on wage packets. This was usually the job she did on Thursday afternoon. The idea of doing it a day early was in order to get ahead of herself. Tomorrow, she would bring in her suitcase. That way, there would be not be the delay of calling home for luggage. Ruth and Miss Crawford would finish work at twelve on Thursday and be straight off to catch the train to Scarborough.

She was not anxious, Ruth told herself. Everything she could do to put on a good show, she had done. This evening, she would have one more voice and deportment session with her coach, Miss Boland.

Ruth had seen photographs of Miss West Riding and Miss East Riding. They were both pretty, especially Miss East Riding, who was connected to Scarborough Brewery. There would be a lot of people cheering her on. Miss West Riding came from Sheffield. The other two girls' parents would be there. Ruth felt a pang, wishing her mother could have come.

Ruth wrote pay packets in order of departments. She came to Cooperage. It always felt strange writing her father's name. Slater Parnaby. Each time she did this, it hurt her heart to see how much her father earned, that he had always been on good wages. In the years when they were growing up, he gave their mam so little, and he would snatch something back in the middle of the week if he ran short of booze money. Growing up, Ruth missed nothing. When she looked back now, knowing how much it cost to pay rent and insurance, and buy food and coal, Ruth wondered how Mam managed to feed them. Now Ruth understood that it was because Mam went short. When she said, 'Oh, I've already eaten,' she spoke with such conviction that for a long time Ruth and George believed her.

The knock on the office door brought Ruth into the here and now. She put the wage packets in the drawer. 'Come in!'

It was the man who had brought the adding machines and went snooping about checking accounts. Mr Sykes.

'Miss Parnaby, Mr Lofthouse asked me to leave word for you and Mr Beckwith. Would you go to the boardroom at three o'clock? Mr Lofthouse has an announcement to make.'

'Oh, it won't be me, Mr Sykes. It will be heads of departments. Mr Beckwith will bring the information back.'

She did not want to go, resenting the interruption, needing to finish her work and be off in good time for the coaching session.

'Mr Lofthouse particularly wants you to come, Miss Parnaby.'

'Very well, Mr Sykes.'

Mr Sykes closed the door behind him. Bloody nuisance, Ruth said to herself.

That was that then. Miss Boland hated her to be late. She would say to Ruth, 'You need to be here before curtain up. It's ridiculous that you are not being given your due time off work.'

Ruth would not let this boardroom interruption put her behind schedule. In her thoughts, she was already in Scarborough. They would take their luggage to the boarding house, go out for a fish supper. Ruth would have an early night, in a bed that did not dip in the middle, ready for the contest on Friday.

At five minutes to three, Ruth and Mr Beckwith made their way to the boardroom. Mr Beckwith was very quiet, as if he knew something.

They took their seats and had to wait for the slowcoaches.

Mr and Mrs Lofthouse came in on the dot of three. It must be something unusual for her to be here, Ruth thought.

Ruth heard Mr Lofthouse say the words, "shocking accident", and then the name, "Miss Crawford".

Ruth felt a lurch inside. Her body went limp. It was like when the stuffing came out of her toy dog and his legs dangled and the stitches in his paws came away. She tried to make herself listen to what else Mr Lofthouse had to say but it did not sink in.

Ever since Ruth left school and came here, with her hair still in plaits, Mrs Crawford had encouraged her, and looked out for her. It was Miss Crawford who came in with the college prospectus and pointed out the courses Ruth must take. It was Miss Crawford who persuaded Mr Lofthouse to meet the costs when she went to classes and to give Ruth time off with full pay for college attendance.

Ruth could hear her now. 'An investment in Ruth will be an investment for the company.'

People were asking those questions, what happened, where, when, how.

Not Miss Crawford, Ruth said silently to herself.

When Ruth had the mad idea of sending her photo into the paper for the brewery queen contest, she told Miss Crawford and no one else.

Miss Crawford said, 'Why not? Just do it and see what happens. If you don't do it, you'll always wonder. Oh, and don't say you sent the photo in yourself. Kid on that it's from your George, then you won't be accused of having a big head.'

Ruth did not want to hear any more from Mr Lofthouse. All she knew was that Miss Crawford was gone. She felt the tears coming. Don't show yourself up in public, she said in her head.

Mr Beckwith passed Ruth his hanky.

When Ruth won Brewery Queen of the North Riding, Miss Crawford said, 'We won't push the point just yet that you must have six months' leave of absence. Let Mr Lofthouse have time to get used to the idea.'

Ruth glanced around the boardroom. Without looking, she knew the old man was there for the announcement, being head cooper.

When Mr and Mrs Lofthouse left the room, Ruth felt the old man's hand on her shoulder. She expected a taunt or a sneer.

She froze, and then shrugged him off.

He spoke softly. 'I'll clean meself up, take the afternoon off and go with you to Scarborough. We might spot a nice little business there. Idiots spend money at the seaside buying sticks of rock, buckets and spades, souvenirs to take home. If we put your winnings in a pokey swag shop stuffed to the rafters, we'll be King Midas and Miss Moneybags.'

When she did not answer, he said, 'I want you to do well, lass. I won't stand in your way.'

He could be like this. Part of Ruth wanted him to come, wanted him to be a proper dad whose pipe dreams did no harm. There was too much in the way for that to happen. Ruth remembered her mother's words: 'I never know who Slater will be when he wakes in the morning.'

Sometimes, Ruth let herself think that one day he would change.

Ruth put Mr Beckwith's hanky in her pocket. She would wash it and return it.

'Thanks, Dad, but I'll manage. Miss Crawford arranged everything. The boarding house is booked. I know where to report on Friday morning.'

'Suit yerself.'

'You'll come in the coach on Friday, with George and the others?'

The old man sneered. 'Ah wouldn't be seen dead with that pathetic bunch. Only just you think on, we share the prize for the good of the family. You wouldn't be working here if not for me, either you or George, but we won't be wage slaves forever.'

Ruth realised her mam was wrong. The old man did not change from one day to the next. He changed moment to moment. Like as not, he would cause trouble at the boarding house. He would get drunk and make an offer to buy them out when his ship came in.

Chapter Thirteen

I was outside, lifting my suitcase into the dicky seat when Sykes's car drew up.

It was somehow reassuring to see that he had reverted to his comfortable style of the dark suit.

'Hey-up,' Mrs Shackleton.' He got out of the car and stretched. 'Something tells me you want me to be quick.'

He was right. 'William and Eleanor are in a bit of a state by the sounds of it. I'd like to be there in time to make a few enquiries before I see them.'

'Right then.'

We went inside, through to the kitchen.

Mrs Sugden had oxtail soup on the table. The three of us sat down.

Over the soup, Sykes gave us a brief account of everything that had gone on, beginning with the lack of security and the way that Joe Finch the drayman made free with the premises. He concluded with the death of the secretary and her failed attempt to talk to Lofthouse on Tuesday.

I asked a few questions, wanting to be clear. 'Joe Finch was the one who got into a fight with Slater Parnaby, the brewery queen's father?'

'That's right, only it might be more correct to say that Slater Parnaby got into a fight with Joe Finch. Parnaby's a man who likes trouble.'

'Did the police find any fingerprints on the contaminated barrels?'

'None that couldn't be accounted for. All the culprit had to do was remove the bungs and slip in contaminated titbits.'

'What about James Lofthouse? Is he still in Germany?'

Sykes produced a sheet of paper from his briefcase. 'I have a copy of his itinerary, but he hasn't kept to it. He added Vienna.'

Mrs Sugden perked up. 'You know that Miss Merton is fluent in German. She went on walking tours there before the war.'

Miss Merton is our former neighbour. She keeps house for her brother. They live close by, in the university Vice Chancellor's residence.

'How would she be able to help?' Sykes asked.

'She knows people, in the embassy, the consulates, and has German friends. I'm sure she'd make some telephone calls, starting with places James Lofthouse has been staying.'

Sykes passed the itinerary to Mrs Sugden. She was about to take it into the dining room, having a dread of food being spilled on documents.

It may take a while for Miss Merton to book a call to Germany, but the Vice Chancellor's residence was on a telephone line regarded as important. 'Mrs Sugden, ring Miss Merton now. Give her the most recent details of James's itinerary, say it's urgent and we would be forever grateful for information about where he is now. I'll call by on my way to Masham.'

I moved the soup plates and brought across the potted meat sandwiches.

Sykes took a sandwich. 'The Barleycorn Annual General Meeting looms. Mr Lofthouse is nervous about it.'

'Why?'

'He has lost confidence, which could be for all sorts of reasons, but it does seem as if the company is being got at. He needs the support of the Tebbits and they are not playing ball. I checked on the distribution of shares. William gave Eleanor five percent of his shares when they married. Between them William and Eleanor have forty-five percent. Wandering James Lofthouse has ten percent. Mrs Tebbit and her son Rory have forty-five percent, she twenty, Rory twenty-five.'

I did a quick calculation. 'So, without James, there could be deadlock if the Tebbits don't agree with a course of action William decides on?'

'Yes, and the other way around of course.'

As Sykes gave me the account of his time at the brewery, I realised I was right in thinking that William Lofthouse had not told me everything when he called to see me on the day of his friend's funeral. He did not want to face what might be a coming storm for his precious brewery.

When Sykes told me of the cancellation of orders by the two pubs and a small brewery. I asked, 'Do you think they are connected?'

'It seems likely. They all stem from Ripon. I'd need to look into that more closely.'

'All of this puts a sinister slant on the secretary's death, wouldn't you say, Mr Sykes?'

Sykes agreed. 'I wish you'd met Miss Crawford. I felt she was on the point of saying something significant on Tuesday, when Lofthouse wouldn't listen to her.'

'Could you make a guess as to what it could be?'

He shook his head. 'I don't know what she might have heard, but I can guess where she heard it. On Monday evening she went with her neighbour, Mrs Rigg, to the Oddfellows supper meeting in Ripon. The next day she tried several times to talk to Mr Lofthouse, but he shut his ears. It's almost as if he suspected she might tell something that would make him take his head from the sand.'

I stood. 'Time for me to go.'

'Here's what I've jotted down, and a bit of a map.' Sykes gave me a sketch, showing the road where Miss Crawford was knocked down, the lane where she lived. He marked Miss Crawford's cottage on the lane, Mrs Rigg's cottage, and the Murthys' house on the main road.

Sykes walked me to the car, saying, 'I'll get myself to the library and the newspaper offices, see what else I can find out about the Tebbits.'

'Yes, and let's hope Miss Merton's friends in Germany can locate the errant nephew.'

Sykes leaned into the car. 'Talking about absences, that reminds me. Mr Lofthouse will need to find replacements for Miss Crawford and Ruth Parnaby. Ruth has gone on working, but in the contract Mrs Lofthouse signed, it was agreed that the brewery queen should have leave of absence.'

Mrs Sugden came out to wave me off. She had picked up that Mr Lofthouse has a tight fist and asked, 'Does Mr Lofthouse need telling it won't be two for one when it comes to fees?'

'The original contract letter was clear, Mrs Sugden.'

Eleanor, without needing to be asked, had said she would arrange for a cottage to be made ready for me.

'Mr Sykes, come in the Rolls for the garden party. You'll come won't you, Mrs Sugden?'

'I'll see. I'm not a great one for garden parties. I don't have the right sort of hat.'

'Rosie will help you choose a hat,' Sykes said. 'But is it a good idea to let Mr Lofthouse see the Rolls? He might think we don't need paying.'

'If William sees the Rolls, our modest invoice will come as a pleasant surprise.'

Chapter Fourteen

One of Jim Sykes's skills is giving directions and drawing maps. I was glad of this as I found my way to West Tanfield, and the lane where Miss Crawford had lived. I passed the house with the steep garden that Sykes had described as belonging to Mr and Mrs Murthy.

Although I was keeping an eye out for the lane, it appeared too quickly, after the overgrown hedgerow. Having overshot it, I carried on a little way, looking for a place to pull off the road.

An odd sight on my right made me slow down. I pulled onto the verge.

A well-made, white-haired woman held a spade. She stood on the grass by the side of the road. I got out of the car and went across to her. She was every inch the countrywoman, with a broad weather-worn face, pale blue eyes and a mass of white hair caught up by combs and pins. Her foot was on the spade, now pushed so far into the ground that it stood on its own. She had dug a semi-circle shaped channel, soil piled around the edge.

This must be the site of Miss Crawford's death. Flowers were crushed, the ground disturbed.

'Hello' seemed an odd thing to say, given that I was interrupting her, but I said it anyway.

'Hello,' she said back.

'My name's Kate Shackleton. I'm a friend of Mrs Lofthouse.'

'They haven't been near,' she said, 'and I thought they would have.'

Quick white lie. 'Eleanor asked me to come because Mr Lofthouse has taken the death of his secretary very hard. He is poorly.'

She gave the slightest of snorts. 'They're going ahead with the garden party. I expect they'll say Miss Crawford would have wanted them to.'

My first thought was to plead ignorance of that, but my second thought led me to speak up for them, and to make their excuses. If in doubt, plead ignorance. I did both. 'I don't know about that, except that they thought long and hard about cancelling. They will be making a tribute to Miss Crawford and considering the best way to commemorate her loyalty and her service.'

The woman seemed placated. There were bulbs on the ground. She had come to do some planting. I recognised that need, that need to do something when grief brings a standstill. 'Mrs Lofthouse asked me to talk to Miss Crawford's friend, Mrs Rigg.'

The woman relaxed her hold on the spade. 'You're talking to her.'

'How do you do, Mrs Rigg? I'm very sorry for your loss.'

'I wish they'd just find the so-and-so that did it.'

'Oh, they will! The Lofthouses will make sure of that. Now, shall we plant those bulbs? What are they?'

'Daffodils from her own garden and mine.' She looked at my gloves. 'You'll get mucky.'

'They're driving gloves, and soil is clean dirt.' I began to place the bulbs. 'What time did Miss Crawford usually set off for work?'

'Eight o'clock on the dot.'

'What time was the accident.'

'That's the shocking thing. If she'd been on her own timetable it never would have happened. It was more like half past nine.'

'How awful.'

'Almost as if it were decreed. She was so punctual.'

'Do you have any idea why she may have been late that day?'

'No.' Mrs Rigg began to replace the soil and patted it down.

I needed to look round Miss Crawford's cottage, without appearing nosy. 'I sometimes leave myself a note the night before, about what I have to do the next day. I wonder if Miss Crawford did the same.'

'It wouldn't surprise me.'

'Shall we have a look?'

'The police have been in. I didn't go in this morning, but I should. She wouldn't want milk turning sour.'

We brought the sadness into the downstairs room that was both parlour and kitchen, yet it felt as if the sadness waited for us. The room was neat and clean, with tapestry cushions on the wooden armchair and footstool. The bookcase held a family bible, *Pilgrim's Progress*, histories, novels by George Eliot, Elizabeth Gaskell and Anne Brontë and Ponsonby's *English Diaries*.

'Miss Crawford kept a diary,' I said.

'How do you know?'

'From her bookcase. And I'm judging that she was that sort of person.'

'You're right about that. She kept it here, on this little table, next to the fireside chair.'

'But it's not there now?'

'Why do you ask?'

I told her about William's distress that he had not listened to what Miss Crawford wanted to tell him. 'Normally, one would never read another person's diary, but I am wondering whether something happened, or she learned something that she particularly wanted to say, and if so whether she wrote that in her diary.'

Mrs Rigg opened the writing desk. 'It's not here. Now you have me curious.' She indicated a pile of typewritten papers. 'Someone's been at this. Look how untidy this is. Miss Crawford is so neat with paperwork.'

'What is the typing?'

Mrs Rigg straightened the papers. 'Mick Musgrove's rhymes. Mr Musgrove is an elderly man who used to work at the brewery.

He knows lots of traditional rhymes about ale, the cup that cheers, all that sort of thing. Miss Crawford took down his dictation in shorthand and typed them. They're to be bound and kept in the library for posterity.'

'What a good idea.'

'Miss Crawford was like that. She went to see him when he was at death's door. He came back to life when someone wanted to hear him recite. He's on his allotment most of the day now. He grows the sweetest carrots I ever tasted.'

She went to the stairs. 'I'll just see if that diary is on her bedside table. If there was something she wanted to say, it should not go unheeded.'

I could tell by the slowness of her footsteps as she came down that there was no diary.

She shook her head.

'Mrs Rigg, when you went to your Oddfellows supper on Monday, was there anyone that Miss Crawford spoke to, a person who might have mentioned something to do with the Lofthouses, or the brewery, that she would have wanted to pass on?'

She thought for a moment. 'I can't think of anything.'

'Nothing at all unusual or different?'

'She did seem a little thoughtful, as we came back. Of course, you can't talk in that car of Mr Murthy's because you can't hear yourself.'

'Is there anyone in particular at the Oddfellows that Miss Crawford was friendly with?' I asked.

She looked at me as if I had asked a stupid question. 'We're all friendly. That's what the Oddfellows is, Oddfellows Friendly Society, friendship and mutual help society.'

She thought for a moment and held up a finger. 'Ah!'

'What?'

'Something and nothing. When Mr Murthy brought us back, Miss Crawford stayed in the car with him, wanting a word. She had never done that before.'

'Do you know what it was about?'

She shook her head. 'I thought nothing of it at the time. All that comes to mind is that Mr Murthy is executor of Miss Crawford's will. Perhaps she had a premonition?'

'Thank you, Mrs Rigg. You've been most kind. I'll go back and talk to the Lofthouses.'

We left the house. Mrs Rigg locked the door, moved to put the key under the plant pot, and then changed her mind. 'I'll hold onto this, since someone has been in and upset her papers and taken her diary.'

'That's a good idea. And Mrs Rigg, this might seem an odd question, but can you think of anyone who would have wished Miss Crawford harm?'

'Odd you should ask me that. Sergeant Moon asked the same question. No one would have wanted to harm Miss Crawford.'

Chapter Fifteen

The imposing old house on Ripon High Street bore the Oddfellows nameplate. I rang the bell and waited. Just as I was about to go to the side of the house, to find another entrance, the door opened, revealing a lanky, smiling man. His welcoming look made me feel sure we must have met before, until I brought to mind Mrs Rigg's words about this being a friendly society.

'Hello, I'm Mrs Shackleton, Kate Shackleton. I'm here on behalf of Mr Lofthouse at the Barleycorn Brewery, Miss Crawford's employer.'

'Hello, Mrs Shackleton. I'm Geoffrey Lincoln, manager, or caretaker if you please. Do come in.'

He and I had not met before. I would have remembered that warm-as-toast voice, and the tendency to promote or demote himself, to manager or caretaker.

We stepped into a hallway hung with portraits of gentlemen in ceremonial robes, medallions and antique headgear. 'Our Oddfellow forebears,' he explained. 'We'll go into the reading room. Can I get you anything?'

'No please don't trouble.'

He led us through the house into a book-lined room with a view of a well-kept garden, and a birdbath occupied by a robin. We sat by the window.

'Miss Crawford's late father was a member in long-standing.

Miss Crawford has been honorary secretary since the war, so highly thought of, such a lovely lady.'

'She will be greatly missed at the brewery.'

We said those much-repeated words that are to hand for such an occasion. He told me that the Oddfellows would be there to do whatever may be useful and helpful.

'We intend to put on the funeral breakfast. She will be buried at the Cathedral.'

I gave a non-committal reply. Miss Crawford would not have discussed her funeral with her boss. It would be Mr Murthy, her executor, who would have that information.

I skirted round Mr Lincoln's questions, and came to my own.

'Mr Lincoln, on Tuesday, the day after your supper meeting, there was something Miss Crawford wanted to say to say to Mr Lofthouse. He had to leave the office before they had time to talk. In retrospect, Mr Lofthouse thought Miss Crawford had been unusually distracted or concerned. Did you notice any difference in her manner on Monday evening?'

He bit his lip and frowned. 'Can't say I did. Some people can be the wrong side out one day to the next, but not Miss Crawford. She was always the same, well-mannered, thoughtful. She paid attention to people, if that does not sound a peculiar thing to say.'

'Did she talk to anyone in particular, any person who might have said something that would be of interest in relation to her work, or whether she intended to call somewhere this morning before going to work?'

'Not to my knowledge. My wife is the one for chatter, but she is out shopping.'

'When will Mrs Lincoln be back?'

'It could be a little while. She calls to see her mother.'

'Then I'll be on my way, Mr Lincoln.' I stood. 'If there is anything else you think of, perhaps you'd be kind enough to contact me through Mr Lofthouse.'

The doorbell rang. Mr Lincoln sprang to his feet. 'That might be Marjorie, loaded with shopping. Excuse me.'

I heard him talking in the hall, and a softer voice with an Indian lilt answering him. Mr Murthy? The man who had given a lift to Miss Crawford and Mrs Rigg. Please bring him in, I said silently.

Mr Lincoln did bring in his visitor, introduced us, and excused himself to put on the kettle.

Mr Murthy was a small man, immaculately dressed and with a courtesy that would not let him sit down until I did. Quickly, I sat down. 'Mr Murthy, I know of you through Mrs Rigg. I'm here on behalf of Miss Crawford's employer.'

'Ah, my condolences to Mr Lofthouse.'

'I'll pass that on.'

'I have written to him. The letter is in the post.'

'You are Miss Crawford's executor?'

'I am.'

'May I ask you a question, on behalf of Mr Lofthouse?'

'Please do.'

'Miss Crawford was on the point of telling Mr Lofthouse something she regarded as important on Tuesday. Sadly, the matter was left over until Wednesday, when it was too late. I know that she stayed in the car a few moments to speak to you when you drove the ladies back to West Tanfield. Normally I would not enquire about another person's conversation but if you can tell me anything that would put Mr Lofthouse's mind at ease, I should be grateful. Mrs Rigg thought it may be in connection with Miss Crawford's will.'

'Under the circumstances, I can tell you. It was not in connection with the will. Apparently, Mrs Lincoln told Miss Crawford that she saw, or thought she saw, James Lofthouse coming out of a public house in Ripon. Rory Tebbit, who works at the bank, is a friend of James. Miss Crawford thought Rory would know whether James really had come back and was perhaps planning to surprise his uncle.'

'And had he come back?'

Mr Murthy showed no emotion other than a slight gesture, opening his palm. 'I have always held Miss Crawford in high regard. It was uncharacteristic of her to ask such a thing. It was not my place to enquire into the comings and goings of others.'

'Was that your answer to her, that it was not your place to enquire?'

He sighed. 'I am afraid so. Do you think the matter was important?'

'It is not my place to answer that question, Mr Murthy.'

'Touché.'

'But am I right in thinking that after today's tragic incident you thought better of it, and you did ask Rory Tebbit about James and that Rory did not deny it?' It was a shot in the dark, but Mr Murthy was surprised into admitting that I was right.

'Did Rory say that James's return was to be a surprise, for the garden party on Saturday, and did he ask you to keep the secret?'

'How do you know that?' Mr Murthy asked. 'Why does it matter now?'

I knew that because Miss Merton had made enquiries based on James's itinerary. She found out that James left Hamburg ten days ago.

It mattered because Miss Crawford's shrewdness may have led to her death.

Chapter Sixteen

By the time I reached Masham, the brewery had closed for the night. I drove to Barleycorn house, a Georgian mansion built by one of William's ancestors who wished to be close to his brewery yet enjoy extensive gardens and fine living.

A maid opened the door. She was clearly expecting me. 'Mrs Shackleton?'

'Hello, and yes.'

'Mrs Lofthouse is in her sitting room, please come through. There's a telegram for you.'

Eleanor almost fell on me with a cry of relief. 'Am I glad to see you!'

'Is something wrong?'

'I was beginning to think you'd changed your mind, had a better offer! Let's have an early supper. I'm guessing you haven't eaten, because I haven't.'

'You're right. I can eat whatever you put in front of me, and a glass of wine, too.'

'Good.'

The maid was waiting for instructions. Eleanor said, 'Yes to the food, Beryl.'

Eleanor waved towards the big comfortable chairs by the fire. 'Kate, you must be frozen after that journey.' She went to the cocktail cabinet.

'Where's William?' I asked.

Eleanor poured wine. 'I packed him off to bed. Honestly, Kate, I've never seen him so upset. He's recovering from jaundice and he needs a holiday, but he daren't take one.' She handed me a glass of wine and sat in the opposite chair. 'It was a stroke of genius, your suggestion that I visit Mrs Tebbit. Would you believe that she hadn't seen the invitation to the garden party?'

'Rory kept it from her?' I asked.

'How do you know about Rory?'

'From Jim Sykes.'

'You and he make a great pair, Kate. Scotland Yard watch out.'

'Oh, they are watching out!'

'Mrs Tebbit hadn't seen the AGM correspondence either. Both are now in her diary. And I'm to call her Gwyneth, which is a great relief, Kate. I did wonder how people would take to me, second wife, younger woman, all that sort of thing.'

'Then you've won over Mrs Tebbit.'

'So it seems. I began by telling her about poor Miss Crawford of course, and how cut up we are. She hadn't heard about Miss Crawford's death. She was desperately sad, and so sympathetic. She knew her you see, not just from Barleycorn meetings but from the Cathedral. They both did all sorts of charitable works and fund-raising.'

Now Eleanor had made me curious. Given Mrs Tebbit's penchant for bright shiny objects, I wondered whether she ever went home with a church candlestick up her sleeve, or whether religious institutions were exempt from her list of targets.

'I'm so glad, Eleanor. She's the right sort of person for a garden party, in spite of her tendencies. And I expect she understood why it must go ahead.'

'She did. We went to the florist together. She helped me choose flowers, including a memorial bouquet and card for Miss Crawford that will have pride of place in the marquee.'

She suddenly spotted the telegram on the mantelpiece and stood to pick it up and pass it to me. 'Here I am rabbiting on and this may be important. I'll give you some privacy to read it. If it's someone urgently requesting your presence, tell them they are too late.'

'No need to leave the room, Eleanor. It will be from Mr Sykes.'

'I'll go tell William you are here. He will be very relieved that you are both on the case and he can stop worrying.'

I was right. The telegram was from Sykes. He confirmed the information Miss Merton had given me. He had also trawled his sources to find out more about the Tebbits and James Lofthouse. The telegram read,

Confirm James left Hamburg by ferry ten days ago STOP James's father was William's elder brother STOP Had the elder brother lived James would have inherited STOP Family connection between Lofthouse and Tebbit families long standing STOP James and Rory at school together

Sykes had not counted the pennies when sending the telegram. The STOPs made it absolutely clear that James must feel entitled to a much greater share of the brewery than his twenty percent. I had to read the last two sentences twice: Lofthouse and Tebbit families long standing connection. James and Rory at school together.

The sabotage of the beer, the lost orders, and possibly even Miss Crawford's death formed a deeply worrying pattern. First bring your opponent to his knees, and then make the next move.

What would the next move be? I was now willing to believe that Mrs Lincoln had been correct when she thought she saw James in Ripon. James and Rory Tebbit were friends. If it came to a tussle on the Barleycorn board, James, Rory and Mrs Tebbit could out-vote William and Eleanor.

What puzzled me was why James did not simply come home and wait to take over, as his uncle expected. It made no sense.

Eleanor came back. 'William feels better after his rest. He's now worrying about me.'

The maid wheeled in our supper on a trolley. 'I thought we'd eat in here, Kate.'

'Perfect.'

'It's steak and ale pie and chips. Just what I've been fancying.'

Beryl the maid beamed. 'Well, Mrs Lofthouse, it'll keep your strength up.'

I suddenly felt the need for another glass of wine. James wanted to take no chances. As Eleanor had made me aware when we met at the café in Ripon, she was pregnant. Her maid Beryl knew. Did James know that his young Aunt Eleanor was in that interesting condition? Uncle William might last another twenty years, leaving a son and heir who would come between James and his expectations.

Eleanor and I settled ourselves at tables by the fire and tucked into the food.

'Eleanor?'

'Kate?'

'Are you keeping well?'

She beamed. 'Very well, and I hardly show do I? My mother didn't. Neither did my sister, for ages. Of course, depends what size dress I put on in the morning.'

'Well I'm very happy for you.'

'Thank you.'

I tried to make it sound the most natural question in the world. 'Does James know about the baby?'

'Yes. He was writing long, chatty letters before he ran out of ink. William is hopeless, leaves it to me to reply. It just slipped out, as things do when you write a chatty letter. He's delighted for us.'

I could imagine that delight. James wanted to be in charge, and not just in charge but to regain what he saw as his rightful ownership. Eleanor and her unborn child could be in danger. I knew that a cottage was ready for me, but should I ask to stay here at Barleycorn House? Staying here, I could keep an eye on Eleanor.

Staying at the cottage, I would be free to come and go, investigate, be a free agent. That is what I must do. But if anything happened to Eleanor, I would be to blame for not warning her. If I did warn her about James, she would not want to believe me. I had no evidence that James was involved in anything other than the subterfuge of planning a surprise visit home on the day of the garden party. Yet the catalogue of things going wrong at the Barleycorn pointed in that direction.

As we ate, it came to me that the best thing to do would be to get William and Eleanor out of the way.

'Eleanor, a change of scene would do you and William a world of good.'

'We have been going around in circles but he daren't take time off, not now.'

'Then break the circle, and it would be good for business. Support your brewery queen. Why don't you and William drive Ruth to Scarborough tomorrow? Make it an overnight stay. Be ready to support her in the contest on Friday.'

Eleanor gave a small cry and put her hand to her mouth. 'Oh no! That poor girl. I completely forgot. Miss Crawford was to take Ruth to Scarborough tomorrow, and Ruth hasn't said a word about it.'

'Do you feel up to making the journey?' I asked. A couple of days would give Sykes and me time to find out more. We could be wrong in our suppositions about James, but I did not think so.

'Yes, as long as I'm not sick in the car.'

'Sit on a newspaper, take a basin, a bottle of water and a towel. If you're prepared, you won't be sick. Do go! Put yourselves and Ruth up in the best hotel. Walk by the sea. You'll come back more able to face what life throws at you.'

'If only we could.'

'I'm here. Mr Sykes can be back in no time. Sergeant Moon will find the driver who killed Miss Crawford.'

'Kate, you are a genius. William is fond of telling me what capable people he has at the brewery. Let them get on with the finishing touches for the garden party. I'll go up and see him. Beryl will take a note round to Ruth about the change of plan.'

'Tell William that you and the baby need a walk by the sea, that the baby needs to listen to the waves. If you say the outing is for William's own good, he'll put up an argument against going.'

'You're right, Kate! I'll go to William now.' Eleanor jumped to her feet but stopped at the door. 'It's a lovely idea but there's too much to do!'

'You've a housekeeper. You've Beryl. William will ask one of the men at the brewery to oversee setting up the marquees and so on. Everyone will pull their weight. You don't organise your own art exhibitions. Think of it like that.'

'True. I'd be pretty hopeless anyway. I'd drive everyone mad. And it will be so nice to come back and for everything to be done.'

'That's settled then.' I stood. 'All I need is the use of your telephone and the key to the cottage.'

'Beryl will show you the way to the cottage. The phone is in the hall. Help yourself. Oh, and before you ask, we do have what passes as a secure telephone line. Our operator served in communications during the war. I'm ninety-nine percent sure she doesn't listen. If she does, secrets will go to the grave with her.'

Fortunately, the telephone was in a private part of the hall, in its own telephone box.

I gave the operator my home number and waited for her to connect me. In spite of Eleanor's assurances, I decided not to mention James Lofthouse's name.

Mrs Sugden answered quickly. She must have been waiting for me to ring.

'Any news?'

'I'm finding my way about. Eleanor and I just had supper.'

'What did you have?'

I told her. 'Is Mr Sykes with you?'

'Here and waiting. I'll put him on.'

'Hello!' Sykes dislikes using the telephone and it shows.

'Hello. I do believe our friend is back from the continent,' I told him. 'It's not yet confirmed, but he was spotted.'

'So he is up to something.'

'He hasn't found time to come to Masham yet.'

I could hear Sykes's brain tick, as he decided how to phrase his next comment. 'But do you think the returned prodigal managed to go out for a drive on Wednesday morning?'

I knew what Sykes was asking. The one person in the brewery whom Sykes had called his guide, Miss Crawford, knew the business inside out. She would have been a threat to James. William Lofthouse was blinded by family feelings and sentiment towards James, and Eleanor was the outsider who endorsed her husband's feelings. Miss Crawford was the threat.

'It's possible that he did go out for a drive that day,' I said. My stomach lurched as I pictured a car putting on speed as the driver saw Miss Crawford riding her bicycle.

'Anything else going on?' Sykes asked.

'I hope Eleanor will persuade William that they should take Ruth to Scarborough tomorrow, and have a couple of days away from everything and everyone.' I put the emphasis on everyone. My unspoken question, to Sykes and to myself was, Do I tell the Lofthouses that James is back?

I like to wait until a full story emerges before spilling bits and pieces of a tale, but it was a risk to withhold some vital piece of information. 'There's always the business of who knows what and when,' I said.

There was a silence on the line, and then Sykes said, 'I can see the yea and the nay. Do you have a feeling to go by?'

'Yes, I do.'

'That's it then. Goodnight, Mrs Shackleton.' It might have been my imagination, but I thought his 'Goodnight' sounded edged with anxiety.

'Goodnight, Mr Sykes.'

Beryl was waiting for me to finish the call. 'Shall I show you the way to Oak Cottage?'

I took the key. 'Thank you, Beryl, but don't trouble. Just tell me the way.'

'Pass the school, go along the lane until you see the allotments. Turn left before the allotments. You'll see two joined cottages. The first is Elm Cottage where Miss Boland lives. She's the music teacher. The second is Oak Cottage, the one you want.'

Bearing in mind the axiom don't trouble trouble until trouble troubles you, I may have left without saying another word to Eleanor, but at that moment she appeared at the top of the stairs. 'Kate, William and I are all set for taking Ruth to Scarborough tomorrow. William will tell Mr Beckwith not to expect Ruth at the office. It was a ridiculous idea that she should spend a couple of hours in the wages office on the eve of her big day.'

'That's good.'

Eleanor came down the stairs to see me out.

As we got to the door, I said, 'Eleanor there's something I ought to tell you.'

'You sound serious, Kate.'

'Knowing how anxious William was to have James back, we did a bit of checking on James's itinerary. James left Germany ten days ago.'

'Never! What a monkey. I bet he's in London, and not even a postcard.'

Don't retreat now, I told myself. 'That's possible, although someone at the Oddfellows saw him in Ripon.'

'That's too bad if it's true,' Eleanor said. 'He must know William needs him back. I wrote to him, saying your uncle is unwell and will be glad to see you back.'

That message may have encouraged James to come in for the kill. 'Look on the bright side, Eleanor. If James does show his face tomorrow, intending to surprise, he'll find out that you won't always be here, holding the fort.'

I wanted to tell her to be careful, but that seemed alarmist.

We said goodnight.

As I left Barleycorn House, the town crier was on his rounds, calling the hour, announcing Miss Crawford's death, and urging anyone with information to go to the police station. It was encouraging to see several people at the entrance to the police station, waiting to go in.

Chapter Seventeen

I followed Beryl's directions, driving past the school and along the paved lane that led onto more bumpy ground. Soon it would be dark. Ahead of me I saw fenced allotments. I stopped the car, not wishing to risk damaging the tyres by driving down what Beryl had called a track. From the dicky seat, I took a blanket and lantern, as well as my overnight case. With a bit of luck, my trunk would be at the cottage.

A figure appeared, swinging what appeared to be an axe. As the distance between us closed, I saw that it was indeed an axe.

'Hey-up!' said a deep voice with a growl in it.

Hey-up does not come naturally to me. Good evening seemed too formal. 'Hello,' I said.

We were closer now. I saw that he was an old man in dark clothes.

He spoke. 'I heard a motorcar engine.'

'Yes.'

He raised his axe. 'Where's the spawn of the devil that drives it?'

'You're looking at her.'

'Oh.' He lowered his axe. 'I don't suppose you never ran no one down.'

'I never did.'

'Well then I'll let you off.' He kept a tight grip on the axe. 'Where are you off to?'

'Oak Cottage.'

'I'll carry your case. But if you hear of the man that did for Miss Crawford, tell them Mick Musgrove, that's me, will see him into kingdom come.'

Mick Musgrove. I remembered the name. The axeman carrying my case was poet laureate of ale, whose rhymes Miss Crawford had taken down in shorthand and transcribed.

I let him carry the suitcase, imagining that this might encourage him to lay down his axe. 'Pleased to meet you, Mr Musgrove. I'm Mrs Shackleton.'

'How do. You're to be staying next door to Miss Boland.'

'So I'm told.'

He waved his arm towards a darkened stretch of ground. 'You're standing next to her allotment, or what was her father's allotment. There'll be a good crop of carrots this year.'

We came to the adjoining thatched stone cottages, both with low gates and fences and a square of garden in front. The first had a light in the upstairs window, the second was in darkness.

We reached the second gate. I thanked Mr Musgrove for carrying my case.

'Would you like to hear a rhyme?' He cleared his throat. 'I collect rhymes, for posterity, all with the same theme as you might say.' Without waiting for an answer, he drew a deep breath and began.

'Your doctors may boast of their lotions
And ladies may talk of their tea
But I envy them none of their potions,
A glass of good stingo for me.
The doctor may sneer if he pleases,
But my recipe never will fail;
For the physic that cures all diseases
Is a bumper of good English ale.'

'Thank you, Mr Musgrove. Is that your own rhyme?' The gate creaked as I opened it.

'It wasn't but it is now.' He tipped his cap. 'I make it my job to keep the praise of ale alive.'

'That's a noble task. Now if you'll excuse me, I'll settle in before it gets dark.'

He carried my case to the doorstep and touched his cap. I thanked him, and we said goodnight.

I thought of the typed manuscript that I had picked up in Miss Crawford's cottage and put in my briefcase for safe keeping. She must have spent hours listening to rhymes, writing in shorthand, typing them. How many motorists might the rhymester axe down in revenge for Miss Crawford's death?

I brought in the suitcase, lantern and blanket. The interior of the cottage was more spacious than I expected. This downstairs room looked large and full of shadows. I lit the oil lamp that stood on the table. There was ample furniture, a polished Yorkshire range, dresser, deal table and chairs, a rocking chair and a steamer chair on either side of the fireplace. The fire was laid. I took off my coat and looked for a hook on the back of the door. A royal blue velvet cloak hung there. There was a second oil lamp and candles. Masham has electricity but it did not come as far as this.

Under the window was a sink but no tap. The place appeared spotlessly clean. A door on the far wall, which I thought must lead into the back garden, opened onto two tiny rooms, one a scullery and the other with a tin bath hung on the wall. On a long ledge there was a decorative basin, a jug of water, a tablet of Pears soap and two towels on hooks. On the floor beneath the ledge were three chamber pots, one of them new.

Eleanor had forgotten to mention there would be oil and candlelight, and outdoor plumbing. I had better find my way round before it became too dark.

I went upstairs. The rooms had been partitioned. There were three bedrooms. My trunk was in the bedroom that looked out onto the front garden.

I always enjoyed camping. Staying here would be like camping, but with beds and a roof. Compared to a tent, this would be luxury.

I was blessed with one of those sudden, illogical bursts of happiness. Here I would be, away from the hustle and bustle, from the telephone, the postman, and above all not beholden to kind hosts with their expectations and obligations, and not confined to a hotel where one must be on best behaviour.

A windowless middle bedroom held a single bed and a chest of drawers.

I opened the door to the back bedroom. There were two beds, a wardrobe and a dresser. The curtains were open. On the nearest bed lay a suitcase. There was a shape on the bed under the window. I went closer, feeling like one of the three bears. Someone has been sleeping in my bed. This was not Goldilocks, but a dark-haired girl in a white nightgown, deep in slumber, her arms spread above the counterpane. The royal blue cape behind the door gave me the clue. Ruth Parnaby, brewery queen, had arrived here before me.

I was not yet expected. She would have known about the cottage being made ready, standing empty. Eleanor had invited me to stay there next Saturday, after the garden party.

I must let Miss Parnaby sleep. She would be more surprised to see me than I her. This could have been worse. I might have come upon wizened Mick Musgrove lying there, hatchet by his side, dreaming of murdering a motorist.

Quietly, I went back downstairs. Taking out my writing case and pen, I wrote a note and put it on the table.

Miss Parnaby. You are most welcome to share the cottage. I hope it will give you peace of mind to know that Mrs Lofthouse will be taking you to Scarborough tomorrow and that you need not go into work.

Kate Shackleton.

Carrying my lantern, I went into the garden and soon spotted the well, shared with next door. At the far end of the gardens were two privies, one for each house, each with its surrounding paving stones. More luxury.

Back in the house, moving quietly, I closed the curtains. I looked again at the cloak behind the door. Under it, on a coat hanger, was a satin gown and a gold medallion—Ruth's finery for the contest in Scarborough. Taking what I needed from my suitcase, I noticed that something had been flung on the floor. I picked up a red swimming costume, or rather two halves of a swimming costume. It had been very neatly cut in two.

I locked and bolted the door.

Chapter Eighteen

Last night, I had opened the bedroom window. I was awakened by the sound of the dawn chorus. I looked in on Ruth. She was still sleeping.

I lit the fire and then washed and dressed as quietly as I could. There was a good supply of food, eggs, bread, butter, jam, a jug of milk and a pail of water. I boiled the kettle on a Calor gas ring, made a pot of tea and sat at the table to read Mick Musgrove's *Rhymes in Praise of Ale.*

Miss Crawford had written a brief introduction and listed contents. It must have taken her hours to transcribe and type. This collection deserved to be printed, not simply bound and kept in the library.

By the time I finished reading, I heard a sound upstairs. I cleared the table and set it for breakfast, making a clatter so as to let Ruth know she was not alone. I had seen her, at the trussing, but she had not seen me. I heard her footsteps on the stairs, and then there she was, looking puzzled. 'Hello, Ruth. I left you a note, in case you were up first. There's tea in the pot but we'll have a fresh one when the kettle boils.'

'I heard a sound and thought Miss Boland had come in from next door,' Ruth said.

'Miss Boland probably heard a sound and thought it was you. Oh, and I'm Kate Shackleton. I wasn't due to arrive until the weekend but here I am. You met my colleague, Jim Sykes.'

I picked up Mick Musgrove's manuscript. Showing it to her and praising Miss Crawford's achievement broke the ice and distracted from the slight awkwardness. 'I'll make breakfast. I know you have a journey today, and big day tomorrow. Mr and Mrs Lofthouse will drive you to Scarborough.'

She gave a sigh of relief. 'Thank goodness for that. I thought I'd be going on my own. Miss Crawford booked the rail tickets, and a boarding house.'

'You must have some moral support and help with your hooks and eyes. That's a very elegant dress on the back of the door.'

'I'm to wear that for the parade through Scarborough. We three hopefuls will be on a decorated brewery dray, waving to people. For the contest I'm to take a day dress and a swimming costume.'

I picked the two halves of the swimming costume. 'What happened here?'

'The old man.'

'What old man?'

'Our dad. He took against the event, or against me.'

'Then we must find you a new swimming costume.'

'You'll help?'

'Of course.'

She smiled. 'I can't believe this. It's a bit like the fairy godmother telling Cinderella, you shall go to the ball.'

'Everyone needs a fairy godmother at some point in their life.'

'Miss Crawford was my fairy godmother. I dreamed of her last night. I think she must have sent you.'

'In a way, she did.' I put the manuscript of *Rhymes in Praise of Ale* on the dresser. 'I'm beginning to realise Miss Crawford was a very special person.'

Before we set off for Barleycorn House, Ruth wanted to say goodbye to her coach, the music teacher in the adjoining cottage.

Miss Boland came to the door and asked us in. She was tall, her white hair plaited and pinned up. She wore a long black skirt, a hand-knitted black cardigan and sturdy boots.

'Ruth! I thought you were going to hurry away without coming to see me. I've found the lucky charm I want you to have, so come in a minute, and who's this?'

I introduced myself. 'For the time being, I'm your new neighbour. Kate Shackleton.'

'Celia Boland.' We shook hands. She insisted we step inside.

As in Oak Cottage, the door opened directly into the big room that was both kitchen and parlour. It would have been spacious had it not held a piano, a harpsichord and tables covered with sheet music. While Miss Boland searched a drawer for the lucky charm, I looked about the room. Posters and photographs from her operatic career covered one wall.

Miss Boland found the charm she was searching for, a four-leaf clover crafted into a brooch. She pinned it under the lapel of Ruth's jacket. 'Fasten it, out of sight,' Miss Boland advised. 'And on your travels, always take a length of knicker elastic, a sewing kit and a small pair of scissors.'

Kissing Ruth on both cheeks, reminding her to stand tall, breathe deeply, and do her voice exercises, Miss Boland released us.

*　*　*

At Barleycorn House, the Lofthouses' chauffeur was polishing the Bentley. He waved. 'I've you to thank for the trip to the seaside, Ruth!'

Ruth went into the house to find Eleanor.

I joined William in the conservatory. He put down his newspaper. 'Oh, Kate. I'm glad to see you. They are all going mad. Mr Beckwith has been on the telephone. He expected Ruth in work this morning, and what is he to do about the locksmith's quotation.'

'And what is he to do about it?'

'I told him to go full steam ahead. The man can start on Monday.'

'Is there anything I can do?' I asked.

'Call in on Mr Beckwith, top floor, wages office. Calm him down if he's fraught. He was talking to me about the garden party and Eleanor's list of what's to be done. Well I can't advise him on that.'

'I'll go see him later. Do you trust me to take decisions?'

'I wish you would.'

I explained about the rhymes that Miss Crawford had typed for Mick Musgrove.

'Ah, she told me about that.'

'It seems a shame that after Mr Musgrove and Miss Crawford spent so many hours on a labour of love, a single copy will languish in a dusty corner of the local library.'

'Then it must be done properly, Kate. Might you see to that?'

'I shall.'

Something had come over William. He was no longer counting the pennies. Suddenly it clicked. Eleanor had told him that James was back. He was preparing to be surprised and pleased at the unannounced return.

William folded his paper. 'We're behind with everything this morning. Eleanor and I went along to the place of the accident, you know. Hurt my heart to see it. Eleanor is going to arrange for a plaque, a memorial at the spot.'

'That's such a good idea, William.'

Beryl directed me upstairs. Eleanor had produced two swimming costumes for Ruth to try. While Ruth tried them on, I asked Eleanor to write a short note of thanks to Mrs Tebbit, for helping with the flowers for the garden party.

'Oh, I should have thought of that,' Eleanor said, going to her bureau. 'I can post it.'

'I need an excuse to call and see her,' I said. 'I'll pick up a posy on the way.'

Eleanor scribbled a note on paper so highly scented that it made me sneeze. She asked, 'Should I give Mrs Tebbit something more substantial than a posy? When she and Rory came to supper, she was mesmerised by a hideous green jade frog with emerald eyes. It's in a cabinet in the music room.'

'That would be too extravagant, Eleanor. It would raise suspicions that you want something from her. Besides, I do believe that for Mrs Tebbit, the pleasure is in the stealing. A gift would take away the thrill.'

'Pity,' Eleanor said. 'I know one shouldn't speak ill of the dead, but William's late wife had the most deplorable taste.' She popped the note for Mrs Tebbit into an envelope. 'What do you want to talk to her about?'

'I'm not sure yet. I want to make sure she is on your side, just in case Rory was up to something by not telling her about the garden party and the AGM.'

*　*　*

Once more, I stopped the car outside the Ripon Oddfellows Society premises. This time it was Mrs Lincoln who came to the door. A woman with a round, jolly face, she had a voice to match. 'Ah, you're the lady who called yesterday. I'm so pleased you came back.' Like her husband, she brimmed with friendliness.

'I was sorry to miss you yesterday, Mrs Lincoln.'

'Come through. Usually, my husband is not very good at describing people, but he didn't do too badly with you.'

I followed her into the kitchen which smelled strongly of Brasso. 'I hope you don't mind but I need to get on. I can't start baking until I've finished polishing the chains of office.'

'I appreciate you sparing me the time. Your husband said that you thought you saw James Lofthouse coming out of a pub.'

'I didn't think I saw him. I saw him plain as day, coming out of the White Horse. He had his coat collar up and a scarf on, like someone who'd caught pneumonia.'

Or someone who, trying not to be recognised, made himself more conspicuous.

'How could you be sure it was James?'

'I hate this job, polishing the chains. You've got to get the cloth on each of the links and there's always a bit of polish that you miss.' She spat on her cloth. 'You ask me how I could be sure it was him. I'll tell you. I used to work for the Tebbits, years ago. Rory Tebbit and James Lofthouse were friends, attended the same school. They'd go to each other's houses.'

'So, there could be no mistake?'

'None.' Mrs Lincoln reached the end of the chain and began to polish the medallion. I know James Lofthouse's looks, his long stride and his slouch.'

'What does he look like?'

'Thick blond hair, fleshy cheeks, wide nostrils, pale eyebrows that almost meet and the most charming smile when he's after something.'

'Perhaps he is staying at the White Horse.'

'They don't do rooms. He'll be staying with the Tebbits.'

'It's a puzzle that he hasn't gone to Barleycorn House, to see his uncle. It could be he is planning a surprise.'

Mrs Lincoln snorted. 'I wouldn't want to be on the receiving end of one of his surprises.' She put down her polishing cloth. 'I could get the sack for talking about James Lofthouse. We swear never to discuss anything we overhear at Oddfellows meetings, or to disclose anything that relates to our members.'

'Is he a member?'

'No. The reason I told Miss Crawford was to warn her.'

'What about?'

'I don't know. But I was wrong to warn her because thirty-six hours later, she was dead. And for my pains, I could lose us this job.'

'You've done nothing to jeopardise your job. It was Mr Murthy who told me that Miss Crawford asked about James Lofthouse. Try not to worry.'

She gave a sigh and started to gather up the polished chains.

I have never before recruited a stranger as an informer, but there is always a first time. 'Are you still in touch with people who work at the Tebbits' house?'

'Yes.' Her answer was cautious. She did not volunteer names.

'We may be right, we may be wrong, but it is possible we could help each other.'

I was doing what I should never do, jumping to a conclusion. But somebody had to do it, before the trail grew cold.

'What do you want me to find out, Mrs Shackleton?'

'I want to know where James Lofthouse goes, and what he's up to.'

I stood on the doorstep of the Tebbit house and rang the bell. A maid with a loose strand of hair and a harassed expression opened the door.

'Is Mrs Tebbit at home?'

'She is but she is unwell today. I am not to disturb her, but I could give her a message later.'

'I'm sorry to hear that. Would you please tell her Mrs Shackleton called, to bring a note from Mrs Lofthouse, and these flowers.'

'That's very kind.' She sniffed the flowers. The maid brightened. She smoothed back her hair and took the flowers and card. 'Thank you. That might cheer up Mrs Tebbit. I'm waiting for the lilac to come out. That's my favourite.'

'Mine too! Oh, and while I remember, did Miss Crawford leave her gloves here when she called on Wednesday morning?' I was taking a chance. If the maid knew Miss Crawford had been killed, she would wonder why I was enquiring after a dead woman's gloves.

'No. She couldn't have because she didn't come in. Mr James Lofthouse wasn't at home to Miss Crawford.'

So, James was not at home to Miss Crawford, but the knowledge that she knew he was back must have given James a fright. All he need have said was that he intended to surprise his uncle by arriving back from his travels in time for the garden party.

Sykes had described Miss Crawford as astute. What did she know that caused James's guilty conscience to make him panic?

Short of searching the Tebbits' premises for a damaged car, there was little else I could do here. I needed more information. In the hope of having the police help me with my enquiries, I set off for Masham.

Chapter Nineteen

The door to Masham police station was propped open with a shoe-maker's last. I guessed that was not for the sake of fresh air but to be as inviting as possible to anyone who might have the least shred of information about the car and driver that killed Miss Crawford yesterday.

There was no one at the counter, and so I rang the bell. Sergeant Moon appeared a few moments later.

'Hello, Mr Moon.'

I was glad that Moon and Sykes had hit it off on the evening of the trussing. At least the sergeant knew who we were, and why we were here.

'Hello, Mrs Shackleton. I heard you would be coming,' he said. 'Mr Sykes called in to say he was going back to Leeds for a day or two. Good of you to call in.'

Sykes had told him about a child's drawing of a car. Now it was my turn. I would have hesitated about imparting Mrs Lincoln's sighting of James Lofthouse yesterday, when it was hearsay. Now I had corroboration of a kind from the Tebbits' maid.

'I have some information for you, Sergeant.'

'Everything helps.' He raised the counter and invited me to come through.

I followed him into a small interview room. We faced each other across the standard issue table.

'What is it you have to tell me, Mrs Shackleton?'

'May I ask, are you leading the investigation into Miss Crawford's death?'

'I am. It will only go to HQ if Northallerton become impatient.'

'They may have become impatient at the thought of child's drawing of a car?'

'That child's drawing was a useful piece of information.'

Useful, or more than that? I was curious to know whether the police were checking who owned a Lanchester. Unsurprisingly, he did not tell me.

He waited for me to speak. I must go first in the information stakes.

'On Tuesday, Miss Crawford wanted to talk to Mr Lofthouse. He put it off until the next day, which was too late of course.'

The sergeant folded his arms. 'Mr Sykes told me that.'

'And did you find out what she wanted to say?' I asked.

'We have our ways, but mindreading isn't one of them.' In spite of his sarcasm, the sergeant looked mildly interested. It had not occurred to him to consider trying to find out what a secretary might have needed to say to her boss.

'She wanted to tell him that his nephew James has been seen in Ripon.'

'How do you know? And if you're right, why didn't she come straight out with it?'

The sergeant was asking me two questions, and in a disbelieving voice. This did not inspire me with confidence in him.

'Miss Crawford may have hesitated to speak because Mr Sykes was in the office at the time and she wanted a private conversation.'

I stopped myself from saying that it was because Miss Crawford suspected James Lofthouse of being behind the Barleycorn's recent misfortunes.

'Your source, Mrs Shackleton?'

'Reliable, Mr Moon.'

'James Lofthouse is in Germany.'

'According to our sources, James left Germany ten days ago by ferry from Hamburg.'

The sergeant jotted a note. 'Why would he come back without telling anyone?'

My truthful answer would be that James wanted to create chaos at the brewery in order to change the balance of power and give himself an advantage at the Annual General Meeting when he and Rory Tebbit would swoop in for the kill. Such a blunt reply might push the sergeant into dismissing my information. It would be better if, eventually, he could come up with the answer himself.

I said, 'He would come back without telling anyone either to surprise Uncle William by turning up at the garden party unannounced, or for another reason that demands secrecy.'

He let out a low whistle. 'That's a big leap of imagination.'

Sometimes it is better to take a step back. 'Well, you have my information about James.'

'It is noted, Mrs Shackleton.'

'I hope it may be as useful as Mr Sykes's information about the Lanchester. Has the car been found?'

'Not yet. There are too many places a car could be hidden, abandoned buildings, old barns, stables. We've alerted landowners, farmers, schoolchildren, asking them to look out for a damaged car that must have been driven by a lunatic. No one in their right mind would risk damaging such a car by running a person down.'

'So, it was a Lanchester?'

The sergeant took a breath that lasted long enough to make me think our conversation would be entirely one way. Sykes and I would offer information, Sergeant Moon would scoop it up.

Finally, he said, 'Mrs Tebbit reported the vehicle stolen. It belonged to her late husband.'

That explained why Mrs Tebbit had taken to her bed. I would feel unwell if my car was taken from the garage and used to knock down a cyclist. 'When was it reported stolen?'

He tightened his lips.

'Mrs Tebbit will be coming to the garden party tomorrow. I could ask her, if you'd rather not say.'

'The car was reported missing when I called at the house yesterday, asking to see it. Of course, we don't know when it was stolen.'

'Sergeant, if I had a Lanchester, I would know when it went missing.' This was not entirely true. The Rolls-Royce given to me by a grateful client sits in a garage. I last looked at it in February, when all neighbours were asked to look in outbuildings for a runaway child.

The sergeant explained: 'The Tebbits may not have noticed it was missing. It is not the main car of use. Mr Rory Tebbit has a sports car, and he walks to work, being so close to the bank.'

I could not decide whether Sergeant Moon was being discreet, or whether he was a throwback, one of those men who doff the cap to the gentry and the well-to-do, and look elsewhere for miscreants. That was a shame. I had liked the man, until now.

Our chat was at an end. He said: 'You can tell Mr Sykes that the Murthys' little lad would be a credit to the force. He deserves ten out of ten for drawing and a star for observation.'

'I'll tell him.'

He walked me to the door, saying, 'You have Mick Musgrove's rhymes that Miss Crawford typed for him.'

'Yes. Who would be a good local printer?'

'Enquire of Miss Thistlewaite, the stationer on Park Square.'

That would keep me busy and out of his hair, he thought. I waited for his final question. Surely it must come.

It did.

'Where does this informant imagine that James Lofthouse is staying?'

'He is staying with the Tebbits.'

Sykes had passed Miss Crawford's spare key to me and given me directions to her office. It felt strange and unsettling to enter the austere room that had played such a large part in the dead woman's life. I almost felt her looking over my shoulder as I picked up the telephone, crossing my fingers that Mrs Sugden would answer.

She answered.

'It's me, Mrs Sugden.'

'I knew it was, but I couldn't pick it up and say that could I? I always know when it's you.'

'I need Mr Sykes to come back. There have been developments.'

'He's on his way. He said if you rang to say he would see you at the brewery, or else at half past one in the Falcon. If you get there first, he'll have the roast beef.'

'What prompted him to set off for Masham?'

'Am I allowed to say on the telephone?'

'Just say it.' We were no longer on a party line at Batswing Cottage. To an operator, our exchanges would sound both mysterious and dull.

'He telephoned the Lanchester motor company. They gave him the names and addresses of Lanchester owners who live in the North Riding.'

Chapter Twenty

At noon, I tapped on the door of the wages office.

A voice called, 'Enter!'

'Mr Beckwith?'

'That's me.'

Mr Beckwith was sweating. He looked flustered. His desk was covered with time cards and wage packets.

'Hello, I'm Mrs Shackleton, Kate Shackleton. Jim Sykes is my colleague. Mr Lofthouse asked if I would come and see how you are getting on and whether you need a hand.'

His face lit up. 'Yes, I could do with a hand.'

'Tell me what to do.'

'You can sit at Ruth's desk and fill in the amounts on the wage packets.'

This was not what I had expected but I happily agreed. He gave me a wire basket stacked with timecards, each with an employee's name and department on the top line. 'On the reverse of the card, you'll see the figures you need for the wage packet, which is gross pay, tax, any other deductions and net wage.'

I set the basket down on Ruth's desk.

Mr Beckwith scooped a pile of wage packets into another basket. 'They fell on the floor. Sorry. Sort the departments, and then the names in alphabetical order and they'll match the timecards.'

'I can do that.'

'Are you all right while I go for my break?'

'Yes of course.'

It was a soothing task and did not take long. When Mr Beckwith came back, bringing the scent of his complimentary pint of beer into the room, he was more cheerful.

'You've done it, Mrs Shackleton.'

'Yes.'

'You're almost as quick as Ruth.'

'What else can I do to help?'

'Two lists came over this morning in Mrs Lofthouse's hand-writing, about the arrangements for Saturday's garden party. The assistant brewer has one list. This one's mine.' He read it to me. 'Check with schoolteacher about plan for children's games. See Joe Finch about pony rides. Here's an item I don't relish, recruitment of secretary and wages clerk.' He sighed. 'So, they've decided Ruth has to have her time off. I suppose it's only right.'

I picked up a pencil. 'I'll talk to Joe Finch about pony rides.' Joe Finch was Mr Sykes's "person of interest", the man who delivered more barrels of beer than were officially paid for.

I breathed in the smell of the stables. Joe Finch stood grooming a shire horse, expertly using a dandy brush in short brisk motions. I could have sworn the horse smiled.

I introduced myself. 'And I know you're Joe Finch.'

'Aye, and some of us have to miss the trip to Scarborough tomorrow, but me and Cleopatra, we'd just as soon be here, keeping an eye on things.'

I said, 'Mr Beckwith asked me to see you about the plan for Saturday, regarding pony rides.'

Joe continued his brushing. 'I've worked this out with Ruth. She gives a speech. At the end of the speech, she invites children to follow her to the stables. I introduce my pony, Billy Boy. I'll tell the kiddies what a poor state he was in when he came to me, how I turned him into a beauty, and that he likes children who are quiet and kind. My pal Phil will keep them entertained, showing them the correct way to groom a horse and letting them sit on the cart until it's their turn for a pony ride.'

'That sounds good. I'll tell Mr Beckwith you have it all planned.'

'The thing is, there's two kiddies that have been left off the list. I know that Miss Crawford had invitations with a space for a name to be filled in. I'm wondering will you write their names on the list and give me two invitations. The kiddies I have in mind deserve a treat.'

'I don't see why not.' I took out my notebook. 'And what about the children's parents?'

'The children are Monica and Michael Burns. The parents won't come, John and Elizabeth. They're down on their luck, you see. They'd feel out of place.'

Sykes had told me about the homeless family. I hoped the brother and sister would not feel awkward or be ragged by the other children.

'Will Monica and Michael be able to fend for themselves?'

The horse nudged him to continue the grooming. 'They'll be grand,' Joe said.

'I'll find invitations and leave them at the desk with your name on.'

'Thank you.'

'Mr Finch, there's one person I haven't met and am curious about. Mr James Lofthouse.' There was a brewery full of people I hadn't met, but just one who interested me at present.

Joe kept his gaze on the horse. 'You haven't missed much, not in my opinion.'

'Oh?'

'Mr William Lofthouse, now he's a man who worked his way up, though he didn't need to. Mr James Lofthouse, he came in at the top and never stopped looking down, looking down at others, and up for himself.'

'So, you wouldn't like it if James came back?'

'He'll make changes for changes' sake. He'll get rid of the horses and buy vans. Me, I do as I'm told, but I couldn't live without horses. James Lofthouse has no soul.'

'Some people seem to love him, Mr Finch. Why would that be?' I had no idea whether anybody did love James, but I wanted to provoke Joe. William Lofthouse had given the impression that James was the apple of his eye and his chosen heir. Eleanor had sent money from the brewery queen account so that James could visit Vienna. Mrs Tebbit was giving him houseroom. Yet Joe had taken a strong dislike to the man.

'Love or loathe, all the same to me,' Joe said. 'People see what they want to see. I know what I know.'

'What's that?' I asked. 'You can tell me, Joe. I don't tittle tattle.'

Joe Finch's vehemence surprised me. 'When James Lofthouse knew I helped out at a stud, he wanted me to nobble a horse we were taking care of. He put it in a way he could deny it. There'd be an advantage to me if the second favourite won. We both knew what he was saying.' Joe Finch put the brushes back in place and stroked the horse's neck. 'There's not many bad people round here, but he's one.'

I thought of Ruth's swimming costume, cut in two by her father. 'And Slater Parnaby, what do you make of him?'

'Sniffer Parnaby is mad and bad in his own way. He can't hide it, he can't help it, and he doesn't try. He's good at his job. Fought like a madman in the war and has the Military Cross and Bar to prove it.'

Chapter
Twenty-One

~

Sykes and I sat at a corner table in the Falcon. It is occasionally necessary to analyse our clients, their motives, weaknesses and setbacks. It was an interesting change to do this over roast beef and a mutton chop. Sykes had a pint of Nut Brown, I had finished my sherry.

Sykes, with the benefit of having spent more time at the brewery, had very definite ideas. 'William Lofthouse loosened his hold on the company's reins because he was distracted by his marriage, weakened by jaundice and expected that by now James would have returned and be pulling his weight.'

'So, he slowed down, and now finds it hard to bounce back, especially after the blow of his new brew turning sour.'

'He ought to bounce back,' Sykes said. 'He has Eleanor behind him. She is surprisingly sharp for—' He stopped mid-sentence.

I filled in the blank. 'For a woman?'

'For a woman in business, especially since her father went bankrupt, but I suppose that explains it. Once bitten and all that.'

We ordered rice pudding. When the waitress had gone, taking our compliments to the chef, Sykes said, 'The chef is her mother.'

He re-arranged the pepper and salt pots, something he does automatically when gathering his thoughts. He opened his notebook. 'The cancellation letters from the two pubs and the brewery that decided to buy its casks elsewhere, arrived over a period of two weeks, just before and after James arrived back from Germany. It must have been set up beforehand.'

I could guess who did the setting up. Small wonder that the Lofthouses had stopped receiving letters from James. He had been busy exchanging messages with his chum. 'Rory Tebbit?'

'That would be my guess too,' Sykes said. 'I went in each of the pubs that cancelled, and asked for a Nut Brown. They're already selling Joshua Tetley's bitter. I had a word with the landlord of the White Horse. He told me that customers miss their Nut Brown Ale, but that the switch was "a business decision". He would not go into details. The landlord at the Swan told the same story.'

'Does "a business decision" sound like the sort of explanation a landlord would give?'

'Yes, if he had been talking to his adviser at the bank. The Little Brewery used the exact same words. They, the White Horse and the Swan all have one thing in common. They have their accounts with the Ripon Bank, under the care of Rory Tebbit.'

That was impressive work by Sykes, but he is in his element when it comes to shenanigans. Call me old-fashioned, but I like to think of banks as being above board.

It was difficult to believe that the Ripon Bank manager would not keep a close eye on his staff, and I said so.

'It's hard to believe that Rory Tebbit would be allowed to coerce clients into changing suppliers. I met the manager, Mr Murthy. Miss Crawford and he were neighbours, on good terms. When she asked if Rory Tebbit had mentioned seeing James Lofthouse, Mr Murthy's instinctive response was to pull the trick of not confirming or denying. He struck me as being straight as a die. Although it did annoy me that he probably made Miss Crawford feel humiliated for asking.'

'Mr Murthy was following the rules. Rory Tebbit works under him, to learn the business. He puts his own twist on what constitutes business.'

Both Sykes and I excel in squeezing information, but he takes the cap when it comes to financial dealings. Sykes could run the Bank of England.

I asked, 'How do you know Tebbit advises those two pubs and the Little Ripon Brewery?'

'I enquired about opening an account, and spoke to a helpful young clerk, pretending I knew more than I did. Tebbit is an assistant manager, building up his list of clients. Mr Murthy ought to watch out.'

So that was how Sykes did it, not such a mystery after all. 'Then tell me, so I'll know for future reference, how would an assistant bank manager get away with recommending a switch of suppliers?'

'I'm guessing Rory's three clients are in hock to the bank for an overdraft or a mortgage. That means regular contact with the person who looks after their accounts.'

'Why would Rory Tebbit recommend Joshua Tetley?'

'It could have been any big brewery that offered a discount in order to get a foothold in this area. My contact at the Chamber of Commerce didn't know of any link between Rory Tebbit and Tetley's Brewery. Rory Tebbit would have pointed out the financial advantages of going to a large company. He was not interested in improving Joshua Tetley's business.'

The penny dropped for me. 'So, there need be no financial gain for Rory or James from the pubs switching to another supplier. The idea is to run Barleycorn Brewery into the ground and force William Lofthouse to bow out gracefully. Our good chaps James and Rory will then shake their heads sadly at William's misfortune, step in, and create their empire.'

'And Rory's bank connections will allow him to source a loan on favourable terms. In a few years' time, he would win back the two pubs who switched to Tetley.'

The waitress approached with our rice puddings. Sykes's rice pudding was brown. He thanked her. 'She knows I like a spoonful of cocoa stirred in.'

There was a little thinking time while we ate our pudding.

'It was a careful plan,' I said. 'Miss Crawford upset the apple cart yesterday morning when she went to the Tebbit house to confront James. He panicked. He may have taken the car from the garage and driven off, hoping to see his uncle before she did, and then he saw Miss Crawford on the road. In that moment, the solution presented itself. He could wipe her off the face of the earth, keep his secret, and stick to the plan.'

'How do we prove it?' Sykes asked.

'I asked Mrs Rigg what time Miss Crawford usually left for work. She told me she left at eight o'clock for her eight thirty start. The collision time was put at half past nine. That morning, I believe she left at eight as usual, but cycled to Ripon to confront James. He must have known that he would not be able to bamboozle and charm her.'

Sykes scoffed. 'That wouldn't work with Miss Crawford.'

'I'm guessing that he told the maid to say he was not there. The maid preferred to hint at the truth, and say he was not at home. Miss Crawford then set off for work, prepared to tell Mr Lofthouse what she knew, and what she guessed. James panicked. He took Mrs Tebbit's car and drove after Miss Crawford.'

Sykes nodded. 'The Murthys' little boy said the car drove slowly, stopped, drove quickly. He was keeping her in sight. You could be right. But we would need evidence of sightings, and to find the car, check the car and the bike for damage.'

'If needs be, I'll follow up my Oddfellows' source at the Tebbit house. Servants don't miss a trick.'

Sykes frowned.

'What is it?' I asked.

'If we're right, and James Lofthouse thinks he has got away with manslaughter—'

'Or murder.'

'He and Rory might turn up for tomorrow's garden party with more tricks up their sleeves.'

'Then go see your friend the sergeant, Mr Sykes. Tell him what we know, or even what we think we know. He'll take it better from you.'

Chapter Twenty-Two

⟿

On the journey to Scarborough, Ruth was happy to be sitting in the front passenger seat, next to the Lofthouses' chauffeur. She looked out of the car window, waiting for her first sight of the sea. It felt extraordinary, dizzying, to think of herself at the edge of the land.

The Grand Hotel took her breath away. This was the largest building Ruth had ever seen. A lift took her and the Lofthouses to their adjacent rooms on the top floor. Ruth felt sure she would lose her way going to and from the bathroom. She might forget her room number and make an idiot of herself by asking for help. Part of her wished she and Miss Crawford could have been in the boarding house, looking forward to a fish supper.

She went for a walk on the beach, leaving off her stockings and carrying her sandals so as to feel the sand under her feet.

In the hotel dining room, Mr and Mrs Lofthouse tried to put her at ease and that made Ruth feel worse because it meant that her nerves were showing. Mr Lofthouse looked at the plan for tomorrow, laid out in a brown folder headed Yorkshire Brewery Queen Contest.

He put on his reading glasses and cleared his throat. 'Eleven hundred hours, North Pool in swimming costumes, sashes, tiaras, suitable footwear. Twelve hundred hours, Seafront procession from

North Pool to The Spa. Fifteen hundred hours, Contest and Formal Judging.' Mr Lofthouse took off his reading glasses. 'I've known battles to be less well planned than this.'

Mrs Lofthouse tried to put a stop to him. 'It's all in hand, William. Ruth and I know what we are doing.'

For about ten minutes, Ruth was glad to be alone in her room. After ten minutes, she wished the other contestants were here with her. Miss Jarvis of Scarborough and Miss Blunkett of Sheffield might be feeling just as nervous as she was. They would be up against each other but in it together. Ruth went to bed just after nine o'clock. She woke, thinking it was morning. It was three o'clock. After a long time, she managed to drop back to sleep. Waking with a jerk she knew she had better try on Mrs Lofthouse's swimming costume again, with its vivid colours and bold geometrical shapes. She looked at herself in the big mirror. It was not her style. People would look and say, that's never her own swimming costume. The day dress was pretty but now she realised how old-fashioned it looked.

When she got up the next morning, Ruth saw that her hair was standing to attention in the shape of three deformed fingers and a question mark. It was while she was brushing her hair, a hundred times, that she thought everything might turn out well.

She did the deep breathing Miss Boland had taught her, and her voice exercises, and her stretches. In her mind's eye, she saw her mother.

'Mam, today will go well. You, me, George, we will be together again.' The other girls' mothers would be here today. Ruth had Mrs Lofthouse, who was young and glamorous.

The four-leaf clover brooch was in the pocket of her bag. As instructed by Miss Boland, Ruth pinned it out of sight, under the lining of her cloak, and that made her laugh because it was so silly. Ruth looked at herself in the mirror and said, 'Nobody else will have had an opera singer teaching her how to breathe and providing her with a lucky charm.'

That made her laugh, too, and Ruth felt glad to be alone.

There was a tap on the door. Ruth went to see.

It was Mrs Lofthouse. She said, 'Shall you and I go down for breakfast soon?'

Chapter
Twenty-Three

～

On the day her beautiful daughter would be taking part in the competition in Scarborough, Annie drank her first cup of tea of the day, in the room where she felt safe, where she had felt safe these seven years.

Early each morning, Annie began the day's baking. She had a safe job at Bedale Bakery. Even in dark days, people had to eat, though not all of them did.

She would have loved to see Ruth, to be there, to sit with George, and cheer. But Slater would be there. He would sneer at a charabanc trip to the seaside but enjoy it because he would be able to mock.

She was a safe six miles from the home where Slater had almost strangled her. The children had come running down the stairs, yelling at their dad to stop, stop, stop. George pushed in, grabbing his dad's arms, trying to make him let go. Ruth jumped on her father's back, pulled his hair and sank her teeth into his ear.

Slater flung his children off.

George cried with frustration. Slater mocked him, calling George the big baby. Ruth looked at her father and said, 'I will kill you.'

Annie feared for Ruth, but Slater simply said, 'How will you kill me?'

'I will wait until you are asleep, but your dead self will know who did it.'

Annie stepped in front of Ruth, expecting that Slater would knock her flying.

Slater said, 'For four long years, I waited for a bullet in the head. Do your worst.'

The next day, George said to his mother, 'We have to go away.'

Annie already knew that she was the one who must go away, for the sake of the children. Slater had never hurt them, only her. It wasn't right that they should see his rages. She was the one who set off his rages. If she went away, they would have peace and quiet.

Annie told George and Ruth to write to their Granny Parnaby and ask her to come. It would be for the time being. Annie would save her money. She would find another job, where she could bring the children. They would be together again.

Slater would never expect that Annie could start again, take a job, have somewhere to live, somewhere to bring her children. Joe Finch found Annie the job at the bakery. He saw the sign in the window. He sang Annie's praises to the baker. For the baker's agreement to cash in hand, accommodation, no questions asked, Joe gave the baker a firkin of ale.

The baker did not want children above his bakery.

Joe came to tell Annie that Slater's mother had moved into the house to look after them all. Annie wanted to be with them, but it was not so urgent then. George and Ruth were safe. They were doing well at school, had their friends, came to visit her at the bakery on Sundays.

Joe called on Annie every week, when he made his deliveries on the Bedale round.

Each night she fell into bed, the box bed next to the fire that never died. There was no need to go outside. She would scurry into the bakery shop, with a full tray, and scurry out again.

She heard the customers talking. One customer named her The Scurrier. Mostly they paid her no heed. Another customer, who heard the owner call, 'Annie!' named her Annie-in-a-hurry.

When she came here, she chose a new surname. Scarth. Scarth was the name that came to her lips. Scarth was the name of the person who assisted with the registration of births, marriages and deaths in Mashamshire. Somehow that seemed right. Because if she had not fled, the Mrs Scarth whose name she stole would have another name to write in the book of deaths: Annie Parnaby.

When George and Ruth came to see her, she toasted teacakes.

Sometimes the children hitched a ride on a cart, or they walked one way and caught the bus back.

One year, Granny Parnaby saw to it that George got a bike for his birthday. The children cycled to Bedale.

The next year, Granny Parnaby saw to it that Ruth got a bike for her birthday.

If Granny knew where the children went, with a bottle of water and an apple, she never said.

For seven years, the three of them planned. For seven years, Annie saved what passed for wages. She knew she must not take them out of school, where George was good at woodwork, and Ruth was clever.

Annie knew she had brought something else to the Bedale Bakery. It tucked itself in with her few belongings, hidden in a skirt pocket, dabbed itself with lavender water behind her ears, combed itself into her hair, and ticked its way into her heart. She had brought fear, and the fear grew.

She could step into the yard when she had to. But it was best not to think beyond the high wooden gate, not to go beyond the high wooden gate.

It took a long time for George and Ruth to suspect that Annie no longer wanted to go outside, no longer could go outside. When they wanted her to go out, it was natural for her to tell them they had come a long way. They must sit and rest and have that toasted teacake with melting butter. Besides, it was safest not to go out, in case she was seen, and someone told their father.

Late on the Friday of the Yorkshire Brewery Queen contest, George was at the bakery gate, whistling to let his mother know who it was. He had come from Scarborough. Knowing that the works charabanc would call at a pub or two on the way back, he caught the train, changed trains, got himself to Ripon fast as he could.

As he listened to his mother cross the yard and draw back the bolts on the gate, George wondered if they would all be together again, Mam, himself and Ruth. Because the truth was, he had fallen in love. He had fallen in love with Miss East Riding. Bernadette Jarvis, tall, and slender as a fairy, her skin dark as an Italian's, her straight thick hair with a sheen like polished jet. She was the one. She had something George could not name.

After the contest, Ruth had introduced George to Bernadette.

Bernadette introduced George to her father, Mr Jarvis, Head Brewer at Scarborough Brewery.

George heard himself saying that he was out of his time at Barleycorn Brewery, and a good cooper. Now that Barleycorn was no longer supplying casks elsewhere, he thought that Mr Lofthouse might release him from his obligation.

'All in good time,' Mr Jarvis said. 'You come along with me. I'll treat you to a stick of rock. Let the lassies talk amongst themselves.'

He doesn't want a cooper for his daughter, George thought. He said, 'I've always been interested in brewing, Mr Jarvis. I helped the assistant brewer no end of times.'

The stick of rock said Scarborough, all the way through. George knew this was not just a stick of rock. This was a good omen for his future life.

At least Mr Jarvis had not told George to sling his hook.

Instead of going on to Masham, George would stay the night in his mam's upstairs room. She must come to the Bedale picture house with him tomorrow to see the Pathé News film of the Yorkshire Brewery Queen contest.

Chapter Twenty-Four

～

Sykes and I had waited at the Falcon for the call to tell us that the Lofthouses and Ruth were back. All the lights were on at Barleycorn House. Beryl opened the door, smiling. The gramophone music played 'Spread a Little Happiness.'

William poured champagne. Whatever misgivings he may have had were gone, for the moment. He proposed a toast, 'To Queen Ruth!'

We raised our glasses.

Ruth has a mercurial quality. She gave a brilliant smile as she thanked Mr and Mrs Lofthouse, and then raised her glass to make her own toast. 'To Mr and Mrs Lofthouse, for making this possible.'

Sykes, Ruth and I drank to Mr and Mrs Lofthouse.

Ruth proposed a second toast. 'To dear Miss Crawford who encouraged me every step of the way, from the moment I first came to Barleycorn Brewery. We will always miss you.'

'To Miss Crawford,' we echoed.

I wanted to know everything about how the day had gone. To Ruth, it was a blur. Eleanor gave the best account. She told me of the thousands who turned out to see the parade along Scarborough seafront. Two shire horses, their plaited manes entwined with red, white and blue ribbons, pulled a decorated dray where the queens of the East, West and North Riding, dressed in their finery waved to the crowds from their plank seats covered with velvet cushions.

Misses East, West and North Riding graciously tolerated the gauche Pathé News compère who made the introductions. The judges tried to look serious, and as if they weren't ogling as each girl paraded in her swimming costume. Each entrant said a little about herself, and where she came from. They then walked on individually in their prettiest day dresses and said what they hoped to achieve, and what would make them a good ambassadress for the brewery industry.

Ruth joked. 'It was your bathing suit that won the day, Mrs Lofthouse.'

'Not at all,' Eleanor insisted. 'You spoke so well, and you are the only one of the three to work in a brewery.'

We made our way into the dining room for a light supper. For a time, all anxieties were forgotten.

I was sitting opposite the door. When Beryl came in, I could see from her face that she was not here simply to clear the table.

'Excuse me, Mr Lofthouse,' Beryl said. 'Sergeant Moon would like a private word with you in the library.'

We all knew that it must concern Miss Crawford's death. Sykes and I sat tight. Eleanor wanted to go in with William, to hear what the sergeant had to say. William patted her arm. 'Leave this to me. You'll know soon enough.'

The French clock on the mantelpiece ticked. The fire crackled.

Eleanor stood. 'What on earth can Sergeant Moon be saying that takes so long?'

An uneasiness settled around us. I felt a sense of dread. None of us volunteered reassurance, or an answer we did not have.

Ruth made the first move. 'Mrs Lofthouse, thank you so much for today, and for this lovely celebration, and for letting me stay in the cottage.' She stood. 'Please say goodnight to Mr Lofthouse for me.'

Eleanor said, 'Someone will walk you back.' She moved towards the bell.

'Please don't trouble. It's no distance. I'll go now and see you tomorrow, in good time for the garden party.'

It was another ten minutes before William returned, looking dazed. He remained standing, holding on to the back of his chair for support. His knuckles turned white. 'I have some bad news. Eleanor, you may not be up to hearing this.'

Eleanor got up from her chair. She went to William, saying, 'Sit down. Whatever it is, you can tell me.'

William sat down.

Eleanor turned to Sykes. 'Mr Sykes, pour us all a brandy, would you?'

At the cabinet, Sykes took out the brandy and four brandy balloons. I knew the nature of what was coming, but not the detail. I guessed what this was about and was glad to have told Eleanor that James was back. That news must, in some small part, have lessened the shock.

William took a sip of brandy. When he spoke, it was in a flat monotone. 'James has been arrested, charged with theft of a vehicle, and wanton and reckless driving. The police are considering a charge of manslaughter. He mowed down Miss Crawford.'

'I want to say there must be some mistake,' Eleanor said. 'But there can't be can there?'

'No mistake,' William said. 'James took Mrs Tebbit's car, drove it straight at Miss Crawford. He tried to blame Rory, but Rory was at the bank. James said he hadn't left the Tebbits' house, but one of the staff saw him go to the garage. He then said that he was on his way to see me.'

'Why was he at the Tebbits'?' Eleanor asked. 'Kate, when you told me he was back, I felt sure you must be mistaken.'

My first thought was how stupid James had been. He must have thought himself invulnerable. After all his planning and scheming, to do something so blatant and expect to get away with it was madness.

William took out a cigarette. Sykes lit it for him. William inhaled. 'James is being held at Ripon. He will appear before the magistrates tomorrow.'

'Whatever possessed him?' Eleanor asked. 'He knew how important he was to you. Over all these years, you've brought him along to take over the business.'

'Sergeant Moon tells me that James is looking to me to stand bail and find him a solicitor.' It seemed possible that we would sit in a glum silence, interspersed with talking in circles. I said, 'Mr Sykes and I have been doing some investigating. We found out only today that James was back in the country, though I suspected yesterday when Mrs Lincoln at the Oddfellows claimed to have seen him. I can give you the background. We believe James and Rory were behind what you thought was a run of bad luck. You may not want to hear what we have to say just yet.'

'Yes,' William said. 'I want to hear.'

Eleanor put her arm through his. 'So do I.'

I said, 'William, Eleanor, we'll tell you what we've learned, but it's where you and the Barleycorn go from here that matters.'

The four of us remained at the dining room table for a long time. Sykes gave chapter and verse of his conversations with the landlords of the White Horse and the Swan, and made the link between these two pubs, the Little Ripon Brewery and Ripon Bank's assistant manager, Mr Rory Tebbit. We listed key dates. I referred to the sightings of James, and the fact that Miss Crawford had called at the Tebbit house asking to see him, no doubt wanting to confirm or dismiss her own misgivings or suspicions.

Of the four of us, I have the most legible handwriting. Beryl and the chauffeur were sent to the brewery to fetch foolscap and carbon paper. I wrote down everything that would build the case against James Lofthouse and Rory Tebbit. I half expected William to break under the strain but he bore up with a steeliness that surprised me.

'I want the Barleycorn shares back from the pair of them, James and Rory,' William said. 'Sergeant Moon had the suggestion that if I put up bail and engaged a solicitor, there could be a price. James would forfeit his shares.'

Sykes is usually a master of self-control. Suddenly, his eyes appeared ready to pop. He said, 'Mr Lofthouse, you owe James nothing. Miss Crawford is gone, James and Rory have robbed you of business and income, undermined the brewery, wasted the money you advanced James to visit breweries in Germany and brought discredit on your good name. We have a solicitor who would happily draw up such a ream of charges that your nephew would sit in his prison cell for years, contemplating an empty purse and a bleak future. Mrs Shackleton and I are here to look out for your interests and that is what we will do.'

I was proud of Sykes and immediately backed up his words. 'William, Jim Sykes is right. Set aside any remnants of avuncular feelings. You have other responsibilities, to Eleanor, the baby, your workforce, and loyal drinkers of Nut Brown Ale—'

'—and Ure Milk Stout and the Fireside Brew,' William said, 'and the new brew, when it's ready. That's what I can never forgive, that he was willing to sink the company, after going on two hundred years of hard work.'

'There is also an obligation to your rhymester Mick Musgrove. If James is let loose, Mr Musgrove will take revenge for Miss Crawford's death. He will hack James to pieces with an axe and hang for it.'

William showed admirable decisiveness. 'I won't attend the hearing at the Magistrates' Court tomorrow. James is on his own. I see him now for what he is, selfish and a bad lot.'

Eleanor had been slow to drink her brandy. She poured the remains of hers into William's glass. 'William darling, with the help of Kate Shackleton and Jim Sykes, we will come through this bad dream and wake to a new day and a fresh start.'

We raised our glasses to that.

Chapter
Twenty-Five

On Saturday morning, I opened my bedroom window. Ruth was up first. I could hear her moving about downstairs. With a picture-book blue sky, no whisper of a breeze and not a cloud in sight, this was perfect garden party weather.

I put on my dressing gown and went downstairs.

Ruth was at the kitchen table, with pencil and paper. 'I heard you moving, Mrs Shackleton. There's a jug of heated water for you in the little room.'

'Thank you!'

As I washed in the small partitioned room with its decorative basin and neatly set out toiletries, I could hear Ruth practising her speech for the garden party, stopping, and starting.

'It's no use,' she called. 'I wanted to thank Miss Crawford, but I can't say her name without choking. And I'm so sad for Mr and Mrs Lofthouse.'

'Then stop for now,' I called back. 'Take a walk round the garden. Come back and tell me what flowers are growing.'

When I was dressed, I went into the back garden. Ruth was sitting on a bench. After debating with myself, I decided she ought to know about James Lofthouse being taken into custody for causing Miss Crawford's death.

Ruth was shocked, but not entirely surprised. 'No one liked him. He swanned about getting in the way and being important. We could never understand why Mr Lofthouse set so much store by him.'

'You are the one bright spot for Mr and Mrs Lofthouse just now, so be brave. The brewery is going through a difficult time. Today isn't about passing on sadness to guests. It's about putting on a good show, making sure the brewery thrives, and that everyone has a job there this time next year. Do your Miss Boland deep breaths and be the queen.'

'You're right.' She relaxed a little. 'I'm glad you're here, Mrs Shackleton. If I'd gone next door to Miss Boland—and she's very good, gave me a lot of confidence, and tips—she would have helped me with what to say, but not what to keep quiet about.'

I told her about the two additional children on the guest list, from a homeless family.

'Oh, I know about them,' she said. 'Mrs Finch gives them their dinner on a Sunday. I'll look out for them.'

She went back in the house for her bag. 'I'll be off. All my things are at Barleycorn House. I'm having breakfast with Mrs Lofthouse.'

'I'll see you at the garden party, Ruth. Good luck. Everyone will be on your side and thrilled to bits at your success.'

As I set off for the garden party, I heard a call, turned and saw Miss Boland, music teacher and Ruth's coach, seated at her open window. She beckoned to me.

I walked along the path to the door.

'Thank goodness!' she said. 'I thought I'd be sitting here the whole day!'

'What's the matter?'

Miss Boland said, 'I saw Ruth earlier, but I wasn't quick enough. She was in a world of her own and didn't hear me call. Do come in!'

Miss Boland appeared distressed. She was seated on a tapestry upholstered chair, wearing the same black wool jacket and a long black serge skirt. She would have cut an imposing figure had one leg not been rather awkwardly outstretched onto a piano stool. 'It's my ankle. I went over on it.'

'Let me help.'

'I don't want any fuss,' Miss Boland said.

She pointed to her leg and hitched up her skirt so that I could see her swollen ankle 'I'm a wounded soldier.'

'Oh, Miss Boland, what happened?'

'All I did was go out to meet the milkman. On the way back in, I don't know how I did it, but I missed the step and somehow twisted my ankle.'

'Let me see.' I moved closer, stopping myself from saying that I used to be a nurse. I was a schoolgirl once, but don't go around announcing the fact.

'You can look, but I'll take off my own stocking thank you very much.' She waved me away.

'I'll fetch my first aid box.'

'Please do. And my feet are clean.'

'Let me get you a drink first.' The glass on the table beside her was empty.

'A glass of water would do nicely. There's a jug in the scullery.'

As I went for the water, I looked at the posters and photographs I had only glanced at when I came in a few days ago with Ruth. Evidence of Miss Boland's career covered one wall, with photographs and posters of *La Bohème, Madam Butterfly* and *The Magic Flute.* Two posters featured a much younger Miss Boland. In one she stood alone, arms outstretched, a look of anguish on her face. In the other, she was with a male singer.

I gave her the glass of water and went next door for my first aid kit.

When I returned, Miss Boland had rolled off both stockings, 'For comparison.' For a large woman, opera star size, she had dainty feet with a high arch and long toes. I complimented her.

'My best feature these days!'

'Very useful for standing centre stage and belting out your arias. I see you are a singer.'

'Yes, so if you hurt me, I'll scream tunefully.'

I could still recognise that imposing figure in the woman who now winced as I examined her ankle.

'Sorry. I'm afraid it's a sprain, and you've pulled the ligaments on this side.'

While I attended to Miss Boland's ankle, cutting strips from a roll of plaster, I talked to keep her mind off the ankle. 'Are you teaching Ruth to sing?'

'You're wondering what my lessons have to do with creating a successful brewery queen?'

'I suppose she may need to sing the national anthem, or perhaps there'll be a song about best bitter.'

'She could do that in style. She has a good voice.'

I asked what sort of coaching Ruth needed. 'She seems so self-assured. Does that come from you, or naturally?'

'A bit of both. I concentrate on her breathing, and her projection. She and Mrs Lofthouse write her speeches. I listen to them and give a few tips on posture, where and how to breathe and pause. Remaining composed, walking well, it's all to do with breathing. Nervousness, tension, that can wreak havoc on the throat. As long as a person breathes correctly, she will speak well, and put people at their ease. There is nothing worse than a nervous, choppy speaker.'

I finished strapping her ankle. 'Keep that leg raised. Rest as much as possible. Have your walking stick by you. You will have a significant amount of pain.'

She refused aspirins.

'Tell no one,' she insisted.

'Of course not. Now, have you eaten?'

She told me where to find a fruit cake and cheese, insisting that would do nicely. 'I'm right as ninepence. People may stop sending their children for lessons if they think I'm past it. A hobbler with a stick.'

'Anyone can go over on their ankle.'

I refilled her glass and left aspirins and the water jug close by. 'Drink plenty of water.'

She relaxed back in her chair. 'Oh, I know that. All singers know the need for hydration.' She took a sip. 'It's such a nuisance. Don't get old, Mrs Shackleton!'

'I'll try not to. Now I'm going to the garden party, but I hope you'll have supper with us tonight.'

'That is kind of you.' She waved her stick at a shelf in the corner. 'Reach down a bottle of dandelion wine, my contribution.'

'Thank you. Do you need me to fetch more water?'

She did not. 'But I always tell people staying in Oak Cottage, the water is from a nearby spring not at all stirred up, no rats. Now, what time shall I hobble round for supper?'

'I'm not sure, but Ruth will be here. We'll call for you and lend you an arm apiece.' I put the wine on the table. 'See you this evening. Sorry you'll be missing the garden party.'

Chapter Twenty-Six

⮬

The gates of Barleycorn House were wide open. I walked along the gravelled drive towards the house. In the corner of the tennis court, a band began to play.

Pots of flowers had been placed on either side of the front door. The porch was filled with red and white carnations. The sound of a band led me round to the back of the house and the extensive grounds. In the tennis court, a brass band played.

Ruth's nervousness of this morning seemed to have vanished. She was at the centre of a group, chatting and smiling.

William came strolling across. 'Hello, Kate. Good to see you.'

'And you, William. How are you this morning?'

'Let's keep walking, towards Eleanor's art marquee. People are less likely to stop a walking, talking target.'

'Any more news?'

'I woke up realising that I have been getting James out of trouble all his life. That's what has been hanging over me. I spent months hoping he would come back changed, ready to take on some responsibility. Now I know that is not going to happen, I can shoulder what I need to shoulder and carry on. It's as you said last night, I have Eleanor and the baby to think about.' He laughed.

'What is it?' I had not expected a laugh from him today.

'Eleanor said this morning, not many breweries have their very own queen. I'm warming to the idea. I can't pretend that everything is as it should be. I pity Mrs Tebbit, for having Rory as a son. Do you know what he had the temerity and insensitivity to say?'

'What?'

'That he wouldn't have risked damaging the Lanchester by reckless driving. Whatever it takes, I will get that young man off the Barleycorn board.'

'William, I admire you for still being on your feet and dealing with everything.'

He looked stronger somehow. I was unsure why when another man might have been scraping himself up from the floor, and then I realised. 'William, you know your enemy now. Before, everything must have seemed random and out of your control. You are back on course.'

'Thanks to you and Sykes.'

'You'll pull through. I'm sure of it.'

'Thank you, Kate.' He raised a hand in salute to a man who was approaching us. William said, 'My solicitor. I'll squeeze in a word.'

'Yes, do that. I'll find Mr Sykes. He's bringing Mrs Sykes, and my niece Harriet.'

'Jolly good, Kate. And you see that lady over there, in the purple, talking to Eleanor?'

'Yes, it's Mrs Tebbit. We have met, but a good while ago.'

'Lovely lady,' William said. 'I sent the car for her. Rory had the good sense to keep away.'

There was no sign of Sykes, Rosie and Harriet. I saw that Mrs Tebbit was suddenly standing alone, looking a little lost. Eleanor had been swept up by a group of admirers.

Mrs Tebbit turned away, heading for the house.

I kept my distance, remembering Eleanor's remark that Mrs Tebbit had her eye on a jade frog in one of the cabinets in the music room, an ornament Eleanor disliked.

By the time I reached the music room, Mrs Tebbit was gently closing the door to the cabinet. Eleanor must have left the door unlocked on purpose. I retreated and hovered by the porch, admiring the flower arrangements.

My task was not to unmask a thief or make a citizen's arrest. My task was to be kind to Mrs Tebbit. She was a shareholder in Barleycorn Brewery and needed to be kept on side, in spite of her errant son. It was not hard to feel kindness towards her. She was a plump, pleasant woman with a round powder puff face and a slightly nervous manner.

When others were catching up with friends' news and making new acquaintances, she was secreting a frog about her person.

'Hello, Mrs Tebbit. I'm Kate Shackleton, I'm the person who brought the posy and the note of thanks from Eleanor after you helped her choose flowers.'

She reacted as if I had thrown her a lifeline when she was drowning. 'I'm pleased to meet you, Kate. Anyone who is a friend of Eleanor's is a friend of mine. I'm Gwyneth.' She had mercifully chosen to forget that I once shadowed her at a party, coming between her and her object of desire.

'Shall we go see Eleanor's paintings, Gwyneth?'

'If it's all the same to you, Kate, I'll take a turn around the herb garden.'

'Alone or shall I come?'

'Do come. I am alone too much. My son Rory would have been with me,' Mrs Tebbit explained, 'but he was called away somewhere this morning. He works at the bank. It keeps him very busy.'

Poor Mrs Tebbit. I had a feeling that Rory would not work at the bank for very much longer. Even a person whose father was once on the board, even a person who inherited his father's shares, might not be welcome in an institution that had a reputation to consider.

There were seats in the herb garden. Mrs Tebbit took a small pair of scissors from her reticule and cut sprigs of mint and rosemary. 'Which scent makes you feel most melancholy?' Mrs Tebbit asked.

I said rosemary. She said mint.

Once that was decided, I thought we would make our way towards Eleanor's art tent, but Gwyneth Tebbit wished to confide in me.

'My daughter has a herb garden. She lives in Mortehoe, Devon with her husband and three children. My grandchildren that I've seen only once.'

'That's a shame. When will you see them again?'

'Soon. There is a small house in Mortehoe that I intend to rent. I haven't told my son yet, but I have put the Ripon house up for sale. It's mine, my family house.'

'Thank goodness for the Married Women's Property Act,' I said.

She smiled. 'Rory will know soon enough. I have told William Lofthouse that I will sell him my shares in the brewery. He ought to have a controlling interest, you see. William's grandfather and my grandfather were cousins, and that's how shares came to me and Rory. I take no interest whatsoever in the brewery and if Rory has the least bit of sense, he will now do the same, and leave brewing to brewers.'

She did know something. It may only have been that James Lofthouse took her car, but the police would have talked to her.

'I'm sure William will be glad of the opportunity to buy the shares,' I said.

'It will be better that way. I've always liked William, and his first wife, and now Eleanor. I pitied them for being stuck with James. He was a bad influence.'

I spotted Rosie and Jim Sykes near the art tent. Sykes wore his American gangster suit. Rosie was beautifully turned out in a light wool coat dress. She was pretending interest in a conversation between her husband and a man wearing a cricket club tie. Many women do take an interest in cricket. She and I do not. Rosie turned away and gave a please-rescue-me look.

I introduced Rosie to Gwyneth Tebbit. Together we made our way into the art tent. Rosie had not yet seen Eleanor's exhibition, and was keen to look at the paintings. She was enthusiastic. 'I said to Jim, we might do this kind of thing more often, now that the weather's warming up.'

'Yes, you should.'

Sykes tore himself away from tales of cricket and caught up with us.

Inside the marquee, filtered sunlight and green canvas created a soft light and a peaceful atmosphere. A goodly number of guests were looking at the paintings, which were displayed to advantage, hung on white-painted boards. At first, I had thought there was nothing so vulgar as a price tag. I then noticed a table with mimeographed sheets naming each numbered picture, and the price.

Eleanor was standing by a painting of a wood at twilight. She was deep in conversation with an elderly gentleman who was leaning on a silver-topped cane. It looked as if she was on the point of making a sale.

Sykes surprised me by having developed an appreciation for art. With unusual enthusiasm for him, he wanted to show Rosie a painting of a man fishing, which he had seen in William's office. They both admired it. He picked up a price list, glanced, and soon put it down again.

Rosie liked Eleanor's work too. 'You should have more jobs like this.'

Rosie is a sociable person and was soon drawn into hushed conversation with Gwyneth Tebbit.

Sykes and I left the marquee. We agreed that Eleanor is a canny businesswoman. The garden party was a good way of selling paintings, and of introducing Ruth to some important people.

'Did Harriet come with you?' I asked Sykes. 'I haven't seen her.' Harriet is my niece who has lived with me since her mother remarried. She shows a keen interest in investigations.

Sykes smiled. 'Last I saw Harriet, she was with Ruth. They'd gone to listen to the bandsmen.' He smiled. 'Some good-looking young fellows in that band.'

'Good! I'll welcome anyone or anything that diverts Ruth just now. Did you introduce the two of them?'

'No. I think they just found each other.'

Ruth and Harriet came into sight moments later. It was time for Ruth to deliver her speech.

Waiters circulated, carrying trays of beer in elegant stemmed glasses as well as pint-size.

Harriet came to stand beside me. 'Harriet, I'm pleased you met Ruth,' I said.

'We got chatting. Everyone else here is either old, or a child.'

'Thank you!'

'I don't mean you, Auntie. Ruth and I got chatting because I told her I'd seen her on Pathé News and how good she was. I was asking, which was her brother, because I picked him out in the crowd at Scarborough, and I was right.'

'And have you met him now?'

'Not yet. She hasn't spotted him.'

Ruth stepped up to the podium. 'Ladies and gentlemen, welcome. For those of you whom I haven't met, I'm Ruth Parnaby, your Yorkshire Brewery Queen.' She paused for the applause and cheers and then continued. 'A few months ago, when the contest for North Riding Brewery was first announced, my brother George sent in my photo to the *Wensleydale Express* and everything just snowballed from there.' Another round of applause rippled across the crowd. 'When you arrived here today, you gentlemen may have expected to enjoy a glass of Nut Brown ale, and I hope you will. Ladies, you may never have tried milk stout before, perhaps regarding it as common, but it is uncommonly good. We have samples from three fine family breweries. Please do taste. The liquor—that is what we call the water and minerals mixture—comes from Yorkshire Dales springs and bore holes. The barley is grown by Dales farmers. Nothing artificial is added. All ingredients are natural.' She raised a glass. 'Hops grown in Kent, yeast fermented in our own brewery, a nectar with the flavour of our countryside, and better than any medicine, brought to you here today in casks made by my father and brother.'

'Your George?' someone called.

'Yes, our George.' Ruth smiled. 'I am proud to support all Yorkshire brewers. Please raise your taster glass to this most healthy and patriotic of drinks.'

After Ruth's uncertainty this morning, she had recovered, overcome her nerves and pleased the crowd.

William stepped centre stage, and thanked Ruth. 'My lords, ladies and gentlemen, and especially children, you are invited to inspect our fine shire horses and watch them being groomed. There will be rides on Billy Boy, the Shetland pony. If you don't know the way, just fall into procession behind our very own Ruth, Yorkshire Brewery Queen. Enjoy the rest of your afternoon. Stay close by and you will shortly hear a poem from the Barleycorn's very own versifier, Mick Musgrove.'

As he stepped down, Harriet said, 'Auntie, I'm going to help Ruth entertain the children. There are a lot of them, and there's a wild gang of little posh boys looking for mischief.'

'That's a good idea.' I had thought Harriet might be bored at the garden party. 'Did you meet two children called Michael and Monica?'

'I did, and they're sweet. I want them to have first rides on the pony.'

The first indication that something was wrong came from a wailing child. He did not like the big horses. It was a cheat. Where was Billy Boy the pony? He wanted a ride on the pony.

Harriet quickly came back. 'Auntie, this Joe Finch hasn't arrived with his pony. There's a man called Phil who's letting children brush the horses but it's a pony ride they're expecting.'

'Don't worry. Go keep the children happy, make up a story, or get them to hop across the yard. I'll find Joe.'

I went to the podium. A fellow with grey hair and long grey whiskers was in charge of the microphone. He listened to my request, putting on a tragic face. 'Shocking. We can't have a disappearing pony.'

The elderly microphone monitor stepped up onto the podium and made his announcement. 'Mr Joe Finch, calling Mr Joe Finch and his pony. Please make your way to the stables where the children are waiting.' He paused, scanned the crowd, and repeated his announcement.

I watched, hoping to see Joe emerge from the beer tent. Sykes came towards me. 'I thought it was all going a bit too smoothly,' he said.

'Do you think Joe has had a drop too much?'

'Possible, but I don't have him down as one who'd disappoint bairns.'

'Perhaps he got the time wrong.'

Sykes frowned. 'Rosie and I went for a walk earlier, up to the churchyard. There's a field runs parallel. At the far side of the field, I saw a fellow leading a pony, same markings as Billy.'

'Joe Finch, has he gone off somewhere?'

'It wasn't him, not tall enough. Now I'm wondering. If someone made off with his pony, he'd go look for it.'

'See what you can find out, Mr Sykes. I'll go and see how Ruth and Harriet are getting on. Mr Finch can't be far away.'

Chapter Twenty-Seven

∽

I went to the stables. Ruth stood by the shire horses, telling the children a story. Harriet led a hop skip and jump race across the cobbles. A drayman in his distinctive black trousers, frieze jacket and white cap lifted a little girl onto a cart. A small boy was paying too much attention to a horse's tail.

'Hello,' I said to the drayman. 'Are you Phil?'

'Phil Jopling, that's me.' He lifted the little boy up to sit next to the girl.

'I'm Kate Shackleton, a friend of Eleanor Lofthouse. Have you seen Joe at all today?'

'No, but he was here earlier. It's his Saturday for the rota.'

'What rota?'

'One person comes in, Saturday and Sunday, to check temperatures and make sure everything is as it should be. Joe went into the brewery to do what needs doing. I know because I went to see. He'd ticked and initialled the sheet on the noticeboard, to show he'd checked, and everything was as it should be.'

'He didn't lock the door behind him.'

'He would have left it open for me, to get a beer.'

'Didn't you wonder where he was?'

'Yes. I expected him to be here. I went over to see Yvonne, his wife. She said he'd gone out before she got up this morning. Neither of us worried. Joe is a law until himself. I expected him to roll in at the last minute. When he didn't show up, it was too late to do anything about it. I couldn't go out and rustle up a pony.'

A posse of boys came screeching from a side door of the brewery. This must be the little gang Harriet had told me about. I hurried across, reached out with both hands and grabbed two of them by their collars, which oddly enough gave me a sense of achievement. My first collaring. The rest of the little gang dashed off.

'What's going on?' I asked my captives. 'You shouldn't be in there.'

'It's scary. There's a ghost.'

The other boy contradicted him. 'We saw the door to hell, with skeleton faces.'

'Where?' I asked.

'Down the steps.' He wriggled from my grasp and ran free.

I was overreacting. Now that I had a free hand, I took my remaining prisoner's arm and let go of his collar. 'Are there any children still in the building?'

'I don't think so.'

'Why were you all screaming?'

'It was horrible.' He looked on the point of tears.

Realising I would get no more out of him, I told him to go back to the garden party and behave himself.

He ran.

Something had frightened them. Sykes was right to be concerned about lax security. It surprised me that on a day like today someone had left doors unlocked.

I didn't know how many boys were in that little gang, or whether any were still inside. I went into the dimly lit building and found the light switch. An iron staircase with an ornate bannister led to the basement. With my hand on the cold bannister, I reached the lower level. The boys were right about skeleton faces, but the faces were wartime gas masks on hooks at either side of a door. It appeared to me that they gave a warning. Do not enter!

I had to look, in case one of the children was inside. When I opened the door, my eyes were drawn to large tanks of what must be beer, and a spillage of yeast on the floor. I then looked down at what lay nearest to me. A foot or so from the door lay the body of a man. I moved towards him, but straightaway saw that he was dead. A sudden violent agitation gripped my body. When my head snatched back, I knew that this room was full of gas.

The man on the floor was beyond help. I turned and hurried away, back up the stairs, hardly aware that I was coughing. At the top of the stairs, I vomited. There was a tightness in my chest. My eyes were sore. When something shocking happens, it can either dull the senses or sharpen them. Perhaps it is a way of the material world coming between us and shock. I noticed a scrap of material caught on the bannister edge.

I tried to steady myself, to regain my balance, trying not to see the image of that man. But with my eyes closed, I saw him more clearly. He wore a drayman's uniform. It was Joe Finch.

Like someone in a dream, I stood and made my way towards the outer door, gasping for air. The brightness of the day dazzled me.

As if through the wrong end of a telescope, I saw Ruth and Harriet and the children. Harriet came over.

'Are you all right, Auntie?'

'Yes. Time to take the children back to the garden party.'

'Why are you coughing? Where's your hat?'

'Just lead the children back, now. As soon as they're safely back in the gardens, find Jim Sykes or the police sergeant. Ask them to come right away, with Mr Lofthouse, and to say the watchman needs to lock the doors.'

'Right, and I'll come straight back to you.'

'Discreetly!'

Harriet went across and spoke to Ruth. I waved them goodbye, as if nothing in the world could possibly be wrong.

Harriet and Ruth led the children away.

Phil Jopling was at the other end of the yard. When the children left, he came over. 'What's going on?'

'Don't go in the building.'

I could see that he resented being told what to do. 'I've no reason to go in, missis.'

My eyes were watering. I coughed into my hanky.

'What's up?'

He already knew where I'd been. I could see the horror in his eyes. 'A group of little boys got as far as the basement.'

'Near the fermentation room?'

'I don't know what you call it. Fortunately, none of them was hurt.'

He cursed under his breath. 'If their parents find out we'll be in bother. They could be dead, so could you.'

'What is in there?'

'Tanks. Yorkshire slates. It's where the fermenting happens. The yeast multiplies and bubbles. It gives off a gas, CO_2. It's heavier than air and sinks to the ground.'

'Yes.' I did not tell him that I had seen what that gas could do. In my mind's eye, I saw Joe Finch, sprawled on his back, arms akimbo, wearing the same black trousers and frieze jacket as Phil Jopling, his drayman pal.

'Even after the tanks are emptied, it's still dangerous. Do you want a glass of beer, or a glass of water?'

The answer was yes, but I said no, in case he wanted to go into the building. He might want to take a look around.

Phil Jopling was astute. 'I don't need telling to keep out.' He saw Sykes and Sergeant Moon approaching and turned to go. 'Right, I'll go shut the stable door. I'm done here.'

If there was any blame to be laid, Phil Jopling did not want it laying on him.

William arrived first. 'What's up, Kate?'

I saw that Sykes and the sergeant were close behind him. 'Let me get my breath, William.' I did not need to tell this gruesome story twice. I waited until the three of them were listening.

'I went into the building because a group of little boys got in. They're all out, they're all safe. I opened the door at the bottom of the stairs.'

William gawped, his mouth falling open. 'The fermentation room?'

'Joe Finch is dead. He's lying in there, a foot or so from the door.'

William was ready to dismiss my words immediately. 'You don't know Joe.'

'Yes, I do.'

A wispy-haired man in brown overalls came rolling towards us, rattling a bunch of keys.

William held out his hand. He was trembling. 'Keys.'

The watchman opened his mouth. Words were slow in coming. 'The thing is, Mr Lofthouse—'

'Out of my sight!'

Sergeant Moon said, 'Go sleep it off, Tickler. I'll want to talk to you at the station.' The sergeant turned to William. 'Mr Lofthouse, I need to call the fire brigade.' He opened the door. 'The nearest phone?'

William said, 'In the reception area.'

Briefly, William put a hand on my arm, either to detain me or for support, and then he and the sergeant went into the building.

Sykes and I waited in the now empty yard.

'Get William out of there,' I said to Sykes. 'He's not a well man.'

'What about you? You look ghastly.'

'I'll wait for the fire brigade.' The door was still unlocked.

Sykes groaned. 'Why didn't I insist on better security before the locksmith came? He's coming on Monday.'

There was no point in reminding him that he and I had done more than might be thought possible in the time available. One way to stop Sykes reproaching himself was to give him something else to think about. I told him about the scrap of black material caught on the bannister. 'It could be from Joe's trousers, or from someone else who was here.'

'I'll point it out to the sergeant.'

'Is there any way of checking what time Joe arrived this morning? He was on the Saturday rota for making various checks.'

Sykes opened the door and went inside, saying, 'There's the clocking in point.' He came back a couple of minutes later. 'Joe clocked in at 6 a.m. He didn't clock out. Phil Jopling clocked in at 9 a.m.'

Phil Jopling had now appeared at the other end of the yard. I waved him to come over.

'Mr Jopling, do you know if any other employees were here today, besides you and Joe?' I asked.

'No one else is working today, apart from the watchman. What's going on?'

'There's been an accident,' Sykes said. 'We need to open the gates for the fire brigade.'

Chapter Twenty-Eight

❦

The speedy arrival of the fire brigade took us by surprise. Sergeant Moon must have told them not to have their bell ringing.

Five men got down from the engine. They were wearing heavy duty protective clothing and boots. We watched them put on gas-masks before entering the building.

Phil simply stood and stared. He then came walking towards me. 'It's Joe isn't it?'

'Yes,' I said.

He put his hands to his head, as if he might tear out his hair. 'Joe, Joe, what have you done now?' He followed the firemen to the door.

'Wait!' I stopped him. 'Let the firemen do their work.'

'Does he need a doctor, the ambulance?'

'The ambulance is on its way.' The image came back to me of the body. I did not like to tell him that it was far too late for a doctor, but I saw from Jopling's face that he already knew that.

Moments later, Sergeant Moon came from the building. He spoke to Jopling. 'Is Mrs Finch at the garden party?'

Phil said, 'No. Yvonne isn't one for garden parties.'

'Right. I'll go and see her.'

'Let me come,' Phil said. 'Joe's dead?'

'Wait here for the ambulance, Phil. I'll break the news to Mrs Finch.'

Phil and I waited in silence. I need not have stayed but it seemed right that we should be there, to see Joe brought out.

The ambulance drew into the yard alongside the fire engine. Two stretcher bearers climbed out of the back.

'Where will you take Mr Finch?' I asked.

The older one answered, 'Harrogate Infirmary.' He put on a mask.

The younger one said, 'It'll be Ripon. Pathologist is there today.'

The driver turned the ambulance around, ready to leave the way he had entered.

Phil and I went to stand by the door. After a few minutes he went inside saying, 'I'll hold it open for them.'

Joe's body, covered by a heavy tarpaulin, was lifted into the ambulance. One of the bearers sat alongside the stretcher. The other went round to sit beside the driver. Slowly, the ambulance drove out of the gate and into the lane. It came to a sudden halt. A woman had leapt out in front of it.

She had dark curly hair and wore a blue dress with a square neck. Now that woman was bashing the vehicle's bonnet hard enough to crack her knuckles.

'I want to see my husband! You're not to take him away.'

I hurried towards her. The driver was visibly shaken. He clutched the steering wheel and stared ahead. His mate got out of the passenger seat and walked round.

The woman was sobbing now and shaking. I put my arm around her. Where was everyone? Who had let her come rushing from the house like this?

The ambulanceman spoke softly. 'Sorry, Mrs Finch. We have to take Mr Finch to hospital.'

She made a bitter sound from somewhere deep inside, a cry of rage or pain. 'To make him better?'

'We have to find out how he died. You'll be able to see him.'

'I want to be with him. You're not taking him from me. The sergeant said I could see him.'

'He didn't mean right now. We have us orders, ways we have to do things. It's laid down.'

'I'll lay you down if you don't let me see my Joe.'

Another woman appeared, perhaps a neighbour. She stood watching the exchange between the ambulanceman and Mrs Finch, who was now setting up a chant. 'You will not take him, you will not take him.'

In time with Mrs Finch's chants, the neighbour began a slight rocking movement as if preparing herself for action.

A look of relief came over the ambulanceman's face when he saw Eleanor and two other women approaching.

The driver opened the door and got out. 'This isn't seemly, Mrs Finch. Let us do our job.'

Mrs Finch would not give in. 'What good's a hospital now? Bring him home.'

I put my hand on Mrs Finch's arm. She shook me off.

'Mrs Finch, I believe the driver will wait five minutes. Come with me to my car. We'll follow him.'

The driver hesitated.

'Please, you will wait?' I asked.

He nodded. 'Very well.'

Eleanor had looked suddenly helpless. Now she stood straight and determined. She said, 'Mrs Finch, go with Kate. I'll make sure the ambulance driver waits for you.'

The ambulance came to a stop outside an imposing brick building with the word "Ripon Dispensary" embossed above the entrance.

The driver's colleague stepped from the vehicle and came towards us.

He touched his cap. 'We'll be taking Mr Finch to another entrance, for privacy. Please go through the main entrance. I'll let it be known you are here. Someone will come and find you.'

Mrs Finch and I climbed the few steps to the entrance. There was a waiting area with benches, and beyond that a reception desk. 'You sit down, Mrs Finch,' I said. 'I'll let them know we are here.'

She sat down quietly without a word, still in a state of shock. I took a packet of mints from my bag.

It ought to have been chocolate. It ought to have been a soft-boiled egg in her best egg cup. She ought to be wrapped in a blanket and cocooned by friends and family. Now I wondered had it been a mistake to bring her here, but there had seemed no alternative in the face of her determination.

I knew that Dr Miller was the pathologist at Harrogate and that there would not be another pathologist in this area. I had worked with him for several months during the war. When I asked about him at the reception desk, the porter told me he was on duty. The porter agreed to pass on a message to Dr Miller.

'Please tell him that VAD Nurse Kate Shackleton is here with the widow of Joseph Finch, and would Dr Miller kindly come and speak to Mrs Finch.'

We sat for what seemed an age before Dr Miller appeared. He came into reception, looking hardly a day older than when I saw him last.

'Mrs Shackleton.'

We shook hands. 'Mrs Finch, this is Dr Miller. Dr Miller, Mrs Finch would like to see her husband.'

I stepped aside.

Dr Miller sat down beside her. He reached for her hands, not to shake hands but to squeeze her hands in his. 'Do you mind if we speak here, Mrs Finch?'

'I want to see him.'

'You will. I'm sorry that your husband has died. I'm going to try and find out how he died, so we will keep him with us a little while, if that is all right with you.'

'How long?'

'No longer than necessary.' A junior doctor hovered nearby. Dr Miller waved him closer. 'Would you please take Mrs Finch to see her husband.'

She came to attention, so ramrod straight that it must have hurt. Had she asked me to go with her, I would have done so. She did not ask. This was something she must do alone.

When she had gone, Dr Miller turned to me. 'Did she or anyone mention Mr Finch having been in a fight this morning?'

'No.'

'He's been in a scrap, very recently. Until I do a thorough examination, I won't know whether he was killed by a blow or blows or by the CO_2 from the fermentation room. It's better that she sees him now.'

Chapter
Twenty-Nine

❧

We drove back to Masham in silence. It would have been difficult to talk above the noise of the car engine. I parked outside Mrs Finch's house. In turning off the engine, I switched on a deep and spreading silence.

'Would you like me to come in, Mrs Finch?'

She shook her head.

'Or fetch someone?'

'No.'

'What can I do to help?'

'Find out what happened.' Mrs Finch fumbled with the car handle.

'Let me.' I got out and went to the passenger door, opened it and held out my hand.

Mrs Finch did not take my hand but climbed out, saying, 'Thank you.'

A next-door neighbour appeared and stepped out. 'Yvonne, can I come in?'

'I'm best alone.' Mrs Finch went inside and closed the door.

The neighbour stayed put. 'That's her,' she said. 'Independent. Needs no one, even at a time like this.'

'Do they have children?'

'None of their own. They adopted a lad. He joined the army. Of course, there was always a lame duck on the scene, but that was Joe's doing. A three-legged dog, a bird with a broken wing, two rickety kids that come for Sunday dinner.' The woman seemed reluctant to go back into her own house. She turned to me. 'Them kids will be here tomorrow, expecting a dinner and a pony ride.'

As I prepared to drive away from the house, the neighbour opened the Finches' letter box and called, 'When those two bairns come for their dinner tomorrow, send them in to me.'

I thought that Sunday dinner would be the last thing on Mrs Finch's mind.

The loud ringing of the bell broke the quiet of the evening, followed by an even louder voice. The town crier stood in the centre of the square, ringing his bell, breaking the news that most of the town must now know. 'Oyez, oyez! It is Saturday evening, eight o'clock. Joseph Finch is dead. If you have anything to say pertinent to the death of Mr Finch, go now to the police station. May Joseph Finch rest in peace. God save the king!'

Chapter Thirty

I parked the car on the lane and walked down the bumpy track past the allotments. Miss Boland's cottage was in darkness, but a welcoming light shone from Oak Cottage.

I walked slowly to the door, feeling suddenly exhausted.

Harriet came to take my coat. 'Auntie, you look done in. Mrs Lofthouse said that you drove Mrs Finch to Ripon.'

'Yes, she wanted to see her husband.'

'What happened?'

'An accident in the brewery,' I said. 'I can't really say any more.'

Harriet was about to ask a question and then thought better of it. I made for the washroom. Everyone went so quiet that they must have heard each splash as I washed my face.

When I reappeared, Harriet set a plate of food on the table for me, and a glass of Miss Boland's dandelion wine. I took a drink. It tasted as horrible as it smelled. Fortunately, I had a small bottle of brandy in my trunk. Harriet brought it down and Miss Boland and I had a glass.

Miss Boland asked about Yvonne Finch, and thought she ought to go see her.

With a sprained ankle, Miss Boland was in no state to go anywhere.

I said, 'A neighbour offered to go in, but Mrs Finch said she would rather be on her own.'

166

Ruth was subdued. I felt sorry for her. This ought to have been a triumphant week for her. Instead, there were two deaths of people she knew and cared about.

When there was nothing more to say about what had happened, and they got little out of me, Miss Boland tried to divert us with a forced gaiety. It clearly suited her to be centre stage, and I believe the brandy helped. She talked about how, in the days when her father lived in this cottage, Joe Finch and Phil Jopling used to come here and play cards. In those days, when she took a break from touring with the Merry Opera Company, she had occasionally been persuaded to sing on a Friday night in the Falcon. When it came to closing time, Miss Boland's father, Harry, would bring Joe Finch, Phil Jopling and Slater Parnaby back here to play pontoon.

At the sound of her father's name, Ruth flinched. She must hate the thought that he had been here, in what was now her refuge. She seemed to glance about the room, as if to see whether her father might be lurking here still.

This did not escape Miss Boland. 'Your father was a poor loser, Ruth.'

Miss Boland then took a pack of cards from her pocket. 'We can either sit here and be miserable, or we can play a game of cards and drink to the memory of Joe Finch and my father.'

Playing cards was the last thing on my mind, but when she put it that way, we all agreed to join in. Perhaps it would be good for Harriet and Ruth to be diverted.

Miss Boland knew that there was a button box in the top drawer. She asked Ruth to bring it out. We were each supplied with sufficient buttons for high stakes.

Between games, Miss Boland told us a story. She told of touring America. She described arriving at a little town in Arizona called Holbrook. The opera company enjoyed a fine welcome, but she and her friend Julia were not comfortable about going out at night. They stayed in their hotel. One of the waiters taught them to play poker.

There was a heavy knocking on the door. Ruth bit her lip and gripped her cards so tightly that her hand turned white. 'It's the old man.' Her shoulders stiffened. She wanted to turn around, and began to move, but then stayed still.

'Do you want to be out of the way?' I asked.

She shook her head. 'He knows I'm staying here.'

I went to the door.

Slater Parnaby reeked of beer. He stared at me, and then laughed. 'So, Mrs Lofthouse has brought in reinforcements.' He was carrying a hessian bag. 'You forgot some stuff, Ruth.'

Miss Boland reached for her walking stick.

To defuse the situation, I invited him in. 'Come in, Mr Parnaby. There's tea in the pot, and cake from the garden party.' I stepped aside to make room.

He crossed the threshold and looked about. 'Are you hiding George? He's the only man in Masham not queuing up at the police station to give his alibi for this morning.' He threw the hessian bag at Ruth.

She caught it.

'If you've left any more of your female rubbish behind, it'll go on the fireback, unless you want to pay me storage.'

I closed the door behind him and went to stand by Ruth. 'Do sit down, Mr Parnaby.' I indicated the chair by the fire. Here was a man with a short fuse. If I behaved normally, that might rub off on him. If I treated him as a guest, he may behave like one.

He did not sit down. Whatever I had done seemed to rub off on Ruth. She spoke calmly, putting the hessian bag by her chair. 'Thanks, Dad.'

'For what? For looking after you all your life, until you have a splash of luck and folk who think you're summat you're not?' He leaned in close to Ruth. 'Do they know you've a terror of rats? Has Miss Celia Songstress Boland told you that there's rats in the thatch? You'll hear them scratching. They smell fear.'

That was enough. 'Mr Parnaby, if you can't be civil, please go.'

'Oh, I will. In a minute.' He stared at Miss Boland. 'You! Still playing cards I see. They better watch out.' He sniffed, and sniffed again, just like our bloodhound does but with a great deal more noise.

He was seriously drunk. If he did sit down in the chair by the fire, he would fall asleep. We would have to carry him home, or into the nearest ditch.

He circled the room, sniffing, stopping by each person around the table, starting at Ruth, then Harriet, pausing behind Miss Boland, giving a big sniff moving his head from side to side. He snatched Miss Boland's hand of cards and looked at them front and back. He leaned over her. 'These are just the same cards you played when you took my money. I thought you'd won fair and square. They're marked. I was set up.'

Finally, he came to me sniffing.

I stood still and sniffed back. He smelled of beer and body odour. There was something else, something that I had once put a name to, and then forgotten.

'What can you smell?' he asked.

'Loneliness, even so it's time for you to go home, Mr Parnaby.' I walked to the door and opened it.

He let out a scoffing laugh, and then moved back to Ruth, grabbing her shoulder. 'I can scupper you. I can scupper the lot of you. You've prize money. Where's my share?'

She refused to flinch. 'Dad, there's no need for this. I'll give you a month's rent and board, because I'm not coming back.'

'You're like the rats leaving the sinking ship. Well no one sinks Slater Parnaby. Think on that. If I go down, two people in this room go down before me.'

I felt a chill. Go down for what? Had he killed Joe Finch? Parnaby and Finch had been at each other's throats on the day of the trussing. It was a mistake to let Parnaby in, but I did not want him to think I was afraid. There was a torch on the dresser, and a cast iron poker on the hearth. I would not hesitate to use either.

He leaned close to Ruth and whispered to her.

She turned white.

'Ignore him, Ruth,' I said. With my eye on the poker, I opened the door. 'It's growing dark, Mr Parnaby. Time you went home.'

'Goodnight, ladies.' He left.

What had he said to Ruth that made her so afraid?

Chapter
Thirty-One

Walking back home through the square, Slater Parnaby spat at the Market Cross. They thought they could slip away, one by one. First Annie did a flit. Then Ruth, driven to Scarborough on Thursday with the Lofthouses after she'd slipped from under his nose, moving into Oak Cottage with people who didn't belong. Moving in next door to someone who called herself an opera singer—a cheating gambler who gave cut-price piano lessons and stole from his allotment in her spare time. George didn't come back with the rest from Scarborough, no sign or light of him.

Who was blamed when Annie slung her hook? He took the blame. But Annie was the one who made him mad, just giving that certain pained look that got his goat and made him want to knock her block off.

George, threatening, thinking he's his own man, thinking he'll walk out of the brewery and into something better. Well, much he knows of what's out there in the world. If he goes, who'll be blamed?

Who was blamed after the trussing? He heard them. They meant him to hear. Sniffer Parnaby went too far. George didn't deserve that sort of trussing.

He wasn't going to pretend to be deaf. 'My lad has to be able to take it. Some folk will have a hard life and it's best they know it.'

Slater couldn't pinpoint the moment when everyone turned against him. He was never liked but always respected. He didn't care whether people liked him or not. He had his moments. Complimented for his marrow, his wife, his gent of a son, his bonny daughter—never for himself. No one cared that he fought. He did his duty. Slater knew he was a wronged man. There wasn't a man here didn't keep his wife in order, one way or another. There was no better cooper than himself, but George ran a close second, and who has he to thank for that? His old dad.

They never liked him in this snot-nosed town. He's an incomer. But he married Annie, and they'd say, Nah then, Slater. Hey-up, Parnaby. Once they knew his talent, it'd be Hey-up, Smeller. Hey-up Sniffer. As if he'd stopped existing, except for his nose. Now his own workmates looked through him, and him the head cooper. It was Finch's fault. He'd no business taking George back to his house for his wife to bring out the bath. He'd no business bandaging George's hand as if that hammer did him any real damage.

The trussing gave them all an excuse to come out in the open and show they hated him. Even his own workmates, Tim and Barney. Of course, they said nothing. They knew better than to open their mouths and spit poison into the cooperage. Toffee nose Mr Head Brewer had to poke his measuring stick in. 'There's no written law that a lad should stay on when he's out of his time, but they do. Unless they've a father like you. No one would blame George if he packed his bags.'

'George is going nowhere. You know nowt.'

No one understood what Private Slater Parnaby had been through. No one knew. Bit by bit they were robbing him of his family. Someone helped Annie to skedaddle, and he had a good idea who. Joe Finch, that's who. Well, what goes around comes around. Finch was dead. There'd be another body before this game was over.

They came for Ruth, though, they wanted Ruth. Mrs Loft-house, posh bitch who could lose Slater his job, she'd shipped in that smart-looking woman and the young lass to pal up with Ruth. Ruth shouldn't have fallen for them. She packed her bag as nice as ninepence, kissed him on the cheek and said it was only until after the Brewery Queen finals. But she didn't say when that was. Slater knew how much money Ruth had won. He would have his share, in cash or blood.

Chapter
Thirty-Two

～

It was late when I walked Miss Boland back to Elm Cottage. She used her stick and leaned on my arm.

She had seemed so very independent earlier, but now allowed me to help her up the stairs. She decided that she would have a couple of aspirins after all. I felt angry with Parnaby. We had all been letting the card game keep sadness at bay and enjoying each other's company. He came in and threw a dirty wet blanket over everything. I had been too kind to him, and yet how else could I have dealt with an unpredictable stranger? Eleanor was right. Ruth would be much better away from him, although a mile out of the town was not far enough. Apart from Miss Boland, we were quite isolated.

I waited until Miss Boland had undressed and put herself to bed, and then went up with a glass of water and aspirins. The room smelled of lavender and camphor.

She took two aspirins. 'You can ask me about Ruth's father if you want to.'

'We're all tired.'

'Slater Parnaby was the other card player party at our Friday night gatherings. We were a regular little gambling den, with my father and Joe Finch and Phil Jopling.'

'You didn't play?'

'I was banker and also the one who made sandwiches and poured home-made hooch.'

'I expect they enjoyed it.'

'It wasn't for enjoyment. Parnaby was notorious for leaving his wife short of money. There's plenty of men do that, but this was in the extreme. His weakness was his love of gambling. We'd bring him back here, give him a few drinks, and cheat him blind until my father, Joe and Phil got housekeeping money to give his wife.'

Picturing the scene made me smile. It seemed ridiculous that Parnaby could be cheated, week after week.

'Did he never win?'

'Occasionally, a small amount, to keep him keen.'

'Did he never cotton on?'

'Well you see, he always drank that drop too much.'

'How long did that go on?'

'Until Annie left him. He made a show of searching for her.'

'When was this, how young were her children?'

'George would have been twelve, Ruth eleven. It was one of those situations where Annie Parnaby believed her children would be better off without her, convinced that she was the one who triggered his rages. The grandmother came to stay. She was the only one who kept Parnaby in order when the madness came over him.'

I wanted to ask more questions. Miss Boland looked tired. It doesn't do to be prying without a good reason. My good reason was to be armed with knowledge, in case Ruth Parnaby needed more back up than Harriet could give. That made me press on.

'Why did he walk about sniffing? That seems such an odd thing to do.'

She shook her head. 'He is a strange man. I blame it on the war.'

'Does he bear a particular animosity towards you, or is it simply that Ruth has chosen to come and live next door?'

She thought this over for so long it seemed she would not answer.

'He eventually realised the card games were rigged. He'll be examining those cards he snatched tonight. I brought playing cards back with me from America. There's a pattern of tiny clocks on the back of the cards.'

'Yes, I noticed.'

'If you know how to read them, it will give you the suit of the card, its number and whether it is Jack, Queen, King or Ace.'

Being cheated at cards would not be normally be a motive for murder, but Parnaby had an excess of rage. I wondered where he was early this morning when Joe Finch died.

Miss Boland began to cough. I passed her the glass of water.

She sipped several times. The coughing fit left her hoarse, but there was something more she wanted to say.

'Parnaby is no fool. When Annie left and he took over the housekeeping, he soon realised the pittance he handed over would not have put food on the table. Annie lacked the courage to escape him without help. He liked to control her. He'll know she had help to leave.'

I thought about the card games. 'You and your father helped her?'

'We didn't have access to a horse and cart, or the contacts to find somewhere for her.'

'Joe Finch helped her get away?' I could just as easily have said Phil Jopling, but I somehow had Joe Finch as the leader in that pair.

'I'm sure of it,' Miss Boland said. 'Yvonne Finch knows, but she won't tell.'

It struck me that Annie may not have gone far away, where she knew no one. It suddenly made sense that Joe had a fiddle on the Bedale round. Bedale was about six miles away. If Joe was still helping Annie, and Slater found out he'd been made a fool of, that would be a powerful motive for revenge.

I made sure Miss Boland was comfortable and her glass of water within reach. 'Goodnight, Miss Boland.'

'Goodnight, Mrs Shackleton.'

I went downstairs and let myself out. As I was walking along the path, I thought I ought to tell her not to trouble about lighting the fire tomorrow. One of us would do it for her.

As I opened the door to go back in, I heard her crying, quietly at first, and then great racking sobs that left me feeling helpless. She had held back her grief at Joe Finch's death until she was alone.

Quietly, I let myself out, not wishing to intrude.

Chapter
Thirty-Three

❧

I slept fitfully that Saturday night. Disjointed dreams took me down a set of stairs into a dark place where there was no way out. I woke with the dream image of a body. It was not Joe Finch, but a young soldier in a stinking trench. In the dream, it seemed as if it was my task to bury him. The face on the soldier was Slater Parnaby's. For moments, I lay there frozen in terror, and then came properly awake in the distempered room with blue curtains and the sound of the dawn chorus coming in through the open window.

I went downstairs. It was too early for breakfast, but it gave me something to think about. Under other circumstances, the thought of frying bacon and cracking eggs in someone else's house would give me a holiday feeling.

The ashes from last night's fire were still warm. I poked them through the grate, setting cinders aside. Everything was to hand for fire-lighting, knots of newspaper, chips of wood, a small log, good coal. I boiled a kettle and made a pot of tea for one. It was too early to expect Harriet and Ruth to raise their heads from the pillow.

By the time I washed and dressed, Harriet and Ruth were moving about upstairs. Ruth had said she wanted to go to church. I expected Harriet would go with her.

Our water pail was empty. I carried it out to the well and attached it to the hook. It was a pleasure to find something new and practical to learn and to feel a sense of achievement as the half full pail came up to meet me.

I glanced across at next door. Miss Boland must have been up early and feeling strong. There were a few pieces of washing on her line. Good thing Mrs Sugden was not here. She would be outraged at the sight of washing hanging out on a Sunday.

I went through the back door and deposited the pail in the scullery. There was a rattling noise from outside and I realised it was the milkman with one of those floats they all aspire to. I picked up our can and walked out to the gate with it.

The milkman was a middle-aged man, wearing a brown smock and a tweed cap. He gave me a cheery greeting.

'We forgot to put the can out last night,' I said, handing it to him.

'I'll fill it since you're here, but there's no need to bring it to the gate. My customers just leave the jug or can on the doorstep.' He filled the can. 'How long will you be here?'

'I'm not sure, perhaps a few more days.' Joseph Finch's death meant Sykes and I may be here a while yet. 'And what do I do about paying you?' I asked.

'I knock on the door on Saturday morning, though if you're gone, you're gone. The Lofthouses will settle up.'

When the milkman had rattled his way back up the track, I made more tea and took a cup next door to Miss Boland, along with a piece of cake. She had gone back to bed, though had cleared her grate and left paper, wood and coal in the hearth, ready to light a fire. We chatted, and I advised her that bedrest was the best thing for her today. She did look tired.

Harriet and Ruth were still upstairs. I called out that there was fresh tea in the pot and leftovers from the garden party and that I was going to take a walk.

I hoped a walk might help me think clearly about the events of the day before.

It was no surprise that the milk float rattled. The track to the lane was uneven, with deep ridges where carts had trundled through on muddy days, leaving the ground to dry into bumpy shapes and holes. It surprised me that it had taken Miss Boland so long to twist her ankle. It could be a regular occurrence along here.

In spite of the early hour, Mick Musgrove was at work, raking a patch of his allotment. Beyond him, on the next allotment, was Slater Parnaby. Too close for comfort, but out of hearing. Mr Musgrove waved to me and walked across, treading carefully between narrow mounds of earth. 'Potatoes,' he said, and blew his nose.

'You two are out early,' I said.

'We allus are,' Mr Musgrove said, 'me most days, Slater on the days he's not working in his cooperage.'

'Mr Parnaby works his allotment on Saturdays?'

'The sergeant asked just that question. Slater was here from just after dawn. Believe me, if I thought he'd done for my Miss Crawford, he wouldn't have lived long enough to do for poor Joe Finch. He wouldn't be planting them King Edwards just now. He'd be under them. People don't think it, but Slater's a good lad at heart. Gives me a hand.'

'Did anyone else go by?' I held my breath, wanting the answer to be no.

'Only the milkman, coming back up from leaving your milk.'

As I turned away, I forgot to watch my step and almost stumbled. I tried to shake off the memory of yesterday, the sight of Joe Finch, the horror of the fermentation room and my disturbing dream, but it was as if Joe Finch's ghost joined my walk, ready to trip me at every step.

Turning into the lane, I spotted Sykes, walking towards me. For the eeriest moment, I felt Joe Finch had set Sykes and me on a path towards each other so that we could find justice for him.

'Mrs Shackleton, you're up early. I just thought I'd come and see if your curtains were open.'

'Shouldn't you be having breakfast with Rosie?'

'After what happened, Rosie insisted on going home. I'm just back from taking her for the early bus from Ripon.'

We fell into step and walked along the lane. 'That is such a shame about Rosie,' I said. 'You'll have to make it up to her, when this is all over.'

'She said to tell you goodbye, and that she enjoyed the garden party. After what happened, she would have gone home last night, if I hadn't spent so much time with the Lofthouses.'

'How are they?' I asked.

'Devastated.' Sykes kicked a stone. 'Mr Lofthouse came up with the mad idea that Joe took his own life, out of shame at being found out in a fiddle.'

'It would have been a horrible death to choose. Besides, I don't think Joe would be ashamed of fiddling. He probably saw it as a redistribution of wealth.'

'Because he looked out for the homeless family?' Sykes asked.

'Yes. He also helped Mrs Parnaby by cheating Slater at cards and giving Mrs Parnaby the money she ought to have had for housekeeping.' The image came into my head of Joe in his working clothes, telling me about his dislike of James Lofthouse. 'What if when Joe was out on Ripon deliveries, he also spotted James and became suspicious. It would be inconvenient if word got out that he and Rory were up to something.' Even as I said it, I knew my speculation was unlikely. Unless Rory had stood bail, James was still in custody. It would have been up to Rory to silence the drayman.

Sykes doubted James's and Rory's involvement. 'James panicked about Miss Crawford. She was the real threat. Besides, he and Rory knew the dangers of the fermentation room. Rory wouldn't have taken that risk, especially with someone who might have got the better of him.'

At that moment, the sun came from behind a cloud. It was as if the sudden change in the light brought a revelation. I said,

'Nobody who knew about the dangers of the fermentation room would have killed Joe that way. It was someone who didn't know what they were doing.'

'Not necessarily,' Sykes said. 'If there was a fight, men don't always think straight. It could be that Phil Jopling was tired of being Joe's henchman. Phil was the only other brewery worker on duty yesterday.'

'Not Phil,' I said. 'He's loyal to Joe. If he fooled me yesterday, he deserves to be playing Iago in some top production.'

A gentle breeze blew up. A solitary magpie alighted on a branch.

Sykes said, 'You're probably right. From what little I saw of Phil Jopling, he seems a follow-my-leader sort of chap, and Joe was his leader.'

We had walked into the town and were now close to the church.

The gates stood open. Strange how the atmosphere around us changed as soon as we entered the grounds.

There is something about the tranquillity of a churchyard that stops time. St Mary's is a solid and ancient church with a fine steeple. The bells were chiming for the early service. There may be worshippers in there now, praying for the repose of Joseph Finch's soul. More members of the congregation were arriving. On a day such as this it may be standing room only. I spotted Harriet and Ruth in their Sunday best.

Sykes and I walked along the path.

We paused at the far side of the churchyard. Beyond lay a long, fallow meadow.

Sykes pointed. 'The man I saw with the pony, he was walking away from the town, over there, on the far side of the meadow. I wasn't close enough to get a good look at him or the pony.'

'You said he was the wrong height for Finch.'

'Yes. He was too short.'

I could tell that Sykes now wished he had sprinted across. 'You would have had no reason to go chasing after him.'

'I know, but I wish I had. I described the man's height and walk to Sergeant Moon, about as much as I could do from this distance.

The sergeant had an idea he might be a horse dealer who's had several brushes with the law.'

'That may be the best lead so far. Dr Miller, the pathologist, said there were signs that Joe had been in a fight.'

We watched a rabbit run across the churchyard.

I said, 'Unless Mr Musgrove is covering for him, Slater Parnaby is in the clear.'

'Everyone's first choice as killer,' Sykes said, 'but according to Sergeant Moon, Parnaby was on his allotment all day. He ate his midday meal at the Falcon, a regular Saturday habit, which reminds me that I haven't had breakfast.'

'Nor I, nor Rosie?'

Sykes said, 'She was keen to catch the bus. She asked the chef for a buttered teacake to take with her.'

We turned and walked out of the churchyard, towards the town square. By the time we reached the Falcon, my stomach was rumbling. 'I'm going to come in with you and have breakfast, Mr Sykes.'

'Good.' He held the door open. 'And we'll talk about something else.'

'Do you think so?'

'No.'

I stepped inside. 'I'll leave Harriet and Ruth to sort out their own breakfast.'

'They've hit it off?'

'Yes.'

Sykes led us to his favourite table in the corner, where he could have his back to the wall and see all. He said, 'Mr Lofthouse has asked me to talk to you about my staying on until the inquest, to deal with the locksmith.'

'I should think he wants you to do more than deal with the locksmith.'

'He does and I'd like to help him get back on course, now that he has given up on the idea of James ever becoming his right-hand man.'

'Then you must stay.'

In a sudden moment of anxiety, I imagined William Lofthouse wanting to recruit Sykes to work with him. I have always valued Sykes for his ability, but it occurred to me that if Sykes departed, the Shackleton agency would not be the same.

Chapter Thirty-Four

~

Harriet and Ruth decided they would go out. First, Ruth took some lunch to Miss Boland. Harriet wrote a note for her auntie. It made her feel excited to write it. She was in a strange place, on a lovely day, with a new friend.

Gone with Ruth to the Druid's Temple.

They had just walked up the track to the lane when someone whistled. Ruth said, 'That's our George.' She whistled back.'

Harriet recognised the lad who was wheeling his bike. He was the boy she had seen in the newsreel, sitting on the front row for the contest in Scarborough, gazing at Miss East Riding. Ruth introduced George to Harriet, saying, 'We're both staying in Oak Cottage, with Harriet's auntie. I'm not going back home, ever.'

'Well neither am I. Richard's mam said I can stay at their house for as long as I like.'

This might be the first and last time Harriet could say, 'I saw you on the pictures.'

George groaned. 'Don't remind me! I looked so soppy.'

'You did not,' Harriet lied.

'Where have you been all weekend?' Ruth asked. 'You could at least have put in an appearance at the garden party.'

'I came back from Scarborough on the train. I went to Bedale on Friday night and stayed in the attic room.'

'You've never done that before.'

'I had to build up a certain person to come and see you on Pathé News on Saturday.'

Ruth's eyes widened. 'And did she?'

'Yes!'

Ruth danced in a circle, punching the air like a boxer in the ring, with cries of triumph, 'Yes, yes, yes!'

Harriet was astonished. Ruth always appeared serene, remote almost. Now she was a whirling dervish. 'We'll do it, George! We're almost there.'

He shrugged. 'I said we would.'

Harriet did not know what they were talking about, but they weren't doing it in a way to make her feel left out.

Ruth's mood suddenly changed. 'You won't have heard then, about Joe?'

George stood stock still. 'It's true then? Abe told me, but he's gaga.'

Harriet listened while Ruth told George what she knew about yesterday's events. 'And we were there, George, by the stables, with no idea that poor Joe was lying in the fermentation room.'

George closed his eyes and lowered his head. 'Abe didn't tell me that.'

Ruth said, 'And our old man, he came to Oak Cottage last night. He said you were the only man in Masham not queuing up to give your alibi for yesterday.'

Harriet was still not used to hearing them talk of their dad as the old man.

George coloured up. 'And where was the old man? He was the one wanted to knock Joe's block off after the trussing.'

'He'd fight Joe, but not kill him.' Ruth's joy of a few moments ago had vanished. 'There's only one person he'd like to kill. One day, I might be his second choice.'

'Ruth!' George looked at Harriet, signalling to her not to say too much in the presence of an outsider.

'It's all right,' Ruth said. 'We can trust Harriet.'

'You can trust me because I've no notion what you're talking about.' Harriet felt pleased and proud. She had never expected to make friends here.

Harriet did have a vague notion of what they might be talking about, but it was their conversation and she would keep out. Ruth was saying that their father would like to kill their mother.

George said, 'Where are you two going anyway?'

'The Druid's Temple', Ruth said.

'I'll come with you but I'm not walking.' he said to Ruth. 'Fetch your bike.' He turned to Harriet. 'Would you ride pillion on my bike?'

'Yes,' Harriet said. She'd be happy to ride pillion on his bike anytime. Harriet wished George hadn't looked so moonstruck at Miss East Riding.

They cycled along country lanes, under a blue sky with a single great wash of streaking cloud, passing shabby old thatched cottages and a couple of farmhouses, lots of trees and fields of sheep. After the novelty of being cycled, Harriet wished she could pedal instead of just sticking out her legs to avoid the wheels.

At the edge of a wood, that might be a forest, they stopped and climbed off the bikes. George and Ruth propped their bikes by an oak tree.

They left the bright sunshine for the shade of the wood, going deeper and deeper, startling rabbits and birds, coming across clumps of bluebells and wild garlic. Shortly after that they stepped into a clearing that took Harriet back through time. It was an arrangement of standing stones, like in a picture of Stonehenge, but smaller. These stones were not much taller than George

Parnaby but the place still gave her the shivers. Harriet thought of her dad, a stonemason. Unhewn, that was what he would have called these stones. Four stones edged what looked to Harriet like a mounted gravestone. There were altars where a pagan might make a sacrifice. But most astonishing of all was a brown and white Shetland pony, all alone at the top of the oval. Harriet went closer. The pony was suddenly nervous and backed away, until George came over and patted its neck and said, 'Billy, what are you doing here?'

Harriet watched, to see what they would do. They both went quiet, and seemed scared. Ruth said, 'Look in the hermit's cave. See if someone is hiding, the person who brought Joe's pony here.'

George said, 'You look.' He took something from his pocket. 'I'll stay with Billy. He knows me best.' He patted the pony. 'I saved you a sugar lump.'

Harriet stepped forward. 'Where is the cave? I'll look.' She thought they might be a little wary. She guessed neither George nor Ruth knew Jujitsu.

Ruth pointed out the cave and walked along behind her. 'The old man told us he would leave us here one dark night and the wolves would come.'

So that's how they deal with having a weird father, Harriet thought. They put him at a distance. "The old man", even though he was not so very old, simply crazy and frightening.

Harriet could not see far into the dark cave. George passed a box of matches to Ruth who threw it to Harriet. Harriet struck a match, and another as she went farther in. There was no one there. An eggshell lay on the floor of the cave, recently cracked. Someone had guzzled the egg but not long ago because soft white of egg still bonded to the shell. A discarded tab end felt warm to the touch.

'Whoever it is, they're nearby, waiting for us to go so they can come back for the pony.'

'Or steal our bikes,' Ruth said.

This made them hurry back the way they had come, George encouraging Billy, jollying the pony along because he had no bridle.

The bikes were where they had left them. There was now the question of the pony. George looked through his saddlebag. He felt sure there was a length of rope in there.

'Give me a hand up and I'll ride him,' Harriet said.

George smiled at her, as if she was not all there. 'No saddle, no bridle, no reins?'

Harriet put her head on the pony's neck. 'You'll let me ride, won't you?'

It was that or climb on George's boneshaker and cling on. She knew which she preferred. The novelty had worn off.

The pony whinnied. George made a stirrup of his hands, to help Harriet onto the pony's back.

She was up.

Harriet whispered to the pony. 'We'll show them, Billy. They aren't the only ones brought up in the country.' Harriet never had a pony of her own, but she had known someone who did.

On the journey back, she asked Ruth about the Druid's Temple.

'They call it a folly,' Ruth called to her. 'Early in the last century a landowner, William Danby, designed it. I don't know whether he had nothing better to do or whether he did it on purpose to provide jobs. A lot of people were out of work, like now, so he paid local men a shilling a day to build it.'

'Did anyone live in the cave?'

'Someone was paid a wage to live there for seven years, but after five years he went mad.'

'Who was it?'

George slowed down. 'It was the old man. I'm thinking of having him sent back to complete his seven years.'

Ruth said, 'He's just being silly. If it was dad, he'd have to be a hundred and fifty years old.'

As they came closer to Masham, the talk turned to where they should take the pony, and who should tell the police.

Harriet had the answer. 'We'll take him to the cottage. No one will look for him in the garden. There's a shed where he can spend the night.'

'I don't want to go to the police station.' George began to pedal a little faster. 'I've somewhere else to go.'

'We'll tell Auntie Kate. She'll know what to do.'

The front gate of the cottage was too narrow to lead the pony through. Billy Boy backed away. The place was unfamiliar. Harriet sympathised. The animal did not know where he was being led. Harriet walked round to the back garden and opened the bigger gate.

Ruth and George stayed on the track, talking. Harriet called to them. 'Would one of you fill a bucket from the well? There's plenty of grass for Billy.'

George called back. 'I have to go now. I'm off to see Mrs Finch!' He went, pedalling over the bumps.

Ruth called after him. 'I'll follow on. Don't go in without me!'

But George was already gone, calling, 'Come when you're ready.'

At the sound of voices, Miss Boland came out of her back door, leaning on her stick. 'Where did you find the pony?'

Harriet told her. 'He was at the Druid's Temple.'

'He was taken by the gypsies then. They must have got into the brewery stable.'

Ruth clanked along with a bucket.

Harriet was astonished to see their dog appear, making a fuss of her and then taking a sniff at the pony. The bloodhound then pushed his way through a gap in the fence towards Miss Boland. He was sniffing at her stick, and then leaning back with front limbs outstretched and head down.

Harriet laughed. 'He wants you to throw your stick for him, Miss Boland. He doesn't know it's a walking stick.'

Miss Boland shooed the dog away.

He came back, sniffing again.

Ruth said, 'Your dog would get on well with the old man. They could have a sniffing contest.'

Kate came out to see what all the fuss was about.

Harriet went to fetch the dog. 'How did he get here, Auntie?'

Kate said, 'You missed Mrs Sugden! She came on the coach and brought him.'

'She got tired of walking him,' Harriet said.

'That's not how she put it. Mrs Sugden thinks that in a remote cottage, we need a dog, but I will take him for a long walk tomorrow.'

'Go to Roomer Common,' Ruth said. 'That's where we always went when we were little. The old man took us there before we knew he was mad.'

The dog grabbed Miss Boland's stick again, ran to Auntie Kate and presented it to her ready for throwing. Miss Boland tried not to show how annoyed she was. Auntie Kate took it from him and passed it back, apologising to Miss Boland and asking about her ankle.

Ruth and Harriet went to stand by the pony, watching him drink.

Ruth said, 'We might have saved Billy's life. What if someone was going to sacrifice him at the Druid's Temple?'

Harriet had noticed that in spite of her grand ideas about winning through, keeping her tiara straight and conquering the world, Ruth always expected the worst.

'That's daft,' Harriet said. 'Why would anyone sacrifice a pony?'

'People make sacrifices to the gods, believing their future depends on it.'

'In the olden days, not now.'

Chapter
Thirty-Five

❧

Ruth had set off with Harriet for an official engagement. I had just sat down to look at the Ordnance Survey map when the dog barked. Moments later, there was a knock on the door. Sergeant Moon stood just a little way back from the doorstep. 'Mrs Shackleton, you have a dog?'

'Yes, my housekeeper brought him over yesterday. Do come in, or he won't let us talk.'

'Ah, a bloodhound.' The sergeant stepped inside, patting the dog.

'He failed as a police dog. My father is on the West Riding force. When I was growing up, we had a police bloodhound called Constable. My mother wanted another dog but forgot she would be left with the job of walking him, so this one found his way to me.'

'What's his name?'

This was a little awkward. I hoped the sergeant would not take the name as a slight. 'Well since our first dog was Constable, we thought a promotion would be in order. This is Sergeant.'

'What a good name!'

'There's tea in the pot. Will you have a cup, Mr Moon?' It would be best not to give the sergeant his title while the dog was here. Our dog also likes a drink of tea, in a saucer with milk, no sugar.

'I will have a cup of tea. Thank you.' The sergeant took off his cap and sat at the table.

I moved the Ordnance Survey map.

'You're going for a walk?'

'Yes, to Roomer Common. Ruth recommended it. She used to walk there with her family. I assumed it must have been in happier times, before Mrs Parnaby left.'

The sergeant eyed the cake. 'I was just passing along the lane and thought I'd let you know that someone will be coming to collect the pony later today.'

Sergeant Dog sniffed at Sergeant Moon's leg, lost interest and left by the back door.

I poured tea. 'Does Mrs Finch want the pony back?'

'No, she does not. But we need to take Billy into custody, at our own stables. We've made an arrest for the theft, and we don't want to lose the creature again.'

Sykes was right to suspect the horse dealer. I wanted to know, and it was worth a try, 'Might the thief be facing more than one charge?'

'You wouldn't expect me to answer that, Mrs Shackleton, but I can give you a few tips about how to find your way to Roomer Common. That dog of yours will like it. Doesn't chase sheep, does he?'

'He doesn't chase sheep.' I cut two slices of cake and slid a plate towards him.

'Thank you.' He sugared his tea and stirred. 'So, Harriet and Ruth found the pony at the Druid's Temple?'

'Yes, they and George.'

'Did George say where he'd been on Saturday?'

'I haven't spoken to him.'

'Not important. Everyone who works at the brewery is being asked to account for their movements up to the time of Joe Finch's death, just a matter of paperwork.'

At that moment, Sergeant Dog returned with Miss Boland's walking stick. He dropped it in front of his human counterpart.

'Bad boy!' I said. 'Miss Boland won't get far without that and Sergeant Moon isn't going to throw it for you.'

Sergeant Moon patted the dog. 'Thank you, Sergeant. I'll give it back to Miss Boland, and just say hello, see how she's getting on.' He picked up the stick and leaned it against the table. 'It's unsettling when we have two deaths in so short a time. We have never known anything like this in Mashamshire. Not to alarm you, but I want to make sure you and Miss Boland are locking your doors.'

Chapter
Thirty-Six

~

Harriet did not reckon much to this idea of a procession. A procession called for brass bands and banners, carnations, rows of girls in white satin and boys in uncomfortable jackets.

Combining a procession with beer deliveries must be Mr Lofthouse's way of saving money. He had said this was a good way of ensuring landlords, landladies and bar staff would see Queen Ruth.

Harriet, acting as companion, was to sit between Ruth and Phil Jopling. To Harriet's thinking, the dray ought to have been decorated but that was not possible because it was loaded with barrels.

Ruth was no help. All she knew was that she must wave, and then give a short speech at Bedale House over lunch. The procession had been announced in the newspaper so could not be cancelled out of respect for Joe Finch, as Ruth and Phil Jopling had wanted.

The seat was draped in red velvet. Caesar and Cleopatra's manes had been plaited with red, white and blue ribbons, decorated with white rosettes. Phil adjusted two large black bows that he had attached to the horses' collars, to remember Joe.

Ruth was to sit holding. Cleopatra's reins. Jopling would hold Caesar's. Harriet would be pig in the middle.

'Why didn't we call it off?' Ruth said again as she eased off her rubber boots.

Jopling sighed. 'That's what I said, but there wasn't time to get word to everyone who will turn out, or to cancel the lunch you're to have with bigwigs at Bedale Hall.'

Ruth put on her satin shoes.

Jopling gave Ruth a quick set of instructions regarding the reins, adding, 'Don't fret. The horses know where they're going. They're the real workers. Me and Joe, we just do—did—the heavy lifting.'

People who came out to watch the dray leave Masham did so in silence, for Joe Finch. The horses clip-clopped their way along Silver Street, towards the river.

Ruth suddenly asked Jopling to stop by the draper's shop. 'I need a black scarf. I'm not going to pretend nothing has happened.'

Jopling whoa-ed the horses. 'You do right, lass.'

Harriet knew this was her job. 'Let me pass, Phil.' She squeezed round, hopped down and went in the shop, taking her purse from the deep pocket of her coat dress. When the draper knew who the scarf was for and why, she said, 'She can fetch it back, or settle up later.' But Harriet paid. She had spotted the sign in the draper's window.

Please Do Not Ask For Credit As Refusal May Offend.

As they continued their clip-clopping journey, a stillness settled around the three of them.

By Masham bridge, a group of people had gathered. Several farmers' wives waited, with a batch of children. Ruth knew them all. A sheepdog wagged its tail. The young shepherd with the dog, sheepish as his occupation, watched from behind the hedgerow. Ruth waved and obligingly climbed down, so that the children could take a better look at her medallion. Harriet noticed that Ruth seemed to have the ability to switch something on inside herself when she spoke to "her public". She was good at putting on the right face. Had she learned that from Miss Boland's coaching, or was that switch always inside her? Perhaps Harriet would ask later, if a person could find the words to ask about something like that.

They now seemed to Harriet to be in the middle of nowhere, nothing but fields on either side, cows on one side of the road, sheep on the other, and a solitary farmhand, mending a gate. It reminded her of where she had grown up, and of helping on the land, picking potatoes, blackberrying, even playing the part of a human scarecrow when seeds were scattered.

As they arrived at the first pub, Harriet said, 'Ruth, don't get down and talk to people. For one thing, we'll take all day. For another thing, queens don't do that. It's not dignified.'

Phil unloaded casks. The landlord and his wife came out to say hello, congratulate Ruth, and give her a bar of chocolate. Harriet took the chocolate for safekeeping, in case it melted on Ruth's dress.

At Five Lane Ends, a little crowd stood to watch them go by. Ruth waved. Caesar and Cleopatra kept on trotting.

At each pub, Phil 'took a drink' as invited. After he had supped five pints in five pubs he began to speak kindly about Finch.

'He'd do anything for anyone would Joe. Give you the shirt off his back he would.' From these sudden switches between being extremely morose and then making up for it by joshing them, Harriet realised he was drunk. 'Watch yerselves as we round this bend, girls. I don't want to have to fish you out of a ditch.'

When he became seriously drunk, Phil nodded off, leaving the horses to find their own way.

Harriet took Phil's set of reins.

When the horses stopped, Phil would wake, without realising he had been asleep, make his deliveries and be pretend-jolly about it.

It was just after dinnertime when they arrived in Bedale, half past one by the town clock, Phil now wide awake. They stopped in the main street. Ruth waved to the crowds.

Phil jumped down. He encircled a great kilderkin in his arms. Hugging it to himself, he pushed his way through the crowd and disappeared into a hotel.

A policeman as round as the big barrel came smiling towards them. 'I'm to drive you to Bedale Hall, ladies. Please come with me.'

Suddenly Ruth looked as though she had been slapped in the chops. Her mouth opened. No words came. And then she said, 'We must stay on the dray to the end of the main street. I have to wave to . . . to people.'

'We don't want you to be late for lunch, miss,' the policeman said. 'You can wave from the car.'

'It's not the same, and Mr Jopling will wonder where we've gone.'

'That's all right, miss. Mr Jopling has been informed. You are late, you see, and there's a gathering for you.'

Harriet knew she must speak up. But how do you contradict a policeman who weighs twenty stones and is determined to make off with you? And who are these people who can't keep the dinner warm for half an hour?

Ruth's regal stance wavered. Whatever switch was inside her, she couldn't find it.

Here goes, Harriet told herself. Here's a test for a good companion. What was that word Auntie Kate came up with whenever life became tricky? Compromise.

'Officer, I'm Harriet Armstrong, Ruth's official companion for her appearances. May we compromise on this?' She had never said the word aloud before. 'You can see from here how people are gathered along the street, waiting. At the end of the main street, we shall be pleased to get into your police car.'

She looked at Ruth, who nodded.

Harriet held her breath.

Annoyingly, the constable looked as if he might laugh.

'Very well, Miss Armstrong. I'm sure that will be satisfactory.'

He's glad, Harriet thought. I bet he's been ragged enough about this job of escorting a queen. She could not be sure whether her own words had done the trick, or that Ruth looked suddenly hopeless and close to tears.

Harriet would always remember the ride through Bedale. The street was lined with well-wishers. A light rain fell. Shopkeepers and assistants stood in doorways. Almost at the end of the street, a woman who reminded Harriet of a wild and wounded creature stood outside the bakery. As they came close, she stepped forward, waving a small white hanky.

Ruth called, 'Stop the horses!'

Ruth climbed from the dray, not noticing that she caught her heel and tore the hem of her cloak, and opened her arms to the wisp of a woman. They hugged each other and kissed. Harriet thought she heard Ruth say, "You've come outside".'

Harriet was so proud when Ruth pointed her out, saying, 'This is my companion, Harriet. Everything is going to be all right.'

The woman glanced at Harriet and gave a small smile. Harriet reached out to give Ruth a hand up. Ruth seemed to have forgotten that they were late. There was a dip in the road and the dray jolted. Harriet's innards scrunched up and sent waves of something like panic through her body. Except it wasn't panic. It was that flash that comes with knowing something in an instant, something that your body tells you.

That woman is Ruth's mother.

That night, the darkness in the bedroom was total, so much so that Harriet thought this was what it must have been like before God said, Let there be light.

And then Ruth, who was nearest the window, drew back the curtain. Harriet saw that the sky was full of stars, hundreds of stars, just in that pane of window, without counting any others.

Harriet wanted to know something. She would not be able to sleep until she knew. What was the best way to ask? Did you go all around the houses, talking about your own mother, or did you ask straight out? Was it a cheek to want to know? Yes. Would Ruth want to tell? Probably not.

'Ruth.'

'What?'

'Can I ask you something?'

'If you like.'

'In Bedale, when we went along the main street, and got near the end, and that lady waved to you and reached out, by the bakery, and you got down—'

'What about her?'

'Is she your mother?'

Ruth did not answer for a long time. She drew back the other curtain, revealing more stars. 'What if she is?'

'I just wondered.'

'We're going to be together again, the three of us, Mam, me and George.'

'When?'

'Soon. That was our plan, George's and mine, since she left. George was always going to be dad's apprentice, then he would finish his apprenticeship and get a job somewhere else. I would find work, earn money. Mam never spends anything. She has an escape fund. It used to seem like a dream.'

Harriet heard a distant owl and, shortly after, the bark of a fox. They were both still awake.

'The trouble is, he knows,' Ruth said.

They had lain without speaking so long that it took Harriet a moment to grasp that Ruth was talking about her father and mother. 'Your dad knows your mam is at the bakery?'

'I'm not sure. But he knows we see her.'

'Who told him?'

'He's crafty. He talks to people when it suits him. Someone must have seen us in Bedale. Mam passed me a note today. She saw dad walking along the street, looking about.'

'That doesn't mean he knows.'

'It does. She has an instinct. In her note, she said that Joe will take her somewhere safe. She doesn't know that Joe is dead.'

Harriet thought about this. 'You couldn't tell her there and then, just on the street. If you like, I'll go back with you.'

'I don't know. I don't know what to do. She might think—'

'What?'

'Oh nothing. I'm going to try and sleep now.'

Harriet guessed what Mrs Parnaby might think. That Mr Parnaby had killed Joe Finch.

Chapter Thirty-Seven

Someone was up. I could hear a scraping noise downstairs, the ash-pan being emptied. All went quiet. The back door opened. Either Ruth or Harriet must have had a bad dream to wake so early. I looked at the clock and went back to sleep.

It was an hour later when Harriet brought me a cup of tea. I propped myself up on pillows. 'Couldn't you sleep, Harriet?'

'I've something to tell you, when you're properly awake.'

'I'm awake.'

'I'll tell you when you come down.'

Not that she was rushing me, but she took my dressing gown from the hook behind the door and put it on the bed, saying, 'I'll do you a slice of toast.'

When I had finished my tea, I brushed my hair, and went downstairs. Harriet was sitting by the fire, a slice of bread on a too-short toasting fork. Her right hand had turned pink from the heat. 'There must be a better fork than that.'

Harriet switched hands. 'If there is, I can't find it.'

'Well I won't rattle about looking. We might wake Ruth. I heard you earlier, when you were laying the fire.'

'That's because your room is at this end. Ruth is still asleep. I knew you'd wake.'

'How did you know that?'

'I just knew.' She turned the bread round on the fork.

'One side will do.'

'No. I'll do it properly.'

Whatever it was she wanted to say was taking some working up to. She toasted another slice while I buttered the first.

As we ate our toast, she told me about Ruth's mother who had been living in Bedale, working in a bakery, living in the kitchen, never going out, except into the yard. Ruth had told Harriet it was a miracle that their mother had let George take her to the pictures on Saturday, to see Pathé News, and it was another miracle that their mother had come out onto the main street to watch the procession and wave her hanky, adding, 'She can't go out.'

'Is someone keeping her there?' I asked.

'Ruth said she just can't. I don't understand why. Mrs Parnaby, her name is Annie, came out of the shop door to watch the procession. Ruth said that must have been very hard for her.'

Harriet told me the story. When Annie Parnaby feared for her life, Joe Finch came to her aid. He found a job for her, with a place to stay. Annie told the children the secret, that she would leave, but they would be together again. She said they would have a quiet life without her.

I was pleased that Ruth had confided in Harriet when they had known each other for such a short time. 'How did she bring up the subject?' I asked.

'I brought it up. Ruth's mother put a note in Ruth's hand. It says that when she was taking a tray of buns into the shop, she saw Mr Parnaby on the other side of the street, looking about. She thinks someone has told him where she is.'

'Is there nobody Ruth's mother can trust? Someone who will help her?'

'There was Joe Finch. Ruth believes he may have been going to take her somewhere safe, and now he's dead.'

An alarm clock went off upstairs. This was the day of Miss Crawford's funeral at Ripon Cathedral.

'Should I go with Ruth to the funeral?' Harriet asked.

'You don't need to. You didn't know Miss Crawford. Just walk up with Ruth to Barleycorn House. She'll be going with the Lofthouses and Mr Sykes.'

A log on the fire crackled. Out in the garden, the dog barked. 'That must be the milkman,' I said. 'I've been waiting for a word with him. We could do with an extra pint.'

'I'll go.' Harriet got up.

'No, I want a word with him.'

When I went back inside, Harriet asked, 'What did Sergeant Moon want yesterday? Was it just about the pony going to the police stables?'

'He stayed for a cup of tea. Oh, and he looked at the map with me. I took Sergeant Dog for a walk to Roomer Common.'

Ruth came down the stairs, dressed in black, ready for Miss Crawford's funeral. She looked pale and miserable but picked up on our conversation. 'What did you think to common, Auntie Kate?'

I was glad to have been adopted as Ruth's auntie. 'It was a good walk.'

'Did you look out for the demolished cottages I told you about?' Ruth asked.

'Yes, but I didn't see them, probably on account of them having been demolished.'

'If we go there, I'll show you the landmark.' She stood in front of the mirror to put on her hat. 'Next to an oak tree, there's a bit of wall left. The old man was always cheerful on that walk. He had us searching for gold coins. When one of the cottages was demolished, a stash of coins was found hidden in the thatch.'

'Did you ever find any?' Harriet asked.

'No. The old man probably still goes up there looking.' She went back upstairs, saying, 'I need that black scarf. I can't believe that I'm going to Miss Crawford's funeral.'

Harriet said, 'What will you do today, Auntie? You're not doing much investigating, are you?'

'You'd be surprised. Which reminds me, did you happen to find out anything about the children from the homeless family who came to the garden party?'

'Michael and Monica? I didn't ask. Why do you want to know?'

'I hate to think of children, a family, sleeping rough.'

That was true, but I also wanted to know whether Joe continued to let them sleep in the stables, and whether they may have seen something on Saturday morning.

The one person who might know the whereabouts of the children was Mrs Finch. She regularly gave them their dinner on Sundays. It was an imposition to visit her, days after bereavement, but I would do it.

When I drove her home from Ripon Dispensary on Saturday, she had said, 'Find out what happened.'

We were three days on and there had been no information of any kind. It was time for me to start making more enquiries about what happened to Joe Finch.

Chapter Thirty-Eight

～

Annie knew that if it had not been for Joe, she would not be here, or on this earth. Slater would have killed her.

She took a tray of perfect small white loaves from the oven. Apart from baking, she had always done things wrong. She said yes when she should have said no. It seemed easier to agree when you had no definite opinion and others seemed so certain. She was good at baking, bad at life.

Even Joe had tired of her, it seemed. Or was he ill? Had he taken that new job and just gone?

Will you marry me? Slater had said to her, all those years ago.

She wasn't good-looking, neither was he. It was a never-ending wonder to Annie that they produced such bonny children. But Annie's sister was pretty, so it was in the family. When first Annie and Slater met, he seemed kind and considerate. She hesitated when first he said they should marry, perhaps because of the occasional sharp word. He persisted. When Annie's mother had that awful sickness, he came with flowers. They sat by the bed. Slater said to Annie's mother, 'I'll take good care of Annie. Your daughter will be safe with me.'

Slater was a man with a trade, a man who would provide. Annie's mother died happy. The die was cast.

When asked why he had applied for a job in Masham after working in a big city, Slater said he wanted a change.

Of course, he got his name on the rent book before the ink dried on the marriage licence.

It shamed him to have a working wife. Nor did he like Annie to stay behind after church to 'gossip', as he called their conversation. She must come straight home. According to him, their neighbour, Mrs Finch, was stuck-up and not worth bothering with. It was better that Annie should keep herself to herself. He kept himself to himself. People only turned against you.

It took the children, it took George, when he was so little, to say, Let's go away, mammy, before he kills you.

She stayed, for the children, until she realised that George was right. Slater would kill her. He would hang. Her children would be orphans. She must do one good thing in her life, save that life, to live another day. She must save her children from being the little witnesses to horror and save them from trying to come between their parents, to ward off Slater's blows.

Annie told Ruth and George that when she had gone, they must write to grandma to come. His mother would come like a shot, to have a better roof over her head. They would be cared for. The old woman knew how to put him in his place. She'd made him, she'd shaped him, she knew what he was and what he had become.

George could not understand why he and Ruth could not come with their mother. Annie told him that they would be together, but not yet.

The children came to see her, walking all the way, pretending they had gone to the woods, or out onto the moors. George became good at fixing bikes. Now, after all these years, the plan was taking shape. They were grown, George a tradesman, Ruth a wages clerk, and a queen.

But perhaps too much time had gone by. They had waited too long. Annie feared her children would grow away from her before she had time to hold them again.

On Monday, Annie was so thrilled to see Ruth that she forgot about Joe. When the dray moved on a few yards, Ruth and the other girl climbed down, to be given a ride in a car.

Phil did not come to say why Joe was not with them.

George stayed at Annie's on Friday night. He told her about Ruth's success. He told her about the loveliness of the runner-up, Miss East Riding, Bernadette Jarvis of Scarborough. On Saturday, when Annie finished the last batch of baking, George insisted she go with him to the cinema. She would see Ruth on Pathé News. Annie spent the day in dread of going outside, of leaving the yard. When she carried a tray through to the shop, her hands shook.

There was no putting George off. Annie held his arm as they walked to the cinema. They had to sit through everything twice. 'Ruth introduced me to Bernadette,' George said during the interval. 'Mam, she isn't just beautiful, she is funny and kind and congratulated Ruth and jollied along Miss West Riding who looked so disappointed.'

George had fallen in love. They had left it too late for the plan to be together. George would find a girl. If not Miss East Riding, he would find someone else who looked like her. Ruth would take her pick. She would make a good match. A well-placed man would not want a useless mother-in-law cluttering up a perfect life.

Chapter
Thirty-Nine

A stillness hung over the town square. The slate grey sky and the stone buildings bleached the small world of colour. Rain drizzled, stopped, drizzled again. For a brief moment, it seemed that everyone may have left town while my back was turned. It was a relief when a woman opened her door and came out carrying a shopping basket.

At first glance, all the houses looked alike, with their neat curtains, scoured steps and doors painted a standard green. Which one belonged to Mrs Finch? Where had I dropped her off after coming back from Ripon Dispensary? My feet took me to a house with a Dutch vase in the window, filled with bluebells. Someone was playing the piano. I knocked.

After a moment, Mrs Finch opened the door.

I had caught her in the middle of something. She had that preoccupied look. It took her a moment to come back into the here and now.

'Mrs Finch, Kate Shackleton, I drove you to the Dispensary.'

She ran her fingers through her hair. 'Of course.'

'I'm sorry to come so early. I took the chance that you would be up. May I come in?'

She opened the door wider and stepped aside. 'It's a change to be asked.'

The house had little by way of ornaments. Cupboards had been fitted either side of the range. A piano stood where another house may have boasted a china cabinet or dresser. Although it had no maker's name, it was not the usual cottage piano that might be fitted into a small space, but almost five feet in width.

She waved at the table. There were three pies, two dishes with lids, and a bottle of tonic wine. 'Neighbours, kind neighbours.'

'I haven't brought anything.'

'Good.' She lifted an old cat from the cane chair by the fire and set it down in a plywood orange box lined with a battered cushion. She waved at the opposite chair. 'Do sit down. Give me a moment.'

She went to the piano and played a few notes, no more than fifteen seconds. She picked up a pencil, took a manuscript sheet from the music stand and made a note.

'You're composing?'

She nodded. 'I suppose you think it odd.'

'Not at all. I'm impressed.' Her husband dies on Saturday, on Wednesday she is composing. I could not remember what I did when I received the telegram about Gerald. Nothing so proper and solid as composing music.

She shrugged. 'Popular songs, that's all. People know I tinker on the piano, play tunes. Nobody knows what comes of it.'

'These popular songs, would I know any of them?'

'Possibly.'

'They're published?'

'Yes, I'm sent a copy of the sheet music. Four are recorded.'

'You're a real composer.'

She smiled. 'I wish that were true. I create ditties. While I'm doing that, I forget myself entirely, and that's a blessing.'

'I've never met a composer.'

'Well now you have. It happened by chance. When we married, Joe did not want me to work. His pride, you see. He could keep a wife, even a wife who needed a piano.'

'It's good that you have that, that interest.'

I guessed that song writing would not bring in a great deal of money. She would miss a man's wage coming in.

'I've kept it to myself. In a small town, it's easy to become a "character". I'd hate that.'

She had nothing to fear from me and I told her so. 'I'm not intending to be a permanent fixture here, so I won't be pointing you out as you cross the square on market day.'

'And now you know my secret vice, what is yours? What brings you to Masham?'

'I'm here because I'm friends with Eleanor Lofthouse, staying at Oak Cottage for a few days. Otherwise, I am a private investigator.'

'Never.' Her eyes widened. 'We must be on the same thought wavelength. Didn't I say something odd when we arrived back from Ripon? I asked you to find out who murdered Joe?'

'When you got out of the car, you said, "Find out what happened".'

'And will you?'

'Something may be revealed at the inquest tomorrow.'

'I can't tell how I feel about that. Nothing is real.'

'Everyone says your husband was a kind man.'

'Oh, he was.' Others had given examples of his kindness. She was not going to expand.

'Joe let a homeless family sleep in the stables at the brewery. It occurs to me that if they slept there on Friday night, they may have seen something on Saturday morning.'

She looked suddenly interested. 'That's possible.'

It seemed to me unlikely that the parents would have come forward. They should not have been in the stables. 'Do you happen to know where that family is living?' I asked.

She shook her head. 'I'm annoyed with myself for not thinking to ask their children on Sunday. I hope they'll come back. I told them to bring their mam and dad.' She bit her lip and paused for a moment. 'From what Monica said, I'm guessing they're in the woods, probably beyond the allotments. She talked about what a fright Michael gave them, pretending he couldn't get down from a tall tree.'

'I'll find them.'

'And is investigating like writing music? The tune comes into your head and it won't let you go.'

'Something like that.'

'You also believe someone killed Joe?'

I said, 'I truly have no idea what happened.'

Yvonne Finch's matter of fact manner set me wondering about her. Whoever was present when Joe died would have had to be ignorant of the dangers of the fermentation room. Joe was more likely to come home and talk about horses than about mash tuns and fermentation.

Mrs Finch's distress on Saturday was real and deeply felt but she could not be ruled out.

'Have you told Sergeant Moon that you suspect foul play?' I asked.

She corrected me. 'I don't suspect it, I know it.' She tapped her heart. 'I know it here.'

'Is there anyone who had a grudge against him?'

'Slater Parnaby, but he knocked on my door, cap in hand, saying sorry for your loss, so I don't think so. Besides, Parnaby has a grudge against almost everyone.'

'What does the sergeant say?'

'He tells me we must wait for the inquest.'

'Was there anything unusual about that morning, any change of Joe's pattern?'

'Joe was a creature of habit. He went to the brewery stables at the same time every morning, before people started work. On Saturday, he was on the rota to do certain jobs in the brewery. But he would have been there anyway, to check on the horses. Someone would have known to lie in wait. I've gone over and over this, trying to work out who might have wanted to harm him. No one rises up before my mind's eye. I can't go that far.'

'He clocked in at 6 a.m. Wouldn't you have expected him back for breakfast?'

She sighed. 'The truth is, we had a falling out. That's what makes it worse than horrible.'

I sympathised, saying how upsetting, and that they would have been back to normal in another day. 'He would have known that.'

'No. We'd hardly spoken since I told him I wouldn't go with him if he took the new job. He loved me, in his way, but what he wanted was someone who would cling to him, who would worship him, like that poor three-legged dog we had for years. I see now that I didn't ask enough of him, apart from wanting him to whistle my tunes. If he could whistle my little ditty, as we called them, and make something of it, I knew it would work. We let each other get on with things. He was immersed in helping his damsel in distress. I steep myself in music. I dream up cheap and cheerful tunes. He blew pipe dreams of Joseph the rescuer.'

'Annie Parnaby?'

She nodded. 'Sergeant Moon has known for years where Mrs Parnaby is hiding. It crossed my mind that I would be a suspect. The jealous wife wreaking vengeance on her husband. Only there wasn't anything to be jealous about. Joe pitied Annie.'

She went to the tap and filled a jug. 'I just caught sight of those thirsty bluebells. Monica and Michael brought them when they came for their Sunday dinner. That's a clue then. The wood beyond the allotments, people call it the bluebell wood.' She poured water into the vase. 'I'm glad you called. Thank you for Saturday. You didn't fuss when I thought I must be going mad. You made sure I saw Joe, before the doctor did his bloody work. I could say goodbye to him. And now, you are not looking at me oddly because I don't burst into tears.'

This was my dismissal. She topped up the vase.

I stood.

Yet I had one more question. 'If you don't mind my asking, how did you and Joe meet? I believe he's not from round here?'

'My parents managed a pub in Whitby with a halfway decent piano. Joe came there on holiday before the war.'

'How romantic. You fell in love?'

I should not have assumed that. But I suppose it was because Whitby was where Gerald and I met.

'No, we were both very young, and just friendly. We didn't stay in touch. When the war came, he joined up. I did war work. I was sent to work on the land, but by some hook or crook found myself delivering barley to the Barleycorn. It was then decided that I should shovel barley into the ovens. Lucky me.'

'Hard work,' I said.

'It was hot, and exhausting, but we were well paid.'

Mrs Finch would know all about the dangers of the fermentation room.

She sat down again. So did I, waiting for her to go on with her story.

'I rented this house, with two other girls. When the war ended, so did our jobs. I wanted to stay in Masham. The piano came with the house. I'd learned to compose, and I'd found a collaborator.' She gave a resigned gesture. 'I knew my job was over when the men came back. Joe was one of them. A lot of the boys who'd worked with horses in the East Riding found their way to breweries.' She smiled at the irony. 'I had one week's work, showing Joe and the others how to do the job I had just lost. He had nowhere to live. I could no longer pay the rent. We did not have a great deal in common, except loneliness and need. A single woman with a male lodger, well, you can imagine. Not exactly love at first sight. But we did care for each other, more than anyone might think.'

She went to the cupboard. 'Among the pies and bread and sausages, an old admirer brought me a bottle of whisky. Have a glass before you go?'

'I will.'

'Good. I thought you might.'

She poured. We clinked glasses and said 'Cheers,' neither of us managing to conjure up a suitable toast. She sat down again. We drank our whisky. 'You mentioned Joe was thinking about a new job. What was it?'

'He had an offer of a job, at a racing stud, with gallops nearby. He wanted us to move. Even for him, seven years was too long a time to go on calling at the Bedale Bakery for a pasty and come home with a Turog loaf. He knew George and Ruth were shaping up at last. Annie would want to be with them.'

'What did you say to the move to the racing stud?'

'I said no. I need to be in a town, near a post box, and within reach of the piano tuner.'

I stood to go. 'I'll let you get on with writing your music. Please don't call your songs ditties, I'm sure they're not.'

She put on a Geordie accent. 'Dinna find fault with ditties, hinny. Why man, a ditty can tear yer heart.'

She got up to see me to the door. 'Thank you for coming. Come and say goodbye before you go, whether or not you find out what happened.'

'I will. Do you need someone with you for the inquest?'

'My mother and sister are coming.' She picked up a manuscript sheet from the table, its lines neatly annotated with musical notes. She slid it into an old envelope and handed it to me. 'Would you put this through Miss Boland's letter box please?'

'You write the music. Miss Boland writes the words.'

She smiled. 'We are unmasked.'

I left the house feeling both impressed and puzzled by Mrs Finch, and also wondering whether she really did refuse to go with Joe to a new place. Joe had told me that he feared James Lofthouse would get rid of the horses, and that he could not live without horses. Perhaps he had not asked his wife to go with him. It would have filled me with rage to have a man who visited another woman every week and then decided to pick up sticks and move.

Perhaps Mrs Finch cared more for her music than her man. Or perhaps she cared so passionately that her feelings were buried deep.

She had given me an idea of where I might look for the homeless family. The bluebell woods. That would be my next call, except that as I left Mrs Finch's house, I saw Sykes coming from the Falcon. He was dressed for a funeral, Miss Crawford's funeral at Ripon Cathedral.

We fell into step. 'I'll walk with you as far as Barleycorn House,' I said. 'What time are the cars leaving?'

'In ten minutes. Some of the staff are going.' I expected that Miss Crawford would draw many mourners. I wished I had met her.

Sykes had seen me coming from Mrs Finch's house. He nodded in that direction. 'She is a possible suspect,' he said. 'Always look at the spouse first.'

'She was deeply distressed on Saturday.'

'That distress could be from the horror of the deed, and fear of being found out.'

'Mrs Finch had a strong reason to keep her husband alive. A woman without a man's wage coming in faces hard times in an area where most jobs are men's work and women earn a pittance, not like the textile towns where women could once earn good money.'

Sykes had clearly given Mrs Finch serious consideration as a suspect. 'The assurance company that recommended me to Mr Lofthouse does very good business in Masham. Their collector calls every Friday night. Working people place great store on their life and death insurance policies. A baby is insured at birth, in case he or she will shortly need to be buried.'

'And Mrs Finch insured her husband's life?'

'She never missed a payment.' He explained that in insurance jargon, pay-outs fall into the categories of pittance, middling, respectable and hefty. 'Mrs Finch will receive a respectable settlement, unless she killed him, or unless he killed himself.'

We had ruled out Slater Parnaby because of his alibi of being on the allotment, in sight of Mick Musgrove. Yet, the feeling nagged away at me that Parnaby was still in the ring as a suspect. I tried out the idea on Sykes. 'Joe Finch had a job offer from a stud. Mrs Finch would not go with him. If Slater found out about that and suspected that Joe meant to take Annie Parnaby with him, that would give Slater Parnaby a motive for murder, especially if he feels he was duped all these years.'

Sykes listened in silence. 'I should think half the town suspects Slater Parnaby of killing Joe Finch. Surely seven years was long enough for Annie Parnaby to make a new life for herself.'

He saw the look on my face and thought again. 'Sorry, but why on earth did she run away? She could have reported Parnaby for cruelty, claimed a separation and an allowance, or hit him over the head with a frying pan.'

'Perhaps she did report him. Who would have listened to her? You must have come across such situations when you were on the force.'

'Perhaps I didn't pay enough attention then.'

I had the sinking feeling that he would not pay enough attention now.

If Parnaby had killed Joe Finch out of vengeance, it might not take Parnaby long to get to his own wife.

We reached the gates of Barleycorn House. I saw Eleanor talking to Ruth. Elderly Mr Musgrove stood a little apart. That Mr Musgrove was Slater Parnaby's alibi for Saturday morning did not inspire me with confidence.

'I'll go talk to Mick Musgrove,' Sykes said. 'He walked all the way to Ripon for James Lofthouse's hearing at the Magistrates' Court. They took his hatchet from him at the door.'

'Did anyone come forward with bail for James?'

'No. He's been transferred to Armley Prison, awaiting trial at the Summer Assizes.'

Chapter Forty

～

The wood beyond the allotments was full of bluebells. One well-trodden path led to another, to more bluebells, and a narrower path. A waft of smoke mingled with the scent of bluebells and led me to change direction, towards the smell of something cooking. A pot hung over a fire that was encircled by flat stones, giving off a whiff of rabbit and greens. The woman in a blue dress and shawl was seated on a large stone reading a newspaper, a girl of about eight years old sat beside her. Conscious of being watched, I looked round, and then up. A boy looked down at me from the branch of an oak tree, so high that I wondered how he had managed it, and how he would get down. The woman let go of her newspaper, which the girl immediately picked up and started to read.

I introduced myself. The woman did not reciprocate but acted as if I must know who she was.

'Have you come about the schooling?' she asked.

'No, I haven't, I'm sorry.'

'Ah.' She looked disappointed. 'I'm trying to get them in school. They'll fall behind if not.'

'Who have you spoken to?' I asked.

'The schoolteacher when I saw her in the yard. She asked my address. I don't know what to do about having no address.'

'There must be a way round that.' I produced bars of chocolate and gave them to her. 'For the children.'

She thanked me.

The boy came down from the tree with the speed of a monkey.

I explained that I didn't know the schoolteacher. 'But I'm willing to make discreet enquiries.'

Her sudden eagerness made me worry about raising false hopes.

'I have their birth certificates, and our marriage lines. A person is at a disadvantage without an address. "The bit of a wood beyond the allotment" won't do.'

'Tell me your names and the names of your children. I'll see what I can find out.'

Panic took over. She stared, open-mouthed, suddenly unsure. 'We're doing no harm. We don't beg. My husband earns when he can.'

'I'm not from anywhere official. I'm staying in Oak Cottage, next door to Miss Boland the music teacher.' I took out my notebook and pencil. 'If you want me to try and help, give me your names.'

She decided to take the chance. 'I can write.'

I handed her the notebook. She hesitated, still unsure whether to trust me.

'We're shunted from pillar to post if we go near authority. We had to run from the last place because they came for the children.'

I had heard such stories before, and of the means test, where someone would be refused relief if they had the luxury of a mirror on the wall that might be pawned or sold. The less people had, the harsher the treatment. This family must be clinging onto life by the skin of their teeth.

'If anyone troubles you, say you have a plan to move into Oak Cottage when it becomes vacant. If you change your mind about me taking your details, just tell me. I'll tear out the page with your names and give it back to you.' I sat down on one of the flat stones that encircled the fire.

'I won't change my mind.' She began to write. Her hand shook. She rubbed her wrist and flexed her fingers before beginning again.

She wrote slowly and carefully, hesitating only when she came to the last line. She handed me the notebook.

They were Elizabeth and John Burns. The children Monica and Michael, which I already knew. The last line was her previous address. They had tramped a long way.

The children were watching and listening.

'You must be Monica and Michael.'

'Yes.' Monica answered for both of them.

'I've just come from talking to Mrs Finch. She said be sure to come next Sunday.'

'Go pick this lady some flowers,' Mrs Burns said. 'She and I want to talk.'

When they had gone, she said, 'They sometimes go up to the allotment. They were afraid of Mr Musgrove at first. Monica said he was Rumpelstiltskin, and Michael thought he must be a goblin. Now he teaches them rhymes. He went off somewhere today, in his suit.'

'Did the children remember to tell you that you and Mr Burns are invited to Sunday dinner with Mrs Finch?'

'They did. Mrs Finch must be an angel. I can't see me making a dinner for strangers if I was in her shoes.'

'You heard about Joe Finch?'

'First I knew something wasn't right was on Saturday night. Joe would usually have opened the gate for us to go in. He wasn't there. There were police about.'

'When did you find out Joe had died?'

'Monica told me, when the pair of them came back from their dinner on Sunday. Why is it the good people are taken first?' She sniffed and was trying not to cry.

I passed her my hanky. 'Keep it. My mother buys me three every Christmas.'

'People can be kind, but not know what to do or say or how to help. Joe was different.' She wiped her nose. 'Joe said what happened to us could have happened to him, to anyone. Bad luck, good luck. All it takes is a bit of the bad. All it takes is for you not to be needed, where before you were. We were let go, both let go.'

'Then it's your turn for some good luck. I'll speak to Mrs Lofthouse at the brewery. She knows the schoolteacher.'

What I wanted seemed hard to put into words. Simply say it, I told myself. Just say it. 'What did you hear about Joe Finch's death?'

'That the police were there, and an ambulance. How did he die?'

'They're not sure. There will be an inquest tomorrow. It seems possible that someone killed Joe on Saturday morning, while there was no one about. He ended up in a cellar room in the brewery. Someone must have been at the brewery, waiting for him.'

She put her hand to her heart. 'I was afraid of this. I've said too much. We were there, but then we were gone. My husband would not have harmed that good man.'

'I believe you. But did you see anyone else?'

'No.' She thought for a moment. 'Joe came in with the pony. He brought him along to the stable and then went into the brewery to clock on. He was upset. He said he'd had a fight with the man who sold him the pony. Joe bought the creature fair and square when it was in a bad way. He took care of it and had it confident enough that it would give rides to the children. And then this fellow wanted it back for the price Joe paid for it.'

'Did you see this man?'

'No. We had to go then. We always go when Joe arrives, to be out of the way.'

'You didn't see anyone else, anyone at all?'

She shook her head. 'Sometimes we see the watchman, but he doesn't see us.'

'Can you remember what you did that morning, before you left?' I thought a specific question might jog her memory.

'I folded the spare horse blankets so no one knows we've been. We leave no trace of us-selves, not wanting to get Joe in trouble.'

'Do you mind if I ask the children if they saw anyone?'

'Ask them. Those two miss nothing.'

I waited for the children to come back. They brought me bluebells.

Monica told her mother that Mr Musgrove's rhymes were going to be printed in a book. He would give her a copy. 'I can read,' Monica said, offering me her own testimonial as she had overheard her mother talking about school.

Apart from that, they were shy with me, not used to talking to strangers.

I asked them about their last morning at the brewery stables, what they remembered, and had they seen anyone.

'This lady has brought you chocolate,' Mrs Burns reminded them.

For chocolate, they were more than willing to oblige with a variety of answers. They had seen horses, spiders, the pony, Uncle Joe. There was one thing on which they both agreed. They had seen a wicked witch in a long black dress and cloak.

This was what I had both expected, and feared, to hear.

They were astute and saw the look on my face.

'We don't like witches either,' Monica said.

'What colour hair did she have?' I asked.

Monica warmed to her story. 'Her hair is silver. Her eyes are red.'

Michael, not to be left out, added that the wicked witch flew away on a broomstick.

This was not conclusive. Whatever Miss Boland's skills, flying was unlikely to be among them. I needed more detail in the picture.

Chapter Forty-One

⁓

It was time for me to talk to Annie Parnaby. She would have finished baking for today. I parked at a little distance from the Bedale Bakery. Not that Mrs Parnaby would expect her husband to arrive by car, but a strange vehicle might make her nervous.

The dark blue blind at the bakery window was pulled down, and the shop door sign turned to Closed. The low wall to the right of the shop was topped by a wooden fence. I faced a high gate that led to the bakery yard. The latch clicked as if it might open, but there was at least one bolt on the bakery yard side. At the other side was a neighbour's backyard, with a normal-size gate and a brick wall between them and the bakery yard. Through the net curtains of the house next door, I could see a figure moving about.

Someone had created a spy hole in the bakery gate. Unless I was very much mistaken, this was Annie Parnaby's hiding place. I did not know what she was calling herself. Perhaps the person moving behind the next door's net curtains did know. If I asked for Mrs Parnaby, I might be giving the game away.

Now I realised this would not be easy. I should have enlisted the help of Phil Jopling, Joe Finch's brewery partner, and partner in deception.

I walked up and down the main street. When dusk fell, the neighbour would close her curtains. I could then go through her gate, vault across to next door, unbolt the gate from the inside—in case I needed a quick departure—and then knock on the bakery door, or tap on the window. Either innocent action might induce terror in the occupant. Besides, dusk was a long way off.

Ruth and Harriet had taught me the Parnaby whistle. A difficulty might be that if it was the family whistle, Slater would also know it.

I thought about this. He would not come to do her harm and announce himself by whistling. Besides, people had different whistle tones.

The next-door neighbour disappeared from view, almost as if I had willed her away. Straightaway, I entered the neighbour's yard by the little gate. The wall between this yard and the bakery wall was taller than it looked from outside. I hitched my skirt, did a great leap, brought one leg across, got stuck, felt the seam of my skirt split, managed to get over, ripped my stockings and badly grazed my shin. The curtains hiding Annie Parnaby were so tightly closed that I would not have seen a candle flicker.

I lifted the letter box, peered at a doormat, pursed my lips and whistled the George and Ruth signal. I hoped she had heard about Harriet or seen her on the dray. 'Annie! I'm Kate, aunt of Harriet who was with Ruth on Monday. We're Ruth's friends.'

No answer. Perhaps she was upstairs.

I stood back, imagining that she might peep through the curtains, to be sure I was alone.

It took a couple of moments for her to do so, from the upstairs room.

I waved.

She retreated. After a short wait, the bolt shot back. Another bolt shot back. A key turned in the lock. She was prisoner, and gaoler.

I entered quickly.

'Is the gate bolted?'

'Yes. I came over the wall.'

She locked the door behind me. 'If you'd come when I had the bread in, I wouldn't be able to let you in. If there's a draught of cold air, the bread doesn't rise.'

'I'll remember that.'

And if I became a regular caller, I should bring my own stepladder for access.

She did not notice my torn stockings, scraped hands, bleeding leg.

Plump and white, she wore her dark hair scraped back into a bun, over a placid, dough-like face. 'You knew our whistle,' Annie said.

I held out my hand. 'Annie, I'm Kate.' Her plump hand felt limp. 'I'm staying at Oak Cottage in Masham. Your Ruth is there, too, and my niece Harriet.'

Annie spoke softly. 'Ruth whispered to me that she'd moved out.'

Under the window stood a small, well-used sofa with big dips on either end.

Annie said, 'You better sit down.'

My own reactions to Annie confused me. I had pitied her from a distance. Suddenly I saw her as a woman who had spent seven years keeping warm and eating pastries. Trusting that my reserves of sympathy would return when the pain in my leg and hand subsided, I sat down.

On the opposite wall was a black-leaded and gleaming chrome fitted range with two big ovens.

The heat was unbearable. We would cook. Tomorrow two roasted women would be discovered, and lamented.

I took off my coat.

She hung it on a hook behind the door. 'Is something wrong, is one of them taken poorly, George or Ruth?'

'No, they're well. Ruth has a practice later with Miss Boland. As far as I know, George is at work.'

Annie stood and poked the fire, and then turned to look at me. Why had I come, she wanted to know.

I had come in the hope of forming a clearer picture of Joe Finch's life. Annie did not know that Joe, her knight in shining armour, had died. When George called, Joe was still alive. Ruth, passing the bakery in procession, would not have whispered the news. Perhaps neither George nor Ruth knew the extent of Joe's involvement with Annie. If I broke the news now, I may get no sense out of her, yet I must do it. 'Annie, I'm sorry to tell you that Joe Finch was found dead in the brewery on Saturday.'

Her dough-like face collapsed in misery. 'Poor Joe. Is that why he wasn't on the dray on Monday?'

'Yes.' I waited, expecting her to ask for details, but she did not. 'You were fond of him. I'm sorry about his death.'

I listened while she told me how good he was, how he had stood by her all these years, asking nothing of her, just being good and jolly, and calling in. Finally, she asked, 'How did Joe die?' She closed her eyes. 'Did Slater kill him? If he found out, it'll be me next.'

'If Slater found what?'

'Where I am, that Joe visited me, that—'

She came to a halt.

'Please be honest with me, Annie. Have you a sound reason for supposing Slater knows where you are?'

'I just know it.'

'Have you seen him hanging about here?'

She twisted her hands. 'I thought so but now I'm not sure. I can feel it. I can feel he's after me.'

I could see why they all wanted to protect her. Her fear went so deep. Perhaps she would never be rid of it. 'You told Ruth you saw him walking up and down the street, but you didn't, did you?'

'I don't know whether I did or not.' She looked into the fire for an answer. 'I had to say something.'

'Did you have to say something because George and Ruth, and Joe, were growing impatient with you?'

'Not George, never George.'

'When you said you had seen Slater, or thought you may have seen him, did you think to yourself that it was time to move away again, to leave here?'

She shook her head. 'I couldn't see as far as that. The day will come. George will find a job in another place, and for me to come with him. Ruth has savings in the Post Office. I have my special savings fund, Joe helped me. He gave me something every week.'

'That was good of him.' That also explained the fiddle on the Bedale round, and why Joe could afford to buy the pony.

'Ruth is sure she and George can find a place for us. That was always their plan. Except, for now, she's tied to Masham, to the brewery, as queen. Slater is the one who should go away, not me. I wish he was dead instead of Joe.'

She looked suddenly exhausted. Leave now, I told myself. Let her have time to take in that Joe has died.

'How did you answer Joe when he asked you to go away with him to his new job?'

She closed her eyes. 'He didn't ask me in so many words. He told me about it. That wasn't the same thing as asking me.'

'But?'

'He said they wanted a cook. I could have done that. I ended up saying I'd think about it.'

'And did you think about it?'

'I tried to. I tried to think it might be best for Ruth and George not to have to worry about me. And I know Joe only ever wanted to work with horses. But it didn't feel right. I said Yvonne should go with him. That's when I knew I was second choice, and why shouldn't I be? He said Yvonne wouldn't go. She'd cook for him. She'd cook for his waifs and strays, but she wouldn't uproot herself to cook for strangers. Two children go to the Finches on Sundays. Yvonne plays the piano and has the children singing.'

'Do you know what music she writes?'

227

'She writes music for songs. Miss Boland writes the words and sends them off. Yvonne should have gone with Joe. She thinks more about her music than she does about him.'

Bakers start work so very early. Here was a woman with few inner resources left to draw on, her hopes and dreams stretched to breaking point, squeezed out by fear. I stood to go.

She took my coat from the hook. 'In fairness to Yvonne Finch, she did consider making the move. Joe told me that. He said Yvonne considered it for an hour and a half.'

'Might you have said yes, to get away from here, to let your children lead their own lives?'

She handed me my coat. 'I might have. I can't remember what I said.'

If Slater knew that Joe had helped Annie for years, if he knew she planned to go away, that would give him a motive for murder. But it would be Annie he would kill.

'Annie, if you want me to come back another time, and for me to help you bring your plan into being, I will. From what you say, you must have savings enough to start a new life.'

She unlocked and unbolted the door to let me out. 'I do have savings. I'm paid poorly here, because of having a roof over my head, but I save my pay and what Joe gives me.'

We went into the yard. Halfway up the yard, she stopped and turned to me. 'Truth is, I can't see myself beyond this gate.' She drew back the bolts. 'After George made me go to the pictures, I was shaking all night.'

'You'd get used to it. Will you come out with me for the time it takes me to cross the road to my car?'

She looked over at the solitary vehicle, saying, 'You've parked so close to the bakery.'

'Slater doesn't know everything. Walk over and back. I'll stay with you. Link arms.'

'I might if you were Ruth.'

'I'm the next best thing. Come on.'

She took three steps and then stopped, suddenly alarmed. 'I haven't locked the door. I could go back and find he's got in.'

'Another time, Annie. You will be able to do it.'

I did not convince myself, much less her.

And then the slightest change came over her. 'I'm standing here. I'm on the pavement.'

'What stops you?'

'The wind might know the answer.' She blew out her cheeks. 'What did Joe die of?'

There was a way for me to not answer. 'There'll be an inquest tomorrow. We'll know then.'

'Just a minute.' She turned and went back inside.

A couple of moments later, she came back with a bag of scones.

Chapter
Forty-Two

～

The doors of Masham Town Hall opened at 9.45 a.m. Those of us waiting for the inquest into the death of Joseph Finch climbed the stairs to a large room on the first floor. Chairs were placed in two columns, allowing an aisle between.

We took our places in a hushed atmosphere of anticipation. Miss Boland and I sat side by side on the second row of the right-hand column. Mrs Finch, on the row in front, was flanked by two women. Miss Boland whispered that they were Yvonne Finch's mother and sister, come from Staithes and Whitby. Next to them sat Phil Jopling and Mrs Jopling.

William and Eleanor sat on the front row of the left-hand column, along with Jim Sykes, George and some of the brewery workmen. Neighbours had turned out in force and took up the rows behind.

On the instant the hand on the round clock moved from one minute to ten to ten o'clock, several dark-suited men stepped smartly into the room and took their places on the row of chairs to the left of the coroner's seat. I counted seven, the minimum number for an inquest jury.

Next came a clerk with wispy hair and rimless spectacles. He pulled out the coroner's chair and flicked a duster across the seat.

He then sat down, without flicking the duster, over his own seat, opened his ledger and drew the inkwell closer.

One juryman examined his hands. The others stared ahead, cutting themselves off from their surroundings and each other. It seemed to me they cloaked themselves with an air of regret and apology, as if on the wrong side of blame. This inquiry into a sudden and suspicious death somehow brought them and the town into disrepute.

When the clerk stood, saying, 'All rise,' I expected him to add, "that is if you don't mind, rising. It won't be for long".

Chairs scraped.

The coroner strode in, somehow lifting the atmosphere simply by looking like a sergeant major in mufti, about to rally the troops. He was tall, big boned, and with so much thick brown hair that he could have donated half to his clerk without missing it.

He sat down.

Chairs scraped again.

The coroner wished us good morning. Someone near the back, imagining herself once more in the schoolroom, echoed his good morning.

The coroner looked in the direction of Mrs Finch and her supporters.

'I extend my condolences to Mrs Finch and family of the deceased. Mrs Finch identified her husband as Joseph Finch, age forty-six. My duty today is to inquire into when and where Mr Finch came by his death. Criminal proceedings may arise from those particulars. Witnesses will be called. Interested persons may question those witnesses.'

He turned to his clerk, who passed him a sheet of paper.

Mercifully, I was not called to give my evidence. The coroner reported that Mr Finch had been missed since early morning, after he brought his pony to the brewery stables. He then went on to say that a garden party guest, who ought not to have been on the premises, unwittingly opened the door of the fermentation room, saw a figure in the room, closed the door and went to raise the alarm.

Miss Boland laid her hand on my arm in a gesture of reassurance.

'We are able to say that Mr Finch died sometime between 6 a.m. on Saturday, 26th of April and 2.40 p.m. that afternoon when his body was found.'

A fireman was called to give evidence. 'John Hawkins, step forward please.'

A round-shouldered man of about forty years old stepped forward. He was wearing a well-brushed suit and highly polished boots. He walked to the podium to the right of the coroner. He gave his name and occupation. 'John Hawkins, Fireman, Masham Police Fire Brigade.'

'Mr Hawkins, I have your statement, now will you tell this court in your own words what you told the police.'

'I was with my fellow fireman Mick Brearley. We received the call at 2.50 p.m. Five of us attended at the brewery at 3.00 p.m. Being warned of the danger of fumes, we donned masks and protective clothing before entering the room in the basement. Fireman Simon Bentley held the door so that we could enter and exit quickly.' He glanced towards the row where Mrs Finch sat. 'We carried Mr Finch from that room. We were very sorry indeed that it was too late for us to save him. I believe he would have died quickly.'

The coroner asked whether the door to the fermentation room was locked.

'No, sir, but a gentleman called Mr Beckwith was on duty, preventing access.'

'Will you please tell the court why such a room is dangerous.'

'Because the process of fermenting creates large amounts of CO_2 gas which is heavier than air and can kill by asphyxiation. Even when the contents have been removed the danger remains until the vessel has been fully evacuated.'

'Thank you, Mr Hawkins. I commend you and your colleagues for your prompt attendance and selfless actions.'

The coroner looked at the row of relative and friends. 'Are there any questions for Mr Hawkins?'

That there were none surprised me. Someone ought to have asked why the building was unlocked.

Dr Miller came to the podium next. He gave his occupation as pathologist and confirmed that he had conducted a post-mortem on Mr Finch. I could tell that he was trying to present his findings in layman's language, for the benefit of the family. He described an abrasion to Mr Finch's left temple and concluded that he had been struck with some force. There were also abrasions to his knuckles, which may have indicated a fist fight.

At this, Mrs Finch let out a cry. 'Never!'

Very gently, the coroner reminded her that she would have the opportunity to ask questions.

Dr Miller continued. 'I did not find any evidence of CO_2 inhalation in Mr Finch's lungs, leading me to the conclusion that Mr Finch was already dead when taken into the place where he was found.'

There was a collective gasp in the room.

Dr Miller had more to say about the bodily injuries and how these indicated a fight having taken place.

The room was suddenly quiet. The coroner allowed the information to sink in before asking once more were there any questions. He looked at Mrs Finch. She shook her head. A woman seated behind the Lofthouses stood up.

'Mrs Strong, Temperance Society. How much alcohol had the deceased consumed?'

There was a cry of "shame", from the back of the room. William Lofthouse turned to look at the speaker. I guessed she may be an old adversary.

Dr Miller said, 'I estimate that Mr Finch had drunk two pints of beer that morning.'

There being no more questions, Dr Miller was allowed to leave.

He gave me the slightest acknowledging nod as he walked towards the door. It left me with a pang for all those times in my life when I have been completely immersed in the lives of others, and then all that is gone.

The coroner glanced at his notes. Phil Jopling was called, Finch's mate and fellow drayman.

He took a deep breath before giving his name and occupation. He clutched one hand in the other, moving slightly on the balls of his feet, as if ready to break into a run and be gone.

'I was asked about how we worked, when we started, how our day began. Joe's day started sooner than mine because of his pony, the pony he rescued. He'd go to the field and fetch Billy Boy and bring him to the stable to see his chums, the horses. And, yes, he'd let Billy have a share of the fodder and no one minded that because he had brought that pony along from a creature that couldn't see for the mane in its eyes, and the blindness in its left eye, and he turned it into a beauty. We were both on duty at the stable that morning, to groom the horses, to look their best for the visitors to the garden party. When I came in at nine, Joe had been and gone. His pony wasn't there, but I thought he could have taken it to graze. I went home for my breakfast.'

The coroner adjusted his spectacles. 'Mr Jopling, the door to the brewery was unlocked. I understand the former night watchman is not able to be here today through illness. Who unlocked the door that morning?'

'Joe unlocked it, sir. He was on the Saturday rota for jobs. I suppose the key would be in his pocket.'

'Thank you, Mr Jopling. You may stand down, unless there are further questions?'

There were none.

The clerk had come to life during Phil Jopling's statement. He hushed the murmurings in the room and with a lift to his voice called Mr William Lofthouse.

William took the stand.

The coroner began with what sounded like a reassurance. 'Let me assure you, Mr Lofthouse, that no verdict of this court may be framed in such a way as to appear to determine any question of civil liability, is that understood?'

'Yes, sir.'

'Nor need you answer any question that may be self-incriminating.'

'I understand.'

'Why was a room that everyone knew to be dangerous to the point of death, not kept locked?'

The woman next to Mrs Finch said, 'Good question.'

Lofthouse looked to Eleanor. She leaned forward ever so slightly. Had she anticipated this question and told him what to say?

'No unauthorised person was ever let into the brewery. Everyone who worked there knew the dangers and knew the rules. It is only when the fermentation is in process that entry would be forbidden.'

'Forbidden but not prevented?'

'I suppose that is correct.'

The coroner made notes. So did the clerk.

'Mr Lofthouse, there is no suggestion that the fumes from the fermentation caused Mr Finch's death, but I shall be making recommendations in regard to that room and to safety procedures in the building.'

'Thank you.'

It was an odd thing to say—a thanks, as if William felt he had been given some recommendation. This was too much for Mrs Finch. I heard her words, but others did not. The coroner asked her to stand, and kindly repeat her words for the benefit of the clerk.

She stood, staring at William, addressing her question to him.

'How does a gypsy or a horse trader, whatever we call him, know that he can hide a foul deed by dragging my husband into the fermentation room? And if he did that, why wasn't he lying there himself—gassed?'

The coroner intervened. 'Mr Lofthouse, bearing in mind that the man Mrs Finch refers to is in police custody for questioning, are you willing to reply to Mrs Finch?'

William took a deep breath. He looked at Yvonne Finch.

'I am willing.' He paused. 'Even in large concentrations CO_2 takes five minutes to kill. A person might hold his breath long enough to escape.'

There were no more questions, but one more witness.

Frank McDonald wore corduroy trousers and a collarless striped shirt. He was weather-beaten from a life outdoors, and frightened too, but reaching for every ounce of bravado in him. In answer to the coroner's questions, he admitted taking the pony, but it was not stealing. He had let Joe Finch have it as a bargain for a shilling. Early that Saturday morning he came for it back, returning the money. He was going to a fair with his horses and wanted the pony for children's rides, which would draw a bit of a crowd. Yes, it was true they got into a fight, McDonald said, 'I swear on my bairns' lives Joe Finch started it.' He pointed to a bruise on his cheek to prove his point.

The coroner quoted the statement Frank McDonald made to the police. 'You say you waited at a distance until Joe Finch let himself into the brewery, and then you broke the lock on the stable door and took the pony.'

'Because ah was robbed of that fine creature for a measly shilling.'

'What was Mr Finch's reply when you offered to buy it back?' the coroner asked.

The bravado fled. Frank McDonald looked at his feet. He mumbled. The coroner asked him to repeat his answer and to speak up. After a pause, McDonald cleared his throat. 'He said he wouldn't part with that pony for a pot of gold.'

McDonald was led away by a constable.

The coroner summed up proceedings and sent the jury to consider their verdict.

We were dismissed and told to stay within hearing of the town crier, or the church bells.

I was on the end of the row and moved to leave. I looked at Miss Boland, but she indicated she would wait.

Walking up the centre aisle, I heard a deep sniff behind me, the kind a man makes when he intends to spit. Without turning around, I knew it must be Slater Parnaby. He and I found ourselves side by side as we left the Town Hall. We walked down the steps together. He had a way of creating an invisible wall about himself, forbidding people to come too close. Something most people might be glad of. I ignored the wall.

'What did you think to the inquest, Mr Parnaby?'

'Bloody useless. Words, just words.'

'Words trying to get to the truth.'

'They'll pin it on the gypsy, and it weren't him.'

He swaggered, and my first impression of a lonely man came back to me. 'What makes you sure it wasn't Mr McDonald?'

'A horse dealer, fool enough to kill for a one-eyed pony? Nah.' He had a point. 'Besides, He smells wrong.'

'What do you mean, he smells wrong?'

'I was near enough for a whiff of him when they fetched him from the cells. He's not a man who wastes time changing his clobber. I'd know if he'd been in the brewery this past week. I smelled it on you though, on Saturday, and on someone else.'

'Why didn't you say something?'

'Because I keep my trap shut.'

At a quarter to three, the town crier rang his bell. 'Oyez, oyez. All ye attending the inquest into the death of Joseph Finch, be told that it will resume at three o'clock in the Town Hall. God save the King.'

The crier had already fastened the notice to the door of the Town Hall. Now he crossed to the Falcon, crying the news, and attached another notice to the pub doors.

The church bells chimed.

Mrs Finch must have had private warning of the resumption. She was climbing the stairs when I went in, her sister and mother beside her.

Phil Jopling and Mrs Jopling were behind me. She greeted me. 'I was glad you took Mrs Finch to the hospital to see Joe.'

'And I'm glad I could help.'

Eleanor and William arrived at the top of the stairs. I waited and went with them into the room.

They made their way to their previous seats on the front row left. I joined them, sitting beside Eleanor. She whispered, 'I'm glad Ruth didn't come. She doesn't deserve to go through this. Nobody does.'

Jim Sykes nodded to me and went to sit by William.

Slowly, the room began to fill. The clerk took his place. The jury filed in.

We all rose for the coroner, scraping chairs, sitting down again, people clearing their throats.

The coroner turned to the jury. 'Members of the jury, have you reached your verdict?'

The foreman rose. 'We have, sir.'

'What is your verdict?'

'We find that Mr Joseph Finch was killed unlawfully, that his death was the result of a crime by a person or persons unknown. We do not have sufficient information to say whether that was murder or manslaughter. We extend our deepest sympathy to Mrs Finch.'

The coroner thanked the jury for their deliberations. He looked at William and Eleanor, and then at Mrs Finch. 'Given the circumstances of Mr Finch's death, and the short time for the police to carry out their investigations, I am adjourning this inquest until a future date. Are there any questions before we close?'

There were no questions.

For several moments people remained glued to their chairs, as if no one wanted to be the first to run away from the oppressive atmosphere in the room, or to make a rush for the door.

Outside the Town Hall, Eleanor said, 'Will you come back to the house?'

Before Sykes could say yes, I said, 'Mr Sykes and I have something we need to do, Eleanor. We'll call on you later.'

When the Lofthouses had gone, Sykes asked, 'What must we do?'

'Give Miss Boland your arm, Mr Sykes. Take her home.'

'Well yes of course.' He paused. 'What else?'

'Miss Boland killed Joe Finch. Would you give us half an hour and then ask Mrs Finch to come? Say that Kate Shackleton has done as she asked.'

'Hang on a minute! Since when are you working for Mrs Finch?'

'When I brought Yvonne Finch home after she had seen her husband's body, she asked me to find out what happened to Joe. I need Mrs Finch to be at Elm Cottage when I question Miss Boland because Mrs Finch is intrinsically connected with Joe's death.'

Chapter
Forty-Three

Miss Boland sat at her kitchen table. I had set the piano stool by her chair, so that she could put up her feet and rest her injured ankle, though it meant sitting sideways on.

She asked me to pass a bottle of dandelion wine and two glasses from the shelf. I passed the wine. She opened it and poured, saying, 'I don't know why I go on making this stuff. I don't think I'll bother this year.'

'You might try dandelion and burdock, for a change.'

'If I'm still here.'

'What did you think to the inquest, Miss Boland?'

'It was thorough.' She took a drink of wine. 'No, I won't make this again.'

'Did anything surprise you, about the inquest?' I asked.

'I don't believe so.'

'Not even that Joe was dead when he found his way into the fermentation room?'

'That might have been a mercy, from what people say about that room.'

A strange mercy, I thought.

She changed the subject. 'I'm glad Ruth wasn't at the inquest. Miss Crawford's funeral was hard enough for her this week.'

'I thought so, too. She and Harriet have gone to Roomer Common. Ruth wants Harriet to see where cottages once stood.'

Miss Boland smiled. 'She has a fascination for that common. I remember going there as a child, when the cottages were still there. Ruth knows a poem about one of the cottages. She'll probably recite it to you.'

'But to go back to the inquest,' I said. 'What about the horse dealer? He looks like the main suspect.'

Miss Boland forgot she no longer liked dandelion wine. She took a great swig. 'He would have to be mad to kill for a one-eyed pony, though of course some people are mad. Some men are born mad. Others have madness thrust upon them.'

'True, though Mr McDonald seemed sane to me,' I said. 'Even George came under suspicion, simply because no one saw him on Saturday. He was being a good lad, taking care of his mother, making sure she would go with him to the cinema and see Ruth on Pathé News.'

'I wish I'd seen the newsreel,' Miss Boland said. 'I couldn't bring myself to hobble to the Town Hall for the showing.'

That did not surprise me. Saturday must have been a trying day for Miss Boland.

There was a tap on the door. Miss Boland stayed where she was. 'Who could that be?'

I stood. 'I'll go see, shall I?'

It was Mrs Finch. 'Hello, I had a message from your Mr Sykes.'

'It's Mrs Finch, Miss Boland.'

'Don't keep her on the doorstep,' Miss Boland said. 'Come in, Yvonne!'

Mrs Finch stepped inside. 'Oh, Celia. Someone said you'd hurt your ankle. I would have come round, under normal circumstances.'

I poured the third glass of dandelion wine for Yvonne Finch. 'Is there something you wanted to tell Mrs Finch, Miss Boland?'

If Miss Boland previously suspected that I knew of her guilt, she was now certain. It showed in her face. She lost that professional music teacher expression. Her face slid into the lines of age that were always waiting. Her eyes lost their gleam to fear. She said nothing.

Mrs Finch took a covered plate from her basket. 'My mother and sister brought food, and neighbours brought food, so I hope you may want this pie.'

Miss Boland looked at the pie. 'Thank you. My father always said, refuse nothing but a good wallop.'

'That didn't work for Joe, did it, Miss Boland?' I turned to her. 'Do you want to tell Yvonne, or shall I?'

Miss Boland said nothing.

I had to make myself continue. This was one of the worst things I ever had to do, and to say. 'Mrs Finch, I asked you here because I believe you told Miss Boland that your husband wanted you to go with him to a new job, away from Masham.'

Yvonne Finch looked from me to Miss Boland. 'Yes I did.'

With the thought that Yvonne may later blame herself for telling her friend, I said, 'And why should you not confide? You were collaborators and friends.' When neither woman spoke, I continued. 'I'm sorry to put it so bluntly, Yvonne, but Joe got a good wallop from Miss Boland when she knocked him down the brewery staircase, isn't that right, Miss Boland? Is that when you tripped and twisted your ankle, hurrying down the stairs to see if Joe had broken any bones? It probably never occurred to you that he might be dead.'

'That is not true. Mr Moon does not suspect me. I don't know why you should.'

'Well then, you must tell me what is true. You went to the brewery to tell Joe that it was unfair, and selfish of him, to expect Yvonne to move away?'

'Yes.'

Yvonne stared at Miss Boland, and then turned to me. 'How did you know?'

'At first, because of the small impromptu lie. Miss Boland, you didn't trip going out to see the milkman. He brings the milk to the door. I found that out early on, when I asked him about paying. He told us not to trouble about bringing the can to the gate, and that he knocks on the door on Saturdays for payment.'

She looked at me. 'Do go on.'

'What you said may have been true, if you had decided to go out and have a word, and so I asked him directly where you tripped. He did not want to say, at first. When he knew I was the person who bandaged your ankle and had an eye to your welfare, he told me that you were coming back from the town square, after going to the post box.'

'What if I were by the post box?'

'But you weren't, were you? You were coming back from the brewery.'

Yvonne Finch looked as if she would speak, but then said nothing. She watched Miss Boland intently and then turned to me, waiting to hear what I would say next.

'The milkman gave you a lift back. He brought his float all the way down the track. Fortunately for you, the allotment holders, Mick Musgrove and Slater Parnaby, had not started work. They were there when the milk float came back in the other direction. You didn't want the milkman to tell anyone, for the same reason you wanted us to keep quiet about your sprained ankle. People in the town might think you were past it, a hobbling old woman, not up to teaching music to their children. I thought that odd at the time, but I know that a woman alone must be careful about the place she occupies in the community. Staying upright is important.'

Yvonne lowered her head. She pressed her fingers against her eyelids. 'When did Joe die?'

Miss Boland said nothing, leaving me to answer. 'Joe died in the early morning, shortly after he opened the pedestrian gates to see the homeless family out of the stable and off the premises. It was the children who saw you, in the brewery yard, Miss Boland. They described you as wearing a long black dress and cloak. I'm sorry to say, and this is nothing personal, they thought you were a wicked witch.'

'Lots of older women dress as I do. It's practical. It's a habit, in every sense of that word.' She leaned forward and reached for her glass, holding it so tightly that the veins in her hand swelled. 'I'm listening, Mrs Shackleton. I'm sure you have more to say.'

'When Slater Parnaby interrupted our card game, and sniffed all about, he sniffed at you, and at me. Again, it was nothing personal, not body odour from poor hygiene. He was smelling at our clothing and our hair, and yours especially, because you had dragged Joe into the fermentation room with its particular smell.'

'That man goes around sniffing all the time.'

'Not everyone he sniffs washes and hangs out their clothes first thing the next morning, in spite of a sprained ankle, and on a Sunday.'

'If, as you say, I went into that room, then how did I come out alive?'

'You're a singer. You know how to hold your breath. You have that lovely scarf to wind around your face, and the nimble feet you are proud of would have had you in and out in less than the five minutes it would take to die. You may even have spotted the wartime gasmask hanging by the door.'

To be too graphic might create images in Yvonne's mind that she would never erase. Miss Boland almost certainly rolled Joe's body onto her cloak and dragged him into the fermentation room.

'I should have known when our dog was behaving oddly. He does not usually deprive people of their walking sticks. There must have been something about your stick that attracted him, a particular smell. In spite of discouraging him, he would not give up. He brought it to Sergeant Moon when we were too dense to understand.'

'Just because a dog picks up a stick—'

'You left a scrap of material behind on the bannister, Miss Boland. It is a heavy fabric, a cape, a cloak?'

Yvonne Finch looked towards the back of the door. 'Where is your cloak, Celia?'

'Somewhere about.'

'Did you roll Mr Finch onto your cloak to pull him into the room?' I asked. Yvonne flinched. She stared at Miss Boland, who answered me without meeting Yvonne's eye.

'Not at all preposterous, Mrs Shackleton, but why would I do such a thing?'

The blood fled from Yvonne Finch's face. She clenched her fists, the knuckles a stark white. 'To protect me? Because I told you Joe was planning to move away, whether I went with him or not. You were angry. You asked me how I would manage. You said I had stuck by him. He should stick by me.'

Miss Boland's hands were in her lap. She placed them on the table, interlaced her fingers, and tapped her thumbs as if marking time.

I felt sure there would be some musical impulse behind her movements, behind all her movements. When it seemed as if she would not answer, I prompted. 'Yvonne is right. You feared that Joe would leave Yvonne for Annie Parnaby. Without a breadwinner, Yvonne would never earn enough to keep herself and write her music, or so you thought. You know all about trying to make ends meet. You hope for pupils. You set your lyrics to Yvonne's music and send off songs to the music publisher, receiving a fraction of what you ought to. How many songs do you have to write to sell one?'

Miss Boland stared at her empty glass. 'We do well.'

'But not well enough. Joe decamping would pull the rug from under Yvonne, that is what you thought. She has been too protected to realise the precariousness of her situation. But you realised. You didn't mean to kill him.'

A long silence held. Eventually, Miss Boland spoke. 'Has your Mr Sykes gone for the police?'

'I don't know.'

'It's all very plausible, Mrs Shackleton, but so would be an entirely different scenario.'

'Such as?'

'I can't straightaway think of one I would want to tell you, but there is no real evidence for anything you have said.'

Miss Boland took a small blue bottle from her bag and poured some into her wine.

I moved the glass away from her before she was able to take a drink.

Miss Boland snatched it back and dropped the glass to the floor where it shattered. 'Oh, I am sorry. Do sweep it before your dog comes in looking for my stick and cuts his paw, and give that bottle a good rinse while you're about it.' She held onto the table to push herself up. 'I'll go lie down now, if someone would kindly pass me my walking stick.'

It was Yvonne Finch who said, 'Sit down, Celia. Spare us a deathbed scene. I deserve to know how my husband died.'

Miss Boland's voice was hoarse, a whisper. 'He was going to leave you.'

'That was between him and me.'

'I know you loved him, not in that stupid soppy way of his. He mistook independence for indifference. I tried to make him see sense. He said it was none of my business.'

'What happened?'

'He called me names, disgusting names. He laughed at our songs. He said the stud would be a new beginning for him, a fresh start. Because they all knew that when James Lofthouse took over from his uncle, he would get rid of the horses and buy vans. Joe said if he couldn't work with horses, he wouldn't be able to breathe.'

Yvonne closed her eyes.

Miss Boland continued. 'Joe went into the brewery. I followed him. I was arguing with him. I told him all the reasons James Lofthouse wouldn't make those changes. By then we were by the staircase. I was holding the head of the bannister with one hand, beating time with my stick as I told him what I thought of him. He snatched my stick, to make me stop. I'm sorry, Yvonne, but I laughed at him. I told him he paraded his kindness, let everyone know what a fine fellow he was. I told him he was a pathetic, sentimental sot and his wife was worth ten of him.'

She would have stopped there, feeling she had said enough. I asked, 'What happened then?'

She spoke quietly, almost a whisper. 'He couldn't bear that there was someone who didn't take him at his own estimation. He raised the stick and came at me. I moved out of the way, but the stick caught me.' She touched her cheek. 'If any blood remains on that stick, it will be mine.'

I must not let her stop now. 'How do you explain that he ended up in the fermentation room?'

'I was at the top of the stairs. I moved as he came towards me. He went toppling down. When he didn't move, I thought he was going to trick me, and would finish me off. After a few minutes, I went down to see. I thought he was unconscious and would have tried to revive him or gone for help. I felt for a pulse. He was dead.'

'He wasn't a violent man, Celia.'

'He was violent that morning, because he knew that I told him the truth.' She brought her hands, in prayer position, to her mouth, and blew through her fingers.

Sykes would be coming back at any moment. He would bring Sergeant Moon. I needed there to be some clarity before that happened. 'You went to remonstrate with him not to kill. If what you say is true, it was an accident. Why didn't you go for help?'

It took her some time to answer. 'Because I don't think like you. It was that shocking moment in the opera, when someone dies, and the action continues. What happened didn't feel real. The character will die again tomorrow. I wanted to wind back to the second act. But Joe was dead. I closed his eyes.'

Celia Boland reached for Yvonne Finch's hand. 'I'm sorry.'

Yvonne pulled her hand away. 'Why drag him into that room?'

'I was thinking of the garden party, of Ruth's speech, Eleanor's preparations. The day would be spoiled.' She took another breath. 'I was thinking of our songs, and of you. I didn't want to be found on brewery premises.'

Yvonne Finch pushed back her chair. 'I can't listen to any more.' She stood and walked to the door, and then she turned back. 'How did you know he was still set on leaving?'

'I was in the draper's, at the same time as Mrs Jopling. People talk.'

Yvonne Finch shook her head. 'That was one of the things we had in common, Celia, we didn't fit here. We didn't join in the gossip.'

Mrs Finch opened the door.

I picked up my coat and hat. 'I'll walk you back.'

'No need.'

'There's every need.' I turned back to Miss Boland. 'Think carefully about what you do next. If what you say is true, Joe Finch's death was an accident. And poison is a horrible way to die.'

'So is a noose.'

'Miss Boland, be alive when I come back from seeing Mrs Finch home.'

Chapter
Forty-Four

❦

Sykes was waiting by the Town Hall.

'Well?' he asked.

'Time for Sergeant Moon to step in.' I gave a brief account of Miss Boland's confession.

'Do you believe her?' Sykes asked.

'Yes.'

He nodded. 'I'll fetch the sergeant. Why did she wait so long?'

'We can ask. I'm not sure there will be a rational explanation.'

When I arrived back at Elm Tree Cottage, after seeing Mrs Finch to her door, Miss Boland was seated where I had left her. She suddenly sprang to life and gave a cry of pain as she stood. 'Where is he?'

'If you mean Sergeant Moon—'

'Who else?'

'I thought you would want some time to put your papers in order. That is what I would want to do, in your situation.'

'Before I am hauled off and thrown in the condemned cell? Well thank you.'

She went to the desk that had been almost hidden under a violin case, several recorders and a pile of papers.

I placed the walking stick beside her.

She grasped the stick, with a grim smile. 'You trust me with it?'

'Don't assume the worst. You described what happened as self-defence, and an accident. Your mistake was not to come clean straightaway.'

She shook her head. 'My word against opinion, accusations, whispers. I know this town, Mrs Shackleton. That is why I left at the age of fourteen and came back only when there was nowhere else to go. My mother was dying. People thought I stayed for my father.' She struggled to her feet, giving a cry of pain as she put weight on her sprained ankle. 'I am not under arrest yet. Once I'm taken, I may never be allowed back.'

She took out a folder. 'Here are some of my papers. I always thought I would have time to sort everything out.'

I asked her the question that was puzzling me. 'Would you have let the horse dealer hang?'

'They have no good evidence against him.'

'That does not always come in the way of a conviction.'

'Without Slater Parnaby's bullying and violence, Annie Parnaby would still be in the family home, Joe would not have played the knight in shining armour and there would have been no rift between Joe and Yvonne. By rights, Parnaby should be the one to swing on the end of a rope.'

'We are not judge and jury, Miss Boland, and you are not going to swing unless you climb on a trapeze.'

She said, 'I thought the police would treat Joe's death as an accident, assuming that he fell, was stunned, went into that room without realising. I didn't take into account a clever pathologist.'

She gave a small cry. 'You said I would have significant pain, and you were right.'

'You can take the arnica ointment.'

'That's very kind of you. To arrange my medication and incarceration.'

'Prison is not inevitable.'

She huffed a scoff as she placed two folders on the table. 'I do have one question for you, Mrs Shackleton.'

'Go on.'

'Why did you take so long?'

'You were my main suspect, but I kept hoping there would be an alternative, a lightning strike moment when I could put you in the clear. Also, I did wonder whether it was a joint effort between you and Yvonne Finch.' I looked at the desk. 'If all your papers are in here, may I pass you a drawer?'

'The one on the left.' She sat down.

I placed the drawer on the table. She took a large envelope from it and handed it to me. It was marked, "Lyrics for Y. Finch".

'Usually Yvonne writes the music first, and I create the lyrics. There are a hundred or so lyrics here. I hope she will be able to adapt her method and find music to fit my words.'

It occurred to me that might be the last thing Yvonne would want to do. How deep did their friendship go? After what had happened, it would take fathomless depths for this collaboration to continue.

She saw what I was thinking. 'Yvonne and I rubbed noses. You might say we were soul mates. I am not sure I'll survive without her.' She instantly became practical, passing me her last will and testament. 'I had it witnessed, by the milkman and Mr Musgrove. He took over tending my father's allotment.'

She handed me another document. Her confession.

'You've thought of everything.'

'Best to be prepared. I really would like time to re-write it if that proves possible. I got a little carried away in the last paragraph. Would you give me an opinion?'

I flicked to the third page of a testimony that began very neatly on page one and then became more of a scrawl. She had been unable to resist the melodrama of that tragic event.

I read the last paragraph.

"I wound my scarf around my mouth and nose. I saw old gas-masks on hooks by the door. I held my breath and went into that dreadful room, dragging on my cloak, holding the door with my shoulder. I had to let go the door. When it slammed shut, I feared I would never get out. We would lie side by side in eternal sleep, an insufficient number for classical tragedy, and too old for Romeo and Juliet."

'I should cross that out, don't you think?'

'Leave it, Miss Boland. It shows your state of mind.'

'Mad as a hatter, eh?'

'No, a doyenne of the opera to the end.'

She took out a fading sepia photograph. 'If ever in the future Ruth can think of me without loathing, please tell her she is the best pupil I ever had.'

The signed photograph showed four young people in costume, two men, two women. Each held a banner with a single word. It read: Merry Opera Company Rigoletto.

'Just the four of you?'

'We toured, doing slimmed-down opera for whoever would book us and give us a stage with piano, travelling the world for our bread and butter, and sometimes a scraping of jam. We thought it would never end.'

Looking exhausted, she pushed herself up from the table and moved towards the stairs. 'Just ten minutes' lie down, and then I will be ready for whatever comes.'

'Miss Boland, please stop playing the tragic heroine. You failed to report a death. You obstructed the coroner. You did not commit murder.' I moved to help her.

'No need.' She paused at the foot of the stairs.

I would have gone up with her but at that moment there was a knock on the door, Sykes's knock. We both stayed put.

'Miss Boland, remember that you were defending yourself.' Taking my time, I walked across the room. The door opened before I got to it.

Sykes stood there, with Sergeant Moon.

Miss Boland turned back and invited them in.

The sergeant looked around the room. 'It's a while since I was in here, Miss Boland.'

'Welcome back.'

'You did a good job with our Stanley,' the sergeant said. 'He's in high demand to thump out a tune whenever there's a party.'

'I'm glad to hear it.'

'Now what's all this about?'

She nodded to me, to pass him the confession. I was right in saying that the flowery last paragraph would show her state of mind. On reflection, a statement with more defence and mitigation would not go amiss. I pretended to misunderstand her nod. 'I'll take care of your lyrics.'

The sergeant waited.

'In the presence of Mrs Finch, Miss Boland told me that she was at the brewery when Mr Finch died. She went to the brewery to talk to him about a private matter and ended in a situation where she was compelled to defend herself.' I turned to Miss Boland. 'Tell the sergeant what you told Mrs Finch and me.'

She did so, with the important words that she was terrified when he hit out at her with her own stick, and she tried to defend herself.

He sighed. 'This is a tragic and serious matter, Miss Boland. I must ask you to accompany me to the station. I am arresting you on the charge of obstructing the coroner in the course of his duty. Do you wish to say anything in answer to the charge? You are not obliged to say anything unless you wish to do so, but whatever you do say will be taken down in writing and may be used in evidence.'

Miss Boland blinked in surprise. She said, 'I have nothing to say at the moment, Sergeant, except that Mrs Shackleton has kindly agreed to change the dressing on my sprained ankle.'

This was another of her lies.

What followed would not have happened in a city, or even a larger town.

The sergeant agreed to wait. He and Sykes would go next door, to give us privacy while I changed Miss Boland's dressing.

Sykes brought a basin of water from the kettle at Oak Cottage, and my first aid kit.

Miss Boland sat down and plunged her feet into the basin. 'Might as well give them both a wash.'

There was a worn towel by the sink. I went to pick it up, ready to dry her feet. 'You will need a solicitor. There is likely to be at least one more charge and that is preventing a lawful burial.'

'I haven't ever prevented a burial.'

'That is the wording for the offence. Usually it is when someone secretes a body for much longer than you did, but in theory you stopped Joe Finch's body from being discovered. Give me your foot.'

'Is it hugely, enormously serious? Will I go to prison?'

I dried her foot. 'It is extremely serious. If there is someone well-connected who will speak up for you, you may avoid prison. Give me the other foot.'

She thought for a moment. 'There is just one person, a family friend. He still sends me Christmas cards.'

'What is his name?'

'Clement Pointing, now Sir Clement Pointing. He was knighted for making lots of money and being charitable.'

'Sir Clement sounds perfect,' I said. 'But you mustn't expect to stay in Masham after this.'

I applied the arnica ointment.

'I never wanted to stay in Masham.'

'You turned your back on the town for years, Miss Boland, but you are one of their own.' The unfortunate Joe Finch, on the other hand, would forever be regarded as a jumped-up hoss boy from the East Riding.

'We don't have long,' I told her. 'Stop feeling sorry for yourself. Do you own or rent your cottage?'

'Own it, for what it's worth. Parnaby was right. It's damp and there are rats in the thatch of both of them.'

I applied the plasters. 'That should see you through the next few days. Do try and keep the weight off.'

'I will if you keep your dog under control and I have possession of my walking stick.'

'Take possession of it now. You'll need it. Here, put your stockings on.'

'Look away. I don't want you to see the veins in my legs.'

I turned away. 'Do you own both cottages?'

'Yes. My great grandfather built them. Eleanor Lofthouse could have found somewhere better for you to stay, but she regards me as a fellow artist and a charity case. I was grateful for the income.'

Once more, I tried to fathom Eleanor. Were we in condemned property because of Eleanor's meanness, or her philanthropy? 'You're fortunate then, to have property.'

'I can't stretch to the upkeep. Cottages like these are being demolished all across Mashamshire, the Urban District Council sends a condemned notice.'

'Then the Council must be kept busy. They may not reach your property for decades. In the meantime, I have tenants for you, a lovely family, parents and two children. He is working as a casual labourer. There would be no difficulty about meeting the rent.'

I said this with more confidence than I felt, but Miss Boland did not ask for proof of earnings.

She said, 'They'd have to be mad to move in here.'

'Your cottage would be a godsend compared with where they are now. You would have an income. The father turns his hand to anything and would likely make improvements.' Although never having met the man, I had seen the neat bender he made in the wood and the symmetrical arrangement of stones around the fire. 'They might move in tomorrow, if you'll let me oversee the packing of your things. I'll make sure your belongings are safe in one of the rooms. Write me a list of what's precious.'

'Everything musical is precious, that's what I want, and my clothes and papers.'

'So, we are agreed, about the rental?'

'You can turn around now, I have my stockings on.'

I turned.

She extended her hand. 'Do we shake hands on the rental arrangement?'

We shook hands.

'How much a week?' I asked.

'Ask Mrs Lofthouse what I can reasonably expect. If you find a permanent tenant for next door too, I'll be in clover.'

'Harriet and I will be here just a little longer. You have Ruth Parnaby as a tenant, for now.' I felt a wave uneasiness. Ruth Parnaby would not feel secure as long as her father was likely to come knocking on the door.

Miss Boland looked around the room. 'I'll never see Yvonne again.'

'Don't ever say never. You'll have a distant link through your tenants. The children have been going to Yvonne for their Sunday dinner.'

'How long will I be in prison?'

'Not long.'

'And where will I go then?'

I took a mimeographed Merry Opera Company programme from her drawer. 'Shall I see if I can track down your friends?'

I looked at the names of this merry band. Celia Boland, Noel Broderick, Delius Jackson and Julia Patterson. 'Do you have addresses?'

She shook her head. 'You may need a ladder to heaven.'

There was a tap on the door. I went to answer and stepped outside to talk to Sergeant Moon and thank him for his patience. 'Sergeant Moon, do you happen to know how to contact Sir Clement Pointing?'

'Oh, yes. He is very generous towards police charities.'

'He is a family friend of Miss Boland's. She hopes he may be willing to speak up for her in court.'

'I'll have to put my skates on then,' the sergeant said. 'After the interview, I'll be taking Miss Boland to be held in custody in Ripon. She'll be up before the Ripon magistrates in the morning.'

I watched as Miss Boland, on the arms of Jim Sykes and the sergeant, was escorted up the lane to the waiting police car. Sykes waved, indicating that he would come back down the track.

The drawer Miss Boland had set on the table contained programmes, fliers and newspaper cuttings, that had fallen out of a scrapbook while waiting to be pasted. The four friends had blasted their arias far and wide. In England they played the Hackney Empire, the Alexander Theatre in Bradford, and clubs and town halls across the country. Perhaps, like Celia Boland, her opera pals had ended up close to where they began. In the hope that one of them might be alive and have a spare bed, I gathered up a selection of press cuttings and biographical material and put it in an envelope, along with a note of ideas for tracing elderly opera singers.

Sykes was waiting at the gate when I locked Miss Boland's door behind me. What stories that house might tell. It seemed indecent to be planning for the Burns family to move in before Celia Boland's hearth grew cold.

Sykes looked glum. 'Which of us will tell the Lofthouses that Mrs Shackleton has solved the mystery of Joe Finch's death and that Miss Boland will languish overnight in the lock-up in Ripon?'

'You tell them, and we did it together, as always,' I said. 'I want to be here when Harriet and Ruth come back from their walk. It will be a blow for Ruth to lose Miss Boland so soon after Miss Crawford's funeral.'

Sykes volunteered to go to the court tomorrow, which took the burden from me. 'Mr Lofthouse may want to go,' Sykes said. 'If not, I'll report back to him.'

He still looked glum. I said, 'Come for a walk with me, before it gets too dark. There's time enough for you to see the Lofthouses, and it will do us good to go to the bluebell wood.'

'What are you up to?' Sykes asked.

'A cheerful errand to an encampment.'

As we walked, I told him about the Burns family and Miss Boland's willingness to have tenants in her cottage. Sykes was pleased for the family. He suggested that we meet the first month's rent and say it was to cover any cleaning or patching up they might need to do.

The joyfulness of that family when we broke the news gave us a lightness of step as we walked back from the wood.

'Where will Miss Boland go when she's let out of clink?' Sykes asked.

I told him of my hope that one of her friends might still be alive and kicking and willing to give Miss Boland houseroom. I gave him the envelope of Merry Opera Company cuttings. 'We're just about finished here, Mr Sykes. How about you see if you can track down Miss Boland's old pals.'

He seemed pleased and relieved. 'Then I'll get off home tomorrow. I'll be better placed to do this tracing in Leeds.'

'Good idea.' I guessed he would have bridges to mend with Rosie after seeing her to the bus last Sunday morning.

We parted, agreeing that this assignment was almost at its end. This ought to be the time to say goodbye and send in the bill yet I felt the last act was yet to come.

Sykes picked up on my uncertainty. 'What's worrying you, Mrs Shackleton?'

'Ruth. She and Harriet went out today and they are getting on very well. Harriet would be a perfect companion for her but there's the spectre of Slater Parnaby. I'd be permanently uneasy.'

'They should move in with the Lofthouses,' Sykes said. 'There'd be plenty of room and they would be safe.'

'If I were their age, I would prefer the cottage. They have their independence. We parted company. I called at Miss Boland's cottage to pick up the pie she would no longer need.'

Chapter
Forty-Five

◢

The lamps were lit in Oak Cottage. Harriet and Ruth were safely back from their day out. They were laughing over Harriet's difficulty in opening a tin of peas with a rusty tin opener. Ruth sliced the pie that Yvonne Finch had brought. Harriet decided that halfway open was enough and she could scoop the peas into a pan. They had been shopping and bought sausages, packets of potato crisps and a tin of jam and cream wafers.

We all sat down to eat.

Our dog barely troubled to greet me. He was by the pantry, tackling a marrowbone.

I felt a sense of relief that swept aside my anxieties about the girls not being safe if I left them. I waited until after we had eaten to tell them the news about Miss Boland, beginning with the signed photograph she had asked me to give to Ruth. In it, young Celia Boland was smiling. She had inscribed the photograph, To Ruth, My Star Pupil.

They listened in silence as I told them of Miss Boland's confession and arrest.

Ruth finally said, 'The old man was right. I thought he was just being cruel.'

'What did he say?' I asked.

'On Saturday night when he was here, he whispered to me. He said Miss Boland murdered Joe Finch. He said he smelled blood on her.'

'She did not commit murder,' I said. 'He was wrong about that. Joe Finch's death was a terrible accident. He fell down the stairs. Miss Boland knew she should not have been there and didn't own up.'

Ruth thought about this. 'Then I will go tell the old man that. I don't want him spreading lies about Miss Boland. What time is her court appearance tomorrow?'

'I don't know. The courts usually begin at 10 a.m. It will depend on how many cases there are, and when Miss Boland's case is scheduled.'

'Then I'll go ask at the police station,' Ruth said. 'If they can't tell me, I'll be at the court for ten o'clock. Will you come with me tomorrow, Harriet? I can borrow a bike for you.'

Harriet agreed. 'What about you, Auntie, will you go?'

'No. Mr Sykes will be there, and perhaps the Lofthouses.' I then told them about Miss Boland letting the cottage to a family.

'Will Miss Boland go to prison?' Ruth asked.

'That depends on the court. If she does, I hope it won't be for long and we'll find somewhere for her to live so that she doesn't have the shame of coming back here. She'll miss you, but she won't be sorry about starting again.'

I could see that both girls thought Miss Boland far too old to begin again, but they did not say so.

They put on their coats and set off for the town.

Chapter
Forty-Six

❧

Harriet did not relish the idea of seeing Ruth's dad, but she did not tell Ruth that. At the Parnaby house, Harriet stood a little to one side as Ruth opened the door and stepped inside, calling, 'It's me, Dad,' and saying to Harriet, 'Come in, we won't be long.'

Slater Parnaby was sitting in a chair by the fire. He was unshaven. His clothes were dirty. He ponged. The house was messy and smelled of what Mrs Sugden would call burnt offerings. The sink was piled high with dishes and pans. Mr Parnaby looked up from reading the paper.

'Talk of the devil,' he said to Ruth. 'I was thinking about you and here you are.'

'Here I am,' Ruth said. 'I've just come to put you right about Miss Boland.'

The floor around him was strewn with newspapers. Harriet saw why. He finished reading a page and then threw it on the floor.

He then stood and said. 'I just made a pot of tea. Sit yourselves down. There's a packet of digestive biscuits.'

Harriet saw that Ruth was about to refuse but Mr Parnaby did not let her get a word in. 'I've had a lot of time to think sitting here all alonio, on my ownio. It was me, my fault. I drove you all away.

That was wrong.' He took two clean cups from the cupboard, put them on the table, poured in milk and stewed tea. 'I'll make it up to you, lass. When I have a business going, we'll pull together.'

Ruth said, 'I don't think that's going to happen, Dad, not now. I've just come to tell you that Miss Boland didn't murder Joe Finch. It was an accident.'

Mr Parnaby scoffed. 'That's just what she would say.' He began to pick up the sheets of newspaper paper and push them into the space between the drawers and cupboard at the side of the fireplace.

Mr Parnaby then picked up a double page and put it in front of Ruth. 'How about this in the *Mole of the World*?' Ruth picked it up and sat down at the table to read.

Harriet saw the headline. 'American Film Star Couple's Child Held for Ransom.' Harriet knew that story. She looked at the date. It was three months ago.

All the while Ruth read, Mr Parnaby talked, wishing he had been different and kept his family together. George had done the right thing going after a job in Scarborough, and on and on Mr Parnaby talked.

Ruth ignored him folded the paper and handed it back. 'The film stars probably did it for the publicity.'

'Some people are shockers,' Mr Parnaby said. 'Some people are money mad. That poor child.'

He talked on. Harriet read the paper's puzzle page and tried to shut out his voice.

Ruth gulped down her tea and took a biscuit. 'We're off now. I'll be going to the magistrates' court tomorrow to see what happens to Miss Boland, but don't go telling people she is a murderess because she is not.'

Mr Parnaby folded more sheets of newspaper, saying, 'I'm saving certain items.'

Harriet could not decide whether to feel sorry for him.

He came to the door to let them out. 'Ruth, come for your dinner on Sunday. I've ordered a leg of mutton. You've a good business head on your shoulders. I have this idea for taking over a tobacconist's shop. I need a capital investment and I want to talk to you about it.'

Chapter
Forty-Seven

~

It was late that night, when Ruth had gone to bed, that Harriet and I sat by the fire.

She asked me, 'Are you tired, Auntie?'

'No.' I poked the fire. A log crackled.

'I liked it on the common,' Harriet said. We looked at where there were old cottages. Ruth recited a poem about one of them. Miss Boland taught it to her, making Ruth speak this poem over and over so as to practise pronouncing her Ts clearly. It's called *The Old Thatched Cottage on the Moor*.'

'Did you learn it, Harriet?'

'Only the first verse. It goes,

"Out on the lonely moors you can see a cottage stand,
It is an ancient cottage, and yet it's sweet and grand,
It has an old thatched roof, and it's just a storey high,
Bonnie little cottage, you're a picture to my eye."'

'I suppose that's what you call heartfelt, and with plenty of Ts to pronounce.'

'There are six verses,' Harriet said. 'You could laugh at it or you could cry. There was a hoard of gold sovereigns found in the thatch of that cottage when it was demolished.'

'What a shame they weren't spent in the hoarder's lifetime,' I said.

But Harriet's biggest revelation was about Slater Parnaby.

'When we called round, Mr Parnaby was so nice you wouldn't believe it. He gave us a cup of stewed tea and digestive biscuits. He looked very scruffy and what's that word? Morose. He said that he was on his own now and that was his punishment for having been bad to them and driven them away, Annie and George and Ruth. He said he wished he had been different, and hoped they would not think too badly of him. He didn't blame George for leaving his job. If he had been George's age and offered a job at a Scarborough brewery, he would have taken it.'

'What did Ruth say?'

'She didn't say anything. I asked her if she thought her father had really changed. She doesn't know. She can't tell.'

The next days seemed so full that they merged into each other. Miss Boland was sentenced to two weeks' imprisonment and a fine. It was strange to think of James Lofthouse and Celia Boland being the Masham Contingent in Armley Prison. James was awaiting trial at the summer assizes. Miss Boland's short sentence allowed little time for her to be found somewhere else to live.

Mrs Sugden caught two buses to help with the packing up of Miss Boland's belongings and the cleaning of the cottage, and stayed on. Beryl from Barleycorn House came to help in the mammoth task.

Before we began work, Elizabeth Burns completed the application form for school places for Monica and Michael. Having lived in a city all her life, she wished for a street name to make the address definite. On being told by Mick Musgrove that the track had no name, she gave it one. The full address was now Elm Cottage, Allotmentside, Masham.

I took the Burns children to the stationer's shop and bought pencils, pens, ink, pencil cases, books and crayons. They were excited to learn that Billy the pony had a new home with the schoolteacher. It was as if Christmas had come early. I also bought two rent books, one for the Burns family and one for Celia Boland so that each could date and tick when a postal order for rent had been sent and received. There was good news, too, for Mick Musgrove. A batch of his *Rhymes in Praise of Ale* was ready for despatch from the printer to the stationer, where it would go on sale. Courtesy of the Lofthouses, there would be free copies for local libraries and a review copy for the *Wensleydale Gazette*. To a crowded room in Masham Town Hall, Mr Musgrove read a selection of verses and signed copies of his book.

On Thursday and Friday, Ruth, Harriet and Eleanor Lofthouse were driven to civic events in Leeds and Pickering where Ruth met local dignitaries. On Saturday, they were driven to Tadcaster for Ruth's parade through the town.

I felt confident about going home on Monday and had arranged with Eleanor that Harriet would be paid a modest wage for staying on as companion to Ruth.

When the girls came back from Tadcaster, Ruth seemed subdued. I asked Harriet, was anything wrong.

Harriet sighed. 'Ruth's brother George is lodging in Scarborough. He will be starting work at Scarborough Brewery on Monday. Ruth is glad for him but didn't think he would be going anywhere so soon. He is talking about finding a place where their mother can stay and that leaves Ruth feeling a little bit out of it.'

'But she must be relieved that her mother will be safe, and Ruth enjoys all the events, doesn't she?'

'Oh yes, and we have a laugh, but she says there is always a fly in the ointment.'

Chapter
Forty-Eight

❦

Ruth said goodbye to Mrs Musgrove. They had sat in the farm-house kitchen for an hour or more. Ruth fed the sickly lamb they had brought in to revive in the warmth. This kitchen was the place Ruth and George were happiest, after their mother left. Mrs Mus-grove had sons but no daughter and she and Ruth always had plenty to talk about. Today they talked about Mrs Musgrove's father-in-law, Mick, who preferred to live in a hut near his allotment, saying he could take care of himself and had no intention of being a 'bur-den' to be bossed about and cossetted by his daughter-in-law. They talked of Miss Crawford who had taken down old Mr Musgrove's rhymes. Mrs Musgrove wanted to know all about this kind woman who had met such a tragic end. When it came time for Ruth to go, Mrs Musgrove said, 'I thought you'd be my daughter-in-law, but you're set for another life.'

Ruth felt sad. She would have liked this life, but perhaps not for long. 'How is Adam?' she asked.

'Well enough. The lass he's courting is a farmer's daughter. I expect we'll get on, but not like you and me.'

They looked out of the window and saw that the darkening sky threatened rain. Ruth left soon after. She wanted to avoid seeing Adam. It was better this way.

The sheep in the field came to watch Ruth pass. She kept to the edge of the fields until she left the farmland behind and set out across the common towards home. She had not walked more than a few hundred yards when she saw the old man. Straightaway, she knew he was lying in wait, and that he was up to something. He waved. She felt a shakiness inside. He had played a part too well when he saw her with Harriet. He had been all friendliness and false regret. He even apologised for scaring them on Saturday night and for snatching her playing cards, acting the part of the repentant father who had done his best but now knew it was not good enough.

Either Harriet was taken in by him, or she was just as good at pretending as Ruth. They did not speak of him when they got back to Oak Cottage.

Now Ruth forced herself to hide a creeping feeling stronger than uneasiness. 'What brings you up here, Dad?'

'Just walking, thinking of the past, wishing I could turn the clock back.'

Ruth thought of the swimming costume that he had cut in two. That was what he threatened to do to their mother all those years ago. He would chop her in two. He would cut her into tiny pieces and feed her to the birds on the moors.

Slater Parnaby did not fool his daughter, but she might fool him. 'It's too late to change the past,' she said. 'You had plenty of chances.'

'Never too late if you have money. Do you remember?' He waved to the spot where the cottages had been, where they had searched for gold coins. Ruth saw the oak tree and the remains of the wall. In her mind's eye she saw George, crying as he raked his fingers through the grass. She saw herself collecting buttercups and heard the old man's praise that at least she collected something that was the right colour. She despised herself for having been pleased by his praise, now understanding that he praised her so that George would be humiliated.

'We were looking in the wrong place,' the old man said.

'What was the right place, Dad?'

'Come with me and I'll show you. You were on the right track all along when you wanted to go down the cellar and your mother said no.'

Ruth felt a creeping horror as she remembered. She was being clever, the clever girl, the brave girl. You could demolish a cottage, but you could not demolish what was underneath.

She thought of the article about the kidnapping of the American film stars' child and she understood that was the old man's way of telling her of his plan.

He made a grab for her hand, and then smiled, his eyes gleaming with what he meant to look like affection. 'We can be friends, can't we? Everyone can turn over a new leaf.' He was not good at a wheedling tone, but he tried. 'You were the one who seriously looked for gold coins. Your mother and George had no faith. You did. We're alike. We want a better hand than life dealt us. We're the ones who will go places.'

She knew her own strength, and his. She knew how fast he could run, a cross-country runner. This was not a popular walk. Ruth tried to stay calm, not let him sense her fear. She would save her strength and outwit him. He would be the one to be found below ground.

Ruth said, 'They'll be sending out a search party if I don't get back soon.'

'You trust me, don't you?' the old man wheedled again. 'You're too precious to come to harm.'

'Dad.'

'Ruth?'

'This is a stupid idea. Let me go now.'

'I'm glad you have the sense not to struggle. You wouldn't win a contest if you were covered in bruises, and there will be a big prize for the Northern Brewery Queen.'

There was still a distance between here and the demolished cottage that Mrs Shackleton had not seen because it wasn't there.

Between here and the oak tree, and the hidden trapdoor, she must take her chance because now it came back to her. This was the place he said he would bury their mother. As the thought came, the old man pulled a teacloth from his pocket. She knew that smell. A boy in her commerce class who knew chemistry and read shocker comics said that chloroform did not work like writers said it did. It would take ever so long, but the old man's arm was tightly round her and the cloth was on her face. She held her breath until he loosened his grasp and then threw the cloth across the ground.

He had left the trap door open. 'Don't make me fling you down there. As soon as Lofthouse pays the ransom, you'll be free, and I'll be gone. All I want is my lump sum. A hundred pounds is nowt to a man like Lofthouse.'

Chapter
Forty-Nine

I was reading the Sunday paper when a heavy and continuous knocking on the cottage door set the window frame rattling. Our dog barked obligingly but stayed in the back garden.

Slater Parnaby was in manic mood, eyes wild, jaw clenched. He held his arms stiffly by his sides, but bounced and tottered, unable to keep still.

'I threw her Yorkshire pudding on the fireback.'

When someone flings words in your face, it takes a moment to translate angry speech into common sense. I knew he must mean Ruth. Yorkshire pudding on the fireback hinted at a missed Sunday dinner.

'Ruth isn't here, Mr Parnaby.'

'Then where is she?'

I stepped aside and opened the door wide. 'You'd better come in. She can't be far away.'

Harriet, having heard the commotion, came downstairs. 'Harriet, Mr Parnaby was expecting Ruth for her Sunday dinner. Did she say anything to you about where she was going?'

'After church, she went up to the farm with Mrs Musgrove.'

'Regretting her foolishness. She'll never find a better lad than Adam Musgrove.' Parnaby's breath grew more rapid.

His face turned red. 'Why didn't you go with her? You're the companion.'

'Ruth and Mrs Musgrove like to talk.'

'You're lying. She'd be back by now.'

'Go up to the Musgroves then. She might be still there.'

'And she might not!' He knew that Miss Boland was no longer living next door, but he went out, vaulted the fence and began to bang on the door of Elm Cottage.

I spoke quietly to Harriet. 'I'll keep him talking. Go to his house, let yourself in. Look for any sign of his having made and thrown away a dinner. Then go to Mrs Finch and Mrs Jopling. Ask if they have seen Ruth.'

I looked out, watching her go. When a surprised John Burns answered Miss Boland's door, Parnaby asked his question. After a reply from Burns that I could not hear, Parnaby vaulted back. 'Vagrants! They didn't let the fire go out and they're in there. Some people have life handed to them on a plate. They don't care two hoots where my lass is.'

Either he was a good actor, or genuinely concerned. I poured him a cup of tea.

He looked round for Harriet. 'Where's that lass of yours gone?'

'To the vicarage. There was some charity meeting Ruth might have attended. These things run on.'

He eyed the sugar lumps, spooned several into his cup and pocketed a handful. 'I didn't like her coming here, not one little bit.'

'You made that clear, Mr Parnaby. She is eighteen.'

'She's eighteen, not twenty-one. She should be under my roof.'

As he drank his tea, he talked about hearing a noise in the dead of night.

'When?'

'Last night. What if someone came in with that chloroform stuff you hear about and they intended to snatch her?'

'But as you say, she wasn't there. She was here.'

'They wouldn't know that would they?'

'Did you catch sight of an intruder?'

'I was half asleep.'

'Was your door locked when you went to bed?'

He snorted. 'I only ever locked it to keep George out when he'd been prancing about at town hall dances and not in by ten o'clock. I don't need to lock it now he's slung his hook.'

'Was there a smell of chloroform?'

'No, and I would have known, no matter how faint.'

I kept Parnaby talking, to give Harriet time to look round his house. It would be just like him to come here with an invented story, solely for the purpose of snooping. 'Perhaps Ruth called to see a friend on the way back. You'll know the names of her friends and where they live?'

He did not, claiming that she was a home sort of girl, never made a big fuss of friends, not in other people's pockets all the time, like some people. 'She wouldn't let me down about summat like Sunday dinner. I tell you she's missing. She's not one for just going off.' His worry now seemed genuine. 'It's one thing a lad slinging his hook because he's taken the huff, and because he's ungrateful for everything that was done for him, but not my lass, not a pretty lass, and one who's been in the papers for all to see. She wouldn't do it. I've never stood in her way. I never stood in her way of coming here.'

I gave him a sharp pencil and the blank Stop Press from the newspaper. 'List the places she might be.'

He wrote, Her Mother, and said, 'Where did you whisk Annie to? I've a right to know.'

'So that's why you're here?'

'I'm here for Ruth. I stopped caring about Annie a long time ago.'

He wrote the names of two girls from school. 'Jealous to death of her the pair of 'em. Oh, and there's the church do-gooders.'

His nose gave several involuntary twitches. Either he was sniffing for his daughter, thinking we had her hidden under a bed, or I was too posh for him, and getting up his snitch.

He had left out Eleanor and William Lofthouse. At my request, he added them to the list.

'The time to worry is if she is with none of these people, or if she is not back by suppertime.' I spoke soothingly. 'Young people never imagine how much worry they can cause.'

He gulped down his tea. 'I can feel in my bones that it's not right.'

'Do your bones tell you where to look first?'

He glared, suspecting that I was being sarcastic. 'Gypsies? They'll steal a pony, they'll steal a dog and seek the reward, they might do the same with a girl.'

He made a note, and a little doodle.

Just as I was running out of ideas, Harriet returned. 'She's not at the vicarage.'

I picked up Parnaby's cap and handed it to him. 'Let us divide the search between us. I'll call on Mrs Lofthouse. It's not four o'clock. Ruth probably lost track of time.'

He seemed reluctant to be dismissed, but then put on his cap. 'I'll go then, go off and make a fool of meself because mi own daughter doesn't trouble to come and see me when she promised.' He paused only to spoon the sludge of sugar from the bottom of his cup and suck it. I picked up the pencil as he moved to pocket it.

We waited until the gate clicked behind him.

Harriet said, 'He might have made some sort of dinner. There was pile of dirty dishes and plates, but not a single clean plate. If he'd expected Ruth there would have been one clean plate for her dinner, wouldn't there?'

'You would think so.'

'Mrs Finch and Mrs Jopling haven't seen her—but he didn't go ask them. Mrs Jopling told me where her two friends live.'

Chapter Fifty

Eleanor and William were in their conservatory, playing backgammon.

William looked exceedingly cheerful. 'Won't you join us, Kate?'

Eleanor brightened. 'Oh, do! You'll be a dab hand. You could take my place.'

I explained why I was here, ending with, 'I'm sure it's nothing to worry about. Harriet has gone to see whether she is with her schoolfriends.'

After her first reaction of astonishment at the idea of Slater Parnaby cooking a Sunday dinner, Eleanor frowned. 'Doesn't Harriet know where she is?'

'Ruth went to the farm with Mrs Musgrove. She must have forgotten the arrangement with her father.'

William insisted we were both fussing too much. The girl needed a life, needed to be able to see her friends without raising alarm. He wouldn't blame her one bit for forgetting to have dinner with her father when the world was full of young admirers.

Eleanor rang for her maid. 'And when we find her, we must keep a closer eye on her, Kate. I know this might sound over-dramatic, but we are so close to the Northern Finals. There is a decent prize for the next stage of the contest. Manchester breweries,' she paused to allow William a withering look, 'Manchester breweries are very much ahead of us. They have put up a prize of fifty guineas for the winner and fifty guineas towards expenses for the brewery concerned.'

This came as news to William. 'What?! Why didn't you tell me?'

'You didn't want to talk about it. You've hoped all along it would come to nothing.'

'I changed my mind. You know I changed my mind. But I wish I'd taken notice of the money involved. People would kill for that kind of money. There could be some Lancastrian assassin crossing the Pennines as we speak. Ruth might be a marked woman. She must be odds-on favourite. I like her and she's the best clerk we've ever had.'

The maid answered Eleanor's call, straightening her cap, making no attempt to disguise the fact that she wished they would get on with their backgammon and leave her be.

'Jenny, please ask Daniel to drive to Musgroves' farm and see if Miss Parnaby is visiting. If so, he is to bring her back. Not as an order mind, but as a polite request, as if we knew about it and wished her to ride back in comfort.'

'Very well, madam.' Jenny now seemed not to mind having been disturbed for such an interesting task.

Backgammon went unfinished. Eleanor refused to contemplate anything other than that Ruth was at this moment being walked back from the farm by one of the Musgrove family.

I now felt two contradictory emotions. The comfort of knowing that Ruth was with friends at a farm a few miles away, and the fear that came from picturing her having fallen on the way back and broken an arm or leg.

It was not until William's driver came back to report that Ruth left the farm four hours ago that my skin began to crawl. He said that two of the Musgrove brothers had gone out with torches.

Before leaving, I used the Lofthouses' telephone to call Mrs Sugden.

I avoided saying, It's nothing to worry about. 'I may not be back tomorrow after all. We haven't seen Ruth since this morning. I'm sure she'll turn up but would you please alert Mr Sykes.'

'He starts another job tomorrow.'

'I just want to keep him informed.'

Mrs Sugden naturally wanted to know whether there was anything she could do, while at the same time knowing there was not. I felt sorry at having given her something to worry about.

Eleanor saw me out. 'Are you all right to walk back on your own?'

'Of course.'

We agreed to let each other know if Ruth turned up.

When I got back to Oak Cottage, Harriet was looking out for me.

'Slater Parnaby was here again. When you sent me to see if he really had made a dinner, I thought he was lying. But he came to say that he searched the woods and the path by the river, whistling for her, asking people to look out for her. She's not with any friends. Now he's gone to the police.'

'I'll drive to Bedale. She may be with her mother.'

'She won't! She saw her yesterday, on our way back from the event in Tadcaster.'

'If she walked back alone from the farm—'

'It's no distance to her. She wouldn't have wanted Adam's dad or one of his brothers to walk her back. They took it badly when she and Adam broke up. Mrs Musgrove is the one who understands.'

I knew that Harriet was more likely to be right than wrong on this. It was time to follow up on Slater Parnaby's report to the police.

Saying little to each other, we walked into the deserted town. I had that scooped-out feeling that comes when you speak of someone in the past tense. When we last saw her, what she was wearing, where she was going.

Sergeant Moon was not on duty. The young constable had contacted him after receiving reports from Mr Parnaby and Mr Lofthouse that Ruth was missing.

I was proud of Harriet. Top to toe, she described what Ruth was wearing, a bottle-green dress, flared at the hem, a small black hat with brim, and court shoes.

'You leave this with me,' the constable said. 'Sergeant Moon will be in shortly. I'll come and see you before the evening's out. Try not to worry too much. Ruth knows her way around. She has a good head on her shoulders.'

When we left the station, Harriet said, 'I'm stupid. She knows I don't like her father, so she didn't tell me she was going to have dinner with him. When she called round to tell him to stop spreading lies about Miss Boland, he asked her to come for her Sunday dinner. She didn't answer him. It's what you said. I judge people and I don't hide what I think.'

'Slater Parnaby could be lying. And remember, Ruth is as strong-minded as you. She may want to keep some things to herself. Has she mentioned any other boyfriend?'

'There's been no one since Adam.'

Harriet and I sat in the kitchen at Oak Cottage, the lamps lit in the windows, front and back, to guide her home. At almost midnight, there was a knock on the door, which I had locked and bolted. The dog barked.

It was Sergeant Moon.

I slid back the bolt and turned the key.

'You do right to lock yourself in, Mrs Shackleton.' He stepped inside. I could see from his face that there was no news.

'Now don't be alarmed, but I'll need an item of Ruth's clothing. This is just a precaution.'

Harriet stood. 'I'll fetch something. Her rubber boot socks?'

'That would be grand,' the sergeant said, 'perhaps a scarf as well. We've two dogs coming.'

At the word dogs, our dog came from his blanket under the table and put his head on my lap.

'Is there anything else we can do, Mr Moon?' I asked. 'Will you tell Ruth's mother?'

'I thought of it, but she'll be sleeping. I'll leave it a few hours. I know what she'll say, that Slater Parnaby has done something to her.'

Harriet came down, carrying a pair of socks and a scarf. 'Mr Parnaby showed Ruth an article from the paper about the kidnapping of a film star couple's child.'

'Did he now?' The sergeant opened a bag for Ruth to drop the socks and scarf in. 'If that's his game she won't be far away. I'll have the town crier call out the news. We'll find her.'

It was raining stair rods when the sergeant left. What started as a light shower would now make searching with bloodhounds near impossible.

Chapter
Fifty-One

⟨～⟩

Ruth saw by the lantern the old man had left that this had been a keeping place, a stone-cold keeping place below the long-demolished cottage. The walls were a yellowing distemper with long streaks of damp where rain seeped through from above. Brick columns supported a deep stone slab by the wall where chopping and cutting must have taken place. It dipped in the centre from years of use. Her father's familiar, carefully folded army blanket was neatly set on the slab and next to it a khaki knapsack. She put the blanket in the dip and hoisted herself up to sit and think what to do. The old man would come back, there was no doubt about it. She was the goose who would lay his golden egg, he thought. He was the goose she would slay. No, he was not that. He was what he had always been, the fly in the ointment. She looked up. There were hooks in the ceiling where meat and game would have hung.

Next to the slab was a long shallow sink. In the corner was a water pump. As her ears attuned to what had at first seemed total silence, she heard the faint sound of murmuring water. The water would be foul. A haven for rats. I will come through this, she told herself. George would have crumbled. Her mother would go mad with terror. I am stronger than the old man, Ruth said. I will better him, but how?

In spite of the blanket and her coat she began to feel the cold. It was as if this cellar had been waiting for a warm thing to encircle, and stab with ice. The old man had been crafty, waiting until George was gone. George would have been onto him. That newspaper article the old man showed her made sense now. Clever Slater Parnaby thought he would extract money from his tight-fisted employer, Mr Lofthouse.

When she was reported missing, and she would be reported missing, the old man would be the first suspect. Harriet would tell the police about the newspaper article.

Now that she was here, Ruth felt she had been waiting for something like this to happen, some great turning point that would change her life and set her free. Instead of giving hints to Harriet, she should have said, if ever I am killed, or my mother is, or we go missing, you must look in the cellar of the cottage that isn't there.

But how could a sane person say such a thing?

Ruth opened the knapsack. There was a crust of bread, a piece of cheese, a rasher of crispy bacon and a bottle of tea. He did not intend her to starve. Not yet, anyway. He had included a candle and a box of matches. All these were good signs. Ruth was not hungry. Mrs Musgrove had fed her, as she always did.

While you have strength, Ruth told herself, try the trapdoor. She slid from the slab, taking the lantern. The light from the lantern cast her own shadow across the floor. He had thought of everything. There was a bucket by the wall, with water in the bottom, to make a suitable lavatory. Tied to its handle by string was a neat supply of newspaper squares.

He wouldn't come back, not tonight. It would be too far and too obvious. He would be at home, acting surprised, upset, outraged that she had left home and gone among folk who cared nothing for her.

Ruth climbed the stone steps, set down the lantern, and pushed at the trapdoor with both hands. It did not budge. She bent down, stood on the top step and put her shoulder to it. There was not the slightest movement. He had weighted it with rocks.

Slowly, and with a sudden hopeless feeling of dejection, she went back down the steps. A voice came into her head. 'It is important for girls and boys to be active and to go on being active.' Ruth was back in the schoolyard. 'Exercises, exercises, we must do our exercises.'

Ruth remembered them. She must keep moving, keep warm and keep her spirits up.

No use screaming, crying, banging the walls, she must save her energy, and think, and pray, and hope, and make her rations and the lantern last.

She placed the knapsack in the centre of the dip in the stone slab, where she could feel her way to it, and she switched off the lantern.

When darkness became total, Ruth shivered. This place was colder than the schoolyard in winter. She heard the voice of Miss Stafford, gathering children together in the yard. 'Exercises, exercises, we must do our exercises. Jump your legs out and back, fling your arms out and back, out and back. Run on the spot, run, run, run.'

Chapter
Fifty-Two

Ten minutes after Sergeant Moon left, Harriet and I still sat by the fire, staring at the same log that was busily burning. This would not do. If I were Annie Parnaby, I would not want a police sergeant to decide that I should sleep until morning and then get on with my baking, not knowing that my daughter was missing.

I stood. 'Harriet, at 3 a.m., I am going to fetch Annie.'

'What about me?' Harriet asked.

'You and Sergeant Dog stay here, lock and bolt the door behind me and only let in Ruth, if she finds her way back, or the police.'

Harriet said, 'I'm not just looking into the fire. I'm trying to see pictures. In the log, I can see a cave, the hermit's cave. He might have tied her up and put her there. And there's Roomer Common, she told you to go for dog walking, and she took me to see the cottage. Is there something in that?'

'I don't know. We can't go there in the dark and the rain, but I can find my way to Bedale.'

Driving in the darkness before dawn, the world looks different, roads feel longer, trees closer than in daylight. I wished I were going to see Annie Parnaby to tell her that everything was all right. Her son, safely in Scarborough, but she would know that. Her daughter safely in Oak Cottage, where she should be. Instead we had no idea where Ruth might be, only guesswork.

At a halfway point, I wondered if Sergeant Moon was right and I was wrong. Annie was not in robust health, mentally or physically. Perhaps she should be left in ignorance until we had definite news, but I was on my way and not prepared to turn back. The hope that lurked was that Ruth may have said something to her mother that would give a clue to her whereabouts.

This time, I parked directly opposite the gate to the bakery, so that my car could be seen. I had not remembered to bring a stool to help me climb over the neighbours' wall.

As it turned out this was not necessary. Annie must have been looking out of an upstairs window and spotted the car.

I heard her draw back the bolts. The gate slowly opened.

She was in nightdress and dressing gown. 'What's wrong?'

I went into the yard. 'Let's go inside.'

I half expected her to say that we would spoil the bread, but we went in.

'Annie, do not panic, do not fear the worst. We are looking for Ruth. She didn't come back to the cottage yesterday.'

'He's got her.'

'That is possible, but we will find her. Can you think of anywhere he would have taken her?'

She blinked and bit her lip. Her breath came in short bursts. When she finally spoke, it was not the wail of despair that I expected. 'I don't know. He's a cunning brute. People, people like you, you can't imagine how bad he can be.'

'If there is anything, however small, that might give a clue as to where he has taken her—if he has her—tell me.'

'I can't think.'

I had broken the news too suddenly.

'But I will think. If I shut my eyes, I'll be able to see her. I picture them all the time. Often, I'm right, or they tell me I am.'

As she spoke, something about her and about the room altered. It was as if a light was switched on, or a window flung open.

'Then will you come back with me?' I asked.

Annie went to the door that led to the stairs. 'I'll get dressed.' She paused and turned. 'That dresser, all that's in it is mine. Take that washed flour bag. Put everything in it.'

I did as she said.

The fire blazed, hot as hell. Orange and red flames licked the fireback, catching the soot. I emptied the dresser as instructed, into the bag that was still dusty with flour. The smell of baking bread grew stronger.

Annie was soon back down, dressed and carrying another large, washed flour bag stuffed with belongings.

'Have you got your money, Annie?' I asked, thinking of the 'escape fund' that Joe Finch had helped her build.

She tapped her middle. 'Aye.' She picked up a large knife from the table. 'And this'll be for Slater Bloody Parnaby if he's harmed a hair of my girl's head.'

I cleared my throat as a waft of smoke curled into the room. It was from the chimney soot but made me realise that we could not leave without telling someone. 'What about the bread?'

'Bugger the bread. He'll smell it burning. Let him see to it himself.'

'Where is he, Annie?'

She tucked the knife in her bag. 'I don't know, but we'll find him.'

'I don't mean your husband. I mean the baker.'

'His house is on the other side of the shop.'

'Come on. I'll tell him we're leaving.' Now was not the time to discuss how the Great Fire of London started. 'What do you call yourself?'

'Annie Scarth.'

'We must tell the baker you are going, and he has to see to the ovens. Otherwise the venerable town of Bedale will be ashes by 6 a.m.'

We went into the yard, and then into the street. She stayed with her back to the gate while I knocked at the baker's house next door.

No answer. I took off my shoe and banged. No answer. I tried again.

An upstairs window opened. The man looking out wore a nightcap. 'What's going on?'

'Mrs Scarth is leaving. The ovens are on. You'll have to see to the bread.'

Annie stepped forward, ready to cross to the car.

The baker saw Annie and started to call to her. We did not stay to listen.

I put the flour bags with her belongings into the dicky seat as she climbed in the front.

The noise of the motor prevented our talking, but there was little we could have said.

Chapter Fifty-Three

~

Ruth now knew her way around this cellar in the dark. She knew the slab, the sink, the water pump, and where she had placed the bucket. When she heard a fumbling at the top of the stairs, the slightest movement of the trapdoor, she snuffed the candle. The knapsack was on her back, with the lantern and what was left of the bread. She had eaten the bacon and cheese, drunk the cold tea and smashed the bottle. She knew exactly where the broken bottle was and would use it.

The trapdoor was raised.

The old man said, 'Ruth? It's your dad. Who else would it be?'

She said nothing, although her breathing sounded to her to be too loud.

His voice became wheedling. 'I know you're there.'

She did not answer.

'You and me must help each other. We're the only ones left.'

She did not know whether he meant that he and she are the ones who did not leave Masham, or were his words more sinister? He had hunted down her mother and brother because they abandoned him.

Ruth cursed the smidgen of light that came from the trapdoor. He must have propped it open. At least she would get out. If she made a dash for it and failed, perhaps neither of them would get out alive.

'I have a difficulty, Ruth, and you are clever.'

She would have liked to say, 'Not clever enough, or I wouldn't be here.' She said nothing.

He came down the stairs, lighting his way with a torch, saying, 'You are clever, but not wise in the ways of the world, which I am.'

He saw her now, and she him. He shone the torch in her face. 'When you were in Standard Two, Miss Stafford said you were good at sums, good at solving puzzles.'

Ruth was blinded by his torch. She said, 'It's too late to be talking to me about a school report.'

He directed the beam of the torch away from her. 'You thought I didn't pay attention. You thought I wasn't proud of you. You were wrong.'

He was good at tormenting. She knew that. He was good at sticking the boot in a weak spot. Don't show weakness. 'Are we leaving now?'

'Not yet. As I said, I have this little difficulty.'

'I have a bigger difficulty, and he is wearing your shoes.'

'I was cursed with a clever girl in the house, but I never stood in your way. Now you have to help me. You want to go to Manchester, don't you, to be in this competition, what is it, Northern Brewery Queen? Everyone in it gets a prize, and the winner gets a very big prize. It would be sad to miss it.'

'What do you want?'

'An answer to this question. How does a person who has sent a ransom note collect the money without being caught?'

She thought for a few seconds, as she touched the bucket with her foot to judge the distance. 'Who has the ransom note?'

'William Lofthouse will open it this morning.'

'Nothing would suit him better than for me to miss the contest. He's fed up of paying out for expenses and not having a wages clerk. If I do win, I'll share the prize with you. Let me go now and no one will know. I'll say I came back a roundabout way, got lost and took shelter.'

'Oh, you'd love that. I wouldn't see you for the dust bouncing off your fancy new heels. Just tell me. Answer that simple question. How will I collect the money and not be caught? I know you'll have an answer. You're the clever one. How do you think it made George feel, when you came top of the class every year?'

She kept her voice steady. 'How do you think it made me feel, watching you taunt him and mock him for not trying harder, and how do you think that made Mam feel?'

'You got your brains from me. He got his from your mam, thick as a barrel and just as hollow.'

The handle clanked as she picked up the bucket, nicely full since yesterday. She had imagined tipping the bucket on his head, shoving it down on his shoulders, but that was not possible, she had to go for his chest, slam bang straight at him. He dropped the torch. She heaved the bucket. He howled as he tilted back. With the remains, she went for what she hoped was his face.

She kicked the torch away and ran past him for the steps, sure of her footing, she had done this over and over to be sure. He had wedged the trapdoor. Even so it was heavy and took all her strength to raise it, and more effort to heave her way out. She saw a sliver of daylight and made one last push.

He grabbed at her ankle. She might have known he could see in the dark, like a rat. She turned and kicked, hitting the mark. He cried out and she heard him falling.

She was out in the air, and though it was a dim dawn, the brightness after the dark made her pause, like being on the edge of a different world. Her instinct was to run, but she sat on the trap door, reaching for the rocks and stones he had placed there, and then set aside.

The trapdoor moved beneath her. She wasn't heavy enough to hold him down.

She picked up a rock and smashed his hand, and then she ran, and he ran after her. And when she stumbled, cursing the wrong shoes, he was there, wearing the right shoes, and dragging her back.

Chapter
Fifty-Four

⁓

As we entered Masham, I weighed up whether we should go to the police station or Oak Cottage and decided on the cottage. We could deposit Annie's luggage and there may be the miracle of Ruth's return. But Annie suddenly called, 'Wait! That's my house.'

We got out, leaving Annie's flour bags of belongings in the dicky seat. Annie tapped the money belt under her clothes. She looked about her. 'Nothing has changed, and everything has changed.'

She stopped and took deep breaths. 'There might be something in the air, some clue.'

This was no time for mysticism. Before I had time to hurry her on, she went to her door.

I looked at my watch and hurried after her. Slater would be there. I was thinking of that long knife she carried.

Annie flung open the door. 'He's not here. I'd know, but I want to look. There'll be something.'

While she went upstairs, I looked about the kitchen. Harriet was right. He had lied about Sunday dinner. There was no cold meat in the pantry, no left-over potatoes, no greasy meat dish. I went into the cellar, to see whether he kept food in the wire press. He did. There was a piece of cheese, and half a loaf. Slater Parnaby had been too busy to think about cooking.

Suddenly Annie was beside me. 'It's too early for him to be at work so where is he?'

'That's what we'll find out. Come on.'

It astonished me that this woman who such a short time ago had seemed incapable of stepping outside, unable to take control of her own life, was now alert to every possibility. This reminded me that I must also be alert. 'We need something of his, so that the police dogs can track him. They tried to find Ruth, but rain got in the way.'

She took a scarf from the back of the door.

We got back in the car and I drove through the deserted town, along the lane, stopping at the top of the track. I heard our dog bark. A moment later, he bounded towards us, Mrs Sugden behind him, offering to take our flour sacks. I made the introductions, noticing that the wind had suddenly gone from Annie's sails.

I had only spoken to Mrs Sugden last night. Even the coaches she prized would not have whisked her here at this time of the day. 'How did you get here?'

'Thanks to our influential friends. Miss Merton was most sympathetic. She persuaded her brother to send his university driver. I wanted him to bring us last night, but he wouldn't drive through the countryside in the dark of night. He drove in the dark of morning instead.'

Harriet was at the door and brought a breath of normality to the situation. 'Oh, Mrs Parnaby, I've been hoping to meet you since Ruth and I went by your bakery on the dray. Come in. I'm sure we'll find Ruth now you're here.'

Annie Parnaby wanted only to talk to Harriet, and to see which was Ruth's room.

Harriet took Annie upstairs. When they came down, Annie held a school exercise book that belonged to Ruth.

She passed it to me, pointing to the poem about a cottage. 'When Slater came courting me, we went to look at the thatched cottages that were being demolished. He said they should keep just one, for us. Later, we would walk there on a Sunday. The cottages were gone, but in the last one, a hoard of gold sovereigns was found in the roof. We used to look in the grass roundabout, to see if any had been left behind. It gave the children something to do.'

'And did you all go?'

The 'Good morning' came from the doorway. It was Sergeant Moon.

Annie made a dash for him and grabbed his arms. 'Any news?'

'Not yet, Annie. We're going out with the dogs. This time we're looking for Slater.'

'So are we,' Harriet said. 'Mrs Parnaby brought his scarf.'

'Were you saying you, Slater and the children walked on the common?' the sergeant asked.

'Occasionally.' She looked at her feet. 'He said one day he would bury me there.'

It came as no surprise that Sergeant Moon politely rejected our offer of help, but I tried. 'Ours is a police dog, and he knows Ruth. None of these dogs do.'

'They don't need to, Mrs Shackleton. We have Ruth's items of clothing, and now we have her father's scarf and a pair of his discarded socks I picked up last night when I went to search the house.'

Harriet opened her mouth to speak and I knew that she was about to share her knowledge of how to conduct a search. Realising he would not want to hear this, she thought of something else to say.

'When we find Ruth, she'll need someone she knows. I am her official companion.'

Not for the first time, I was inclined to back Harriet. She needed to prove herself as a good companion. I spoke quietly to the sergeant. 'She will not set a foot wrong.'

Harriet heard me. 'And what's more, I know the whistle.'

'What whistle?'

'Ruth and George have a signal whistle, isn't that right, Mrs Parnaby?'

'It is.'

'Then whistle, and I'll copy.' Sergeant Moon pursed his lips, ready to whistle. He was bending over backwards to be reassuring, as well as to make sure he had every bit of information he could muster.

Harriet put on her coat. 'Sergeant, it's unlucky to whistle indoors. I wouldn't dare risk it. I must come'

Annie Parnaby folded her arms. 'Her and her dog have to be there. They know the whistle, they know my girl. I would be there, but I'm done in. I wouldn't keep up.'

Harriet persisted. 'I'm fit, I'll walk fast as you like or slow as you like, and I won't be in the way. I promise.'

'Miss Armstrong, we're without a WPC. I am enrolling you as part of the search operation, under my command.'

'Yes, sir!'

'This is only so that when we find Ruth, and we will, you will be there for her. You are not searching.'

'No I am not.'

Harriet can be very believable. She would have her fingers crossed behind her back, saying to herself, 'I won't search, but Sergeant Dog will.'

Only I knew that Harriet had a small cloth bag in each of her coat pockets. One contained the handkerchief Slater Parnaby dropped on Sunday. The other contained Ruth's glove.

Chapter
Fifty-Five

Two dog handlers led the way from the edge of the common. Sergeant Moon was close behind, with the four constables fanning out behind him. Harriet followed on with her dog. They had walked for what seemed an age, with the two official dogs agreeing on the route taken by Slater Parnaby.

These two official dogs worked quietly, beginning to show increased interest in the trail they followed.

Harriet liked to think she was the one who spotted the lone figure on the horizon. It was Ruth's dad, she felt sure. There was something in the way he moved, his speed at spotting them. From this distance she could not be sure, but he seemed to tilt back his head and sniff the air before breaking into a run with straight forearms and elbows tucked in like the men and boys who did fell running.

Sergeant Moon must have seen him at the same time and gave an order.

The dogs and handlers did not divert from their path, but two of the four constables gave chase.

'Is it him?' Harriet asked the sergeant.

The sergeant raised his binoculars. 'It's him. I saw him years ago, doing a cross-country run. If he's still fit, he'll take some catching.' He paused. 'There's something up. He's turning. I don't know which way he'll go.'

Terrible thoughts came into Harriet's mind, but she refused to entertain them. What had Ruth's dad done to her? It would be time for him to go to work. Perhaps he had done nothing. He was setting off back for Masham and the brewery, so that he would clock in on time. Well that would not happen now. Let's find her, she said to herself. Don't give up, Ruth. We're on our way.

The official bloodhounds wanted to follow the way Ruth's dad had gone. The handlers needed time to persuade the animals that they should follow the scent of where he had come from.

While this exchange between men and dogs took place, Harriet took Slater Parnaby's hanky from her pocket and let Sergeant Dog take his best whiff. This led him to move back and forth sniffing the ground to Harriet's left and right. He decided on a course and stuck to it. This put Harriet at a distance from the dog handlers, about the length of three trams.

There was no definite path to wherever the dog handlers were going. Harriet continued on her way. A path emerged, and she was on it. Her heart beat faster. She knew where she was now. They were coming to the cottage that wasn't there, where Ruth had brought her. There was an oak tree that had grown to a great height by a dry stone wall.

Harriet whistled, startling the dogs, the sergeant, the dog handlers and the remaining two constables fanning out behind.

'We're here. At the cottage.'

The dog handlers, who had now fallen behind, stopped so abruptly, they almost bumped into her.

Sergeant Moon, who knew the area best, having grown up close by, said, 'There was a cottage here, years ago.'

They looked down and saw the evidence of it. Sergeant Dog stopped. He barked. He would not budge. Harriet brought out

Ruth's glove. The dog sniffed the glove and sniffed the ground. He wagged his tail and whined.

Harriet felt sick. There was nothing here but ground, grass and stone.

Sergeant Moon put a hand on her shoulder. 'There's been no digging. Don't go to pieces now.'

Sergeant Dog barked.

'Whistle,' Harriet said. 'Everybody whistle!' She whistled.

They copied her whistle, the sergeant, the handlers, the constables. 'Once more!'

This time, very faintly, an echoing whistle came from somewhere just beyond their feet.

The two men bringing up the rear dashed forward on the sergeant's signal and began to move a branch, and another, and to push away stones. They lifted a trap door, and out popped Ruth's head, like a jack-in-the-box.

Sergeant Dog almost pulled Harriet over to get to Ruth, but Sergeant Moon and one of the constables were already helping her out.

Harriet let go of the lead, ran to Ruth and hugged her. Ruth swayed a little, blinking against the light.

Sergeant Moon blew his nose. The dog handlers let go of their dogs' leads, freeing their hands so that they could applaud the rescue.

Sergeant Moon turned to the dog handlers. 'Stay on Parnaby's trail. He knows this area inside out and might give them the slip.'

One of the constables said to Ruth, 'Do you need a piggyback, miss?' He came closer. 'I can do a fireman's lift, until you get your legs back.'

'Thank you, but I want to walk. I'm leaning on you, Harriet. For the first few steps.'

Sergeant Moon took Sergeant Dog's lead.

Ruth's first few steps became the entire way back, with Harriet and Ruth walking arm in arm.

Harriet saw that a small crowd had gathered at the end of the path. She saw her auntie and Mrs Sugden, with Annie Parnaby standing between them.

Harriet let go of Ruth and watched her run towards her mother, who ran to her. They grabbed each other as if they would never let go.

Chapter
Fifty-Six

~

Harriet was upstairs, working out sleeping arrangements.

Ruth lounged in the steamer chair, covered with a blanket. Annie sat beside Ruth, holding her hand. William and Eleanor seated at the kitchen table, wearing their Aquascutum coats, waiting quietly until Mrs Sugden's fussing over making tea and locating the egg timer subsided.

'Come back with us, Ruth,' Eleanor said firmly. 'You can have a proper bath and a rest.'

'That sounds lovely, Mrs Lofthouse, but if it's all the same to you, I'll stay put for now. I've lost track of time. How long is it to the Northern Finals?'

Eleanor said, 'It's next Sunday, but no one will blame you if you want to withdraw.'

William's face fell. 'She's come this far, Eleanor. She'll want to go on.'

We all waited. Under the blanket, Ruth hugged herself and gave a little shake.

William said, 'Of course, Eleanor's right. If you've had enough, you've had enough. Your job is waiting. Mr Beckwith misses you in the wages office.'

Ruth shook her head. 'I will not give up now. I know I look a wreck and I may be beaten by other girls on the night, but I won't let the old man knock me into a cocked hat.'

Eleanor beamed. 'Good for you. We have two first class carriages booked to take us to Manchester. It will be a night to remember. We'll crack open the champagne.'

At that moment, Ruth did not look like a winner, but I admired Eleanor's optimism and determination.

William stood. 'Come on, Eleanor, let's leave these ladies to get on. Mrs Shackleton, if there is anything that you need, just send word.'

'I will.' I got up to walk them to the door.

Eleanor was not to be rushed away. 'Ruth, Harriet, I am taking you both to Harrogate for a few days, and I won't accept no for an answer. We will go to the Turkish Baths, a beauty salon and the hairdressers. We will stay in a delightful boarding house, run by a charming widow. There is an adequate bathroom and long mirrors. The hotels are too impersonal, trying to outdo each other in grandeur. We will have home-cooked food and privacy, and we will shop for clothes.'

Ruth looked to her mother. 'Will you come?'

'Wild horses wouldn't drag me there. You and Harriet go with Mrs Lofthouse and enjoy yourselves. I'll stop here, if that's all right?' She looked to me.

'I may need to go back to Leeds, but Mrs Sugden will stay.'

'I will that. We'll tick over nicely, Mrs—'

'Call me Annie.'

The burst of brave energy that led Annie to run to her daughter seemed now to have evaporated. It would take time for her to get better, but I now felt sure she would. The police would find Slater Parnaby. If there was any justice, he would be put away for a very long time.

The rest of that day and the next went by without any news about Slater Parnaby. A police constable patrolled the track. He had given Ruth the key to the Parnaby house which now stood empty. Neither Mrs Parnaby nor Ruth wanted to live there again.

On the third day, when Eleanor was to take Harriet and Ruth to Harrogate, and I knew I ought to be going back to Leeds, I woke just before dawn. Our sleeping arrangements were now that I shared the back room with Harriet, Mrs Parnaby and Ruth had my bed and Mrs Sugden had the middle room.

Harriet was still sleeping. Mrs Sugden is an early riser, but the tread on the stairs was not hers. She has heavy footsteps, and so does Annie Parnaby. I heard the back door open. It was Ruth, probably going up the back garden to the outhouse, but I felt a stab of anxiety and went downstairs.

Chapter
Fifty-Seven

❧

Ruth had closed the backdoor. I opened it, looked out and saw that
she was dressed, carrying a small knapsack, and wheeling her bike
along the path. 'Where are you going, Ruth? You know the constable's on duty. He's watching out in case—'

'In case my father comes looking for us.' She leaned the bike
against the wall. 'They haven't found him.'

'They will.'

She shook her head. 'I got out of the cellar once by hitting him
with a bucket of slops. He came after me and dragged me back. I
nearly got out the day I was rescued. I hit him with an old brass
candlestick that was on the corner of the slab. I cut his head. There
was a lot of blood. If the police haven't found him by now, it's
because he has crawled somewhere to die, or to survive.'

'Tell the police.'

She shook her head. 'I woke in the night knowing where he is.'

'Where is he?'

'I can direct us there. I've watched the constable. He always
does the same thing, does his walkabout and then goes to the hut
to shelter. If we get to your car, we'll be there in no time. Take me
there, or I'll go on my own. Auntie Kate, I have to know, or I'll

never have peace, none of us will. And bad as he is, I don't want the old man to be hunted by dogs.'

I should have said no, but I put on my coat and shoes.

As dawn broke, I stopped the car by a wood. Ruth lit our way along a path until we came to a small version of Stonehenge. There was a chill in the air and frost on the grass but another kind of chill as we walked between the stones. This was the Druid's Temple Harriet had told me about.

'He is in the hermit's cave,' Ruth said, with such certainty that I thought she must be having some sort of aftershock. She bent down to pluck a handful of buttercups.

We walked until she directed the torchbeam to a dark space in the rock. 'I brought water.'

Ruth was off like a shot, the light of her torch dipping as she hurried along the path. I followed. I must have been mad to bring her here.

She had dimmed the torch, perhaps by turning the beam to the wall. At the back of the cave, Ruth sat beside a figure that looked more like an effigy than a man. She cradled his head, and tried to make him drink, though he looked too far gone to be aware of anything. Perhaps he was already dead.

She was talking to him softly. I thought I heard him speak. But the only words I caught were hers, buttercups and pity. I could not tell how long it was until Ruth closed her father's eyes.

On the way back to the car, she said, 'I had to know. I threatened to kill him when I was little. He said he had waited four years for someone to put a bullet in his head, and no one did. When the constable walked me to our house last night to collect a dressing gown, I picked up the old man's service revolver, and I put bullets in. I brought it, but he doesn't need it now.'

'Did he know you were there?'

'He said, "I thought it would be you."'

Chapter
Fifty-Eight

❧

I was back at home, in Batswing Cottage. All was clean, neat, tidy and very quiet. My house seemed strangely empty. Ruth and Harriet had gone to Harrogate with Eleanor. Mrs Sugden and the dog were still in Masham with Annie.

In the late evening, Sykes called round. He and I sat at the kitchen table. He looked tired. Alongside his current assignment, he had spent hours writing letters, making telephone calls and taking the train to Blackburn in his attempt to trace former members of Miss Boland's opera troupe, drawing on previous addresses, a distant relative, friends of friends, newspapermen, electoral rolls and musicians' organisations.

He had set out his results with impeccable neatness. Those few lines represented a mountain of work and would perhaps result in a new home for Miss Boland.

'This calls for a drop of whisky, Mr Sykes.'

'I'll get the bottle, Mrs Shackleton.'

I read his notes, headed The Merry Opera Company.

Noel Broderick, tenor, residing in a home for elderly, impoverished musicians in Folkestone—vacancies for suitable candidates.

Julia Patterson, contralto, residing in a self-sufficient, artistic community on the outskirts of Abergavenny.

Delius Jackson, baritone—pauper's grave, Blackburn.

Given the decades that had passed since the four members of the Merry Opera Company last performed together, Sykes had done extraordinarily well to trace all three.

I raised my glass. 'To the Merry Opera Company.'

'The Merry Opera Company.' He took a drink. 'I'm glad Miss Boland didn't travel with an orchestra. And we missed Delius Jackson by only six months.'

'Then I must act quickly and find out whether Miss Boland would like to join one of the two remaining comrades before they take a final bow.'

'Please do. I couldn't face hunting for some second cousin twice removed and hoping that he or she had a heart of gold and a spare room, just so that the townspeople of Masham might sleep safely in their beds.'

I was allowed a 'resettlement' visit to Miss Boland in Armley Prison. We sat in a cold, dingy room. She wrapped her shawl tightly round her shoulders and adjusted her spectacles.

Miss Boland had not come up with any ideas of her own as to where her future might lie. She looked at Sykes's findings.

'Poor Delius, in a pauper's grave in Blackburn. His father owned a cotton mill there. You think someone would have put a hand in a pocket.' She sighed. 'He was very popular. Everyone who heard him sing fell in love with his heavenly voice. There was always a rude awakening when the man didn't match up.' She sighed. 'A pauper's grave might be an improvement on where Noel has ended up. "A home for elderly, impoverished musicians." How ghastly. Some people have no tact. Noel and I were close for a long time. We talked of marriage.' She shook her head. 'I will write to him. I don't suppose he knows about Delius. You'd think just one of us might have fallen on our feet.'

'That leaves Julia.'

'Julia, in a self-sufficient, artistic community, whatever that means. It sounds livelier. She was a good sport, though she often took a dislike to people. Sometimes she and I took a dislike to each other, but that's what makes life interesting. And I've never been to Abergavenny.'

Chapter
Fifty-Nine

~

The Midland Hotel, Manchester where we were to stay for the weekend of the Northern Brewery Queen finals, can truly be described as a baroque twentieth-century palace, of red brick, terracotta and polished marble. The hotel's own theatre seats a thousand, not large enough to accommodate the numbers attending Sunday's contest. That was to be held in the three thousand-seater Palace Theatre.

With admirable foresight, huge optimism and not inconsiderable expense, Eleanor had, months earlier, from her own money, booked four rooms for the Saturday night before the contest, and the Sunday night of the event.

We set off on the Saturday, travelling first class. Annie Parnaby could not face going into a dress shop and so had left it to Mrs Sugden to choose outfits for her. Eleanor had arranged everything down to the last detail. Once on the train, she began to fret as to whether the trunk was on board, with her and Ruth's outfits and William's dress suit. She insisted on a porter taking her to the luggage van to check. William and I waited for her in the dining car.

'This is a once in a lifetime event, Kate, and we are in on it,' William said.

'I know. And the Midland Hotel was the place where Mr Rolls met Mr Royce.'

'Really?' William lit up with an excitement I had never before seen in him. 'Look what came of that, eh? Everyone who matters will be there.'

Everyone who mattered included Sykes and Rosie. William had asked me if I had any objection to Sykes being offered a post as administrative director on the Barleycorn board. He would attend all meetings and work twelve days a year assisting in strategies and planning. It was the perfect job to complement Sykes's work with me and I was delighted for him.

Eleanor came back from the luggage van, reporting that the trunk was safe and so were all our suitcases: mine, Harriet's, Mrs Sugden's and Mrs Parnaby's.

The hotel did not disappoint. William came to whisper to me, 'The place is awash with brewers, potential investors, and men with big ideas.'

Saturday evening took on the quality of a fairy tale. We sat at a round table in the dining room. Ruth seemed remarkably calm on this evening before her big night. Harriet said, 'She practises deep breathing. Miss Boland taught her how to be calm before a performance. You'd hardly notice that underneath she is a bag of nerves.'

William and Sykes made their way to the bar, for what they called a bit of hobnobbing. Eleanor escaped to her room, to put her feet up. Harriet, Ruth and I went to see the variety show in the theatre. That was too busy an event for Annie Parnaby's liking. She and Mrs Sugden took to one of the lounges, to admire the décor, and watch people come and go.

On that glittering tie and tails and evening dresses Sunday night, a placard outside the Palace Theatre declared that tickets were SOLD OUT.

Ruth was already backstage.

Eleanor whispered that she was one of the first to book seats. Ours was a block on the second row of the stalls.

Our programme named seven contestants, in alphabetical order of county: Cheshire, Cumberland, Durham, Lancashire, Northumberland, Westmorland and, at number seven, Yorkshire. As the lights dimmed, we were almost too excited to speak.

A child in the row behind queried where did the North begin and end, and what were its edges? Why was Cheshire included and Derbyshire not when both counties edged Yorkshire and Lancashire? It was explained to her that so did Nottinghamshire and Lincolnshire touch the white and red rose counties, but everyone knew they were the Midlands.

A brass band fanfare heralded the start of the contest.

Three judges took their places at the side of the stage. The glamorous editor of a fashion magazine wore black satin. The president of the Society of Brewers and a national newspaper columnist wore formal evening clothes with bow tie and tails.

Minor members of the aristocracy occupied a box, allowing the compère to welcome My Lords, Ladies and Gentlemen.

Although each contestant was a queen of her county, they were introduced as miss, starting with sparkling Miss Cheshire in a gold ball gown.

The questions followed a pattern, probing each candidate's character and personality, each judge asking his or her question. The newspaperman's questioning caused four entrants to hesitate.

At last, Ruth came on stage, to roars of approval from the Yorkshire contingent in the gallery, and cheers from our row.

She was poised, smiling and charming. No one would have guessed what she had recently gone through. It was in the last questions, from the newspaper columnist, that she excelled.

'Please tell the audience what, in these difficult times for our country, has saddened and gladdened your heart?'

Ruth thought for a moment. 'It gladdened my heart that when a destitute family came to live rough in the nearby woods, the father was given a job in our brewery, the mother found school places for her children, and the family now have a home in a cottage, and can start their lives again.' She paused for the applause to die down, indicating that there was more to be said. 'What has both saddened and gladdened my heart is that an elderly man who was part of all of our lives died recently. But I am proud to have been one of the people who took down his rhymes in praise of ale, so that they will never be forgotten. Here is one of Mick Musgrove's short rhymes, to make you smile.'

She took a deep breath and began in the style of a comic monologue.

'They say there's five reasons for drinking,
But more, I'm sure may be got;
For I never could find, to my thinking,
A reason why people should not.
A sixth I'll not scruple at giving,
I'll name it, while 'tis in my head;
'Tis, if you don't drink while you're living,
You never will after you're dead.'

There were cheers and laughter as the compère thanked her, and she left the stage.

Silence fell as the judges leaned in closely to each other, producing their score cards. The brass band struck up the William Tell Overture, which must have made conversation impossible for the judges. Being so close to the stage, I was able to see each one lay out their score cards. The audience remained seated, mostly in silence. Only a few talked amongst themselves as we waited for the result.

The compère returned to the stage and conferred with the judges.

Against a racket of tumultuous applause, the seven contestants came back on stage.

The compère took the microphone. He praised all the candidates, congratulated them, and their breweries.

'And the winner is, Miss Ruth Parnaby of the Barleycorn Brewery, Masham in the North Riding of Yorkshire.'

Ruth stepped forward to receive the crown, and to give a short, surprised speech that she had practised. She was given an envelope containing a cheque, held it tightly and said, 'Thank you, thank you everyone.'

When William Lofthouse was called to the stage, he walked along our row to the aisle almost blindly, into the spotlight, and was ushered onto the stage to accept congratulations and the cheque. He said, 'Ruth came to us as a trainee clerk, at the age of fourteen. The congratulations are all for Ruth, and for my wife, the artist Eleanor Hart, who has championed Ruth every step of the way.'

We gathered back at the hotel and it seemed as if the enormous chandelier sparkled just for us. The waiter opened champagne. Eleanor raised a toast to Ruth, and to her companion, Harriet. William, not normally a demonstrative man, hugged Eleanor.

'I have the name for Barleycorn's new brew. It will be Hart's Artist Brew, in honour of my wonderful wife Eleanor.'

They both looked so happy. I was glad to have been wrong in my early suspicions of Eleanor. She came and sat by me. 'Hasn't it been a glorious evening, Kate?'

I agreed that it had. For a short time, the trials and tragedies of the past weeks receded. 'I'm so glad William has named a brew for you!'

'He keeps asking if I need to go and lie down, but this is one after-show party that I wouldn't dream of missing.'

I looked about but couldn't see William or Sykes.

'Where are they?'

'William and Mr Sykes are chatting to everyone who matters, exchanging business cards. Ruth keeps popping back to tell me about new orders, offers of investment, expanding premises, establishing a bottle plant, making more use of the railways, hiring barges for the Ure, and buying a fleet of vans for the more distant deliveries. If only a tenth of that comes to pass, it will be good times for Barleycorn. I've told William that he must never let the horses go. Ruth backed me up on that. She told me that horses are much more economical on the short runs.'

The next morning, Harriet, Mrs Sugden and I caught a train back to Leeds. William's cheque settling our account had arrived before us, and included a bonus.

Thanks to a good neighbour, our vegetable patch still thrived. Harriet and I went into the garden, to praise Mrs Sugden's tomato seedlings.

Author's Note

The Yorkshire market town of Masham, pronounced Massam, home to the famous Theakston's and Black Sheep breweries, provides the background for this story. In 1930, there was one brewery in the town, Theakston's, which I have replaced with the fictional Barleycorn Brewery. Barleycorn Brewery bears no resemblance to existing breweries in the town, except in the way that all breweries have features in common. Some characters in this story have local names. Any similarity to real persons would be an extraordinary coincidence. Mashamshire has its own specially commissioned Ordnance Survey Explorer map. Walkers, please go by that and not by my locations and distances.

Between the 1920s and early 1980s, Britain's major industries crowned queens, following the tradition of May Queens. Attractive and charismatic young women who worked in, or had family connections with, their industry became its ambassadors, an opportunity that could change lives. There were queens of railways, coal, cotton, wool and textiles, but never breweries. This story remedies that omission.

Acknowledgments

My mother was brought up in the Lloyd's Arms public house. When we were growing up, one of her many jobs was at the Melbourne Brewery. While saving for a typewriter, I worked as a barmaid at the White Horse. I knew how to pull a good pint, and that the landlord went into the cellar to see to the barrels. With such impeccable credentials, the idea of creating an imaginary brewery was not daunting, until I began.

In Masham, I took brewery tours at Theakston's, with Stuart Burrows, and at Black Sheep. At Tetley's Brewery, once part of the Leeds city skyline, I took the Heritage Tour. Tetley's was taken over by Carlsberg who closed the brewery and demolished the plant. The iconic art deco headquarters is now The Tetley, a contemporary art gallery. On Georgia Taylor's tour, I met former Tetley employees. Sylvia and Ted Johnson, Dudley Mitchell and Brenda and Andrew Metcalfe kindly answered my questions.

Robert Lawson, formerly brewer at Tetley's, showed me round Ossett Brewery, of which he is Chairman. He kindly loaned me the old volumes where I found the rhymes in praise of ale.

Thanks to Alan Slomson of the Thoresby Society and to Professor John Chartres who wrote a chapter about Tetley's for the book he and Katrina Honeyman edited, *Leeds City Businesses, 1893–1993*—all of which businesses have since bitten the dust.

Acknowledgments

Thanks to nurse Stephanie Carncross, retired police officers Viv Cutbill and Ralph Lindley and to Karyn Burnham, Sylvia Gill and Patricia McNeil.

John McGoldrick, Curator of Industrial History, Armley Mills Museum, mounted the exhibition Queens of Industry, sparking my interest in this hidden strand of history. He gave me the link to Rebecca Conway's *Making the Mill Girl Modern?*: *Beauty, Industry and the Popular Newspaper in 1930s' England*. The links to this and other background pieces can be found on my website.

My source for Willie Lambert's poem *The Old Thatched Cottage on the Moor*, is *Days of Yore, A History of Masham* by Susan Cunliffe-Lister, 1989, Yore being an old name for the River Ure. J B Priestley's *English Journey* gives a deeply resonating insight into l930s England.

A big thanks to Emma Beswetherick for her spot-on editing, to the team at Piatkus, especially Hannah Wann, Clara Diaz and Brionee Fenlon. Last but by no means least, thanks to Jenny Chen, Rebecca Nelson, and the team at Crooked Lane Books, New York and to agents Judith Murdoch and Rebecca Winfield. It has been my pleasure to work with you all.